Man Hunt

Marisa Mackle was born in Armagh, Northern Ireland. Her books include *Mr Right for the Night*, *So Long Mr Wrong*, *Mile High Guy* and *Chinese Whispers*. They have been translated worldwide and sell in Japan, Poland, Thailand, Turkey and the Czech Republic. She attended Mount Anville Senior School and afterwards graduated from UCD with an honours French and English degree. She worked in Aer Lingus for five years and is currently editing a compilation of short stories called *Party Animal* the proceeds of which will go to animal charities. She is single and lives in Dublin.

Contact Marisa: dodderbooks@eircom.net

Man Hunt

Marisa Mackle

DODDER

First published in Ireland by Dodder Books Ltd, 2006.

Dodder Books Limited
9 Airfield Court
Dublin 4.

A CIP catalogue record for this book
is available from the British Library.

ISBN 0954491351

Cover design by Slick Fish
Typeset by Palimpsest Book Production Limited,
Grangemouth, Stirlingshire.

Printed and bound in Great Britain by
Cox & Wyman Ltd, Reading, Berks

*This novel is dedicated to the memory
of my darling grandmother,
Sheila Collins.*

Acknowledgements

I would like to thank God, St Anthony and St Jude. Also thanks to my family – Mum, Dad, Tara and Naomi. Huge thanks to Tatianna Ouliankina, Emma Roche, Georgina Heffernan, Stephen Rae, David Diebold, Claudia Carroll, Linda Martin, Cathy Kelly, Quentin Fottrell, Sue Leonard, Tom Cruise, Ruth Griffin, Sarah McGovern, Alex Best, Cathy Kelly, Roxanne Parker, Colm Ennis, Sarah Cassidy, Eoin McHugh, Mary Biggins, James Byrne, Alison O' Reilly, Mary Healy from Argosy, Alan Swan, Catherine Daly, Mary Malone, Melanie Finn, Tanya Sweeney, Amanda Brunker and Suzanne McDonald from Hughes and Hughes, Dublin Airport.

Chapter One

The perfect man does not:

1. Drink while I drive.
2. Use my eye cream to massage his smelly feet.
3. Resent asking strangers for directions.
4. Buy the cinema tickets, but refuse to look after popcorn etc.
5. Text people in my company (especially other women).
6. Put me down in public.
7. Hamper my diet by buying me chocolate.
8. Criticise my friends/mother/dress sense.
9. Tell me how different he is from other men.
10. Take the last can of Diet Coke from the fridge.

I'm single again. And this time I'm not accepting the tired old line about all the fish out there. Yes there *are* plenty of fish. But as far as I'm concerned they're still in the sea. At the bottom of it. The only form of sea life I seem to meet these days are the sharks. Dreadful things that hang about nightclubs asking you what you do for a living and what kind of car you drive. Honest to God! Everybody is looking for a good catch these days. Even my cat won't entertain another feline unless he's wearing a Prada collar! Anyway, I'm now at an age where I'm not prepared to give second chances. So stingy men who are 'saving for a rainy day', womanisers who 'can't help loving more than one person', and drunks are not welcome to call. From now on, it's serious. I'm looking for Mr Right.

If I were a man, women would love me. That's because I'd know how to play the game. I'd spend Saturday afternoons in clothes shops with a pleasant, interested smile on my face. And I wouldn't even wonder who was winning the match. Not only would I insist that her bum *definitely* didn't look big, I'd go a step further and say it was practically invisible. I would never ever force my opinionated friends on her and argue that they were 'great guys once you got to know them'. I'd forget about killing myself in the gym because, let's face it, who is attracted to a man who runs on the same spot for 45 minutes and then needs four bath sheets to wipe off the sweat?

If my new girlfriend asked whether my ex was pretty, I would frown and pretend to think about it carefully. Then slowly I would answer 'well, she's fairly good-looking but not a patch on you.'

I would never dream of ringing *any* woman at four in the morning hoping for a bit of action, simply because I had failed to score elsewhere that night. And also I would never hop out of a taxi first calling cheerfully, 'I'll get it the next time.'

If I said I would ring, I would do it. The next day. And I would do it sober, and not wait till the next time I was completely bollixed and out with the lads. I would not inform her that her friend/sister/colleague was stunning before wondering aloud why she was still single. If my girlfriend asked me how many women I'd slept with, I'd pretend not to remember but assure her that it couldn't have been more than five. When she mentioned other people's kids, my eyes would not glaze over. Nor would I reach for the remote control and turn the volume up loud. On the road I would not try to kill us both by trying to overtake every second car, nor would I take it personally if a bigger, more expensive car or a woman driver succeeded in overtaking us.

So where are all the kind, attractive, fun loving guys around town? Where *do* they go incidentally? I mean they must go somewhere. They certainly don't hang out in my local pub anyway. To hang out in my local pub you must:

a) have a beer belly.
b) be losing your hair.
c) wear a check shirt.
d) ignore every woman who walks past.
e) never offer to buy anyone a drink.
f) talk in a loud voice about what a great fellow you are.

God, now that I actually think about it, I wonder why I ever bother going to my local. I've been going for about fifteen years now and always complain that the crowd never changes. No *wonder* I'm still single. I always see the same men week after week, propping up the bar having the same old conversations. Mind you, they probably look at me and say, 'Jesus, why doesn't that old bag ever go anywhere else?' They seem as pleased to see me as I am to see them. Which isn't one bit.

We all ignore each other unless one of us gets really drunk and then starts shaking hands with everyone in the bar, even strangers. I wonder is it the same in other people's locals? I don't know because I only have one local pub. But when I watch *EastEnders* and *Coronation Street* I always think it's quite nice that everybody greets each other. Oh I know they secretly don't like each other, scream abuse at each other, have affairs with each other and then try to kill each other. But it's still pretty great the way they all say 'hello' and stuff when they see each other. In my local pub, we just don't have that same kind of camaraderie.

I live in Dublin. On the Southside. In a leafy affluent suburb where people are brought up to astutely avoid each other and only say 'hello' when the alternative is to cross a busy street and maybe get knocked down. And even then the greeting is always lukewarm, followed with an impertinent 'what are you doing now?' or 'are you still living in the area?' or 'so where are you working now?'

When I was a child people always asked me what my dad did for a living. Now they ask what I do. And what my husband does. Only I don't have a husband. So I don't really like that question. No.

Reading this, you're probably wondering why I still go to the local pub. Well I have my reasons. You can always get a seat and hear yourself talk. You don't have to queue for the toilet and nobody asks you to dance. Also it's handy for a first date as it's only a five minute run to my flat if things don't work out.

Everybody tells me that I won't meet anybody unless I go into town. But in town I can never get a seat and at least one person stands on my foot causing severe bruising. I can never get a taxi home, some man always insults me by saying 'don't worry, he'll turn up eventually', and some drunken woman always tries to start a conversation about make-up in front of the toilet mirrors.

Usually my last thoughts before I leave a pub are that a) I won't be going into town again for a long, long time b) I wish I hadn't spent all that money getting my hair professionally blow dried and, c) Irish men just aren't worth it.

And I usually mean it, I really do, but the following week I find myself back in town, queuing to get into a new trendy pub thinking that tonight things will be different. You see, I don't need lots and lots of men chatting me up, I just need one. One decent man. With a secure financial future and a friendly disposition. A man who is delighted but not *grateful* to be going out with me. I'd prefer not to have to settle. Or panic at a certain age, pick out some random male and think that, well, he's better than nothing.

Despite popular belief, most women are not looking to marry a bank balance. No. Therefore we work for long hours, and commute for even longer hours, determined to be financially independent. However, long hours in the office and car, definitely leaves less time for man hunting.

Personally I have a deep-rooted fear of marrying a man I'm not madly in love with. I always worry that one day I'll wake up, look at my husband and think 'Good God, you're not THE ONE!' And then what'll I do? After all, once you say 'I do', it's not so easy to say 'I don't'. You can't just return your man to the shop the following week and demand a refund. Nor can you trade him in for a newer shinier model. Nor can you ask to have him in a different size or colour. So proceed with caution.

My fear of commitment all began at the age of sixteen when I went to Vienna in Austria to work for a wealthy family. I didn't really intend doing much work of course. After all, it was the summer so I wanted to have fun. But staying with a family would be cheaper than a campsite, I reckoned. And anyway I don't think my parents would have let me just head off to Europe at random.

I couldn't wait to leave school. My agency found me a 'lovely' Austrian family, where all I'd have to do would be to look after a three-year-old girl and help the heavily pregnant mother around the house. I was promised my own ensuite room with a double bed and a television. Having always shared a bedroom with my extremely messy sister, Carly, who used to remove her make-up with *my* face cloth, steal my pony tail holders, and shout in her sleep, I couldn't believe that I was finally going to get a decent night's kip *and* that my personal belongings would be safe for an entire summer. Oh and I was also going to be financially independent. Yes. I was actually going to be *paid* to look after the toddler in Vienna. Hadn't I landed on my feet?

I flew to Vienna via London because at the time there were no direct flights from Dublin. The man of the house was to pick me up at the airport. Very kind of him. Or so I thought.

During my flight the air hostess offered me wine with my meal which I thought was pretty amazing, considering I was still only sixteen. Obviously she thought I was older and I didn't bother to correct her. Of course now I don't like people mentally adding on a few years to my age. But back then it was cool.

At the airport I scoured the sea of strange faces in Arrivals holding cardboard signs. I saw my sign almost immediately. Lara Hope. Yes, that was me. However, the man holding the sign was yuck. To be honest he gave me the creeps. You see, I'm a tall girl and he only barely came up to my chest, which he gave a good gawk before offering me a 'Herzlichen Wilkommen', and standing on his tippy toes, he planted a slimy wet kiss on my cheek.

He had the greasiest head I had ever seen. The only sign of hair was sprouting from his nostrils, and two tufts, like mini hedgehogs, sprang up just above his sticky-out ears. His nose was like something that you'd buy in a joke shop. I kept expecting him to take it off to reveal another one underneath, but no such luck however. My heart sank as he went to lick my other cheek. Jesus, wasn't once enough?

'You are a beautiful woman,' he kept saying over and over again. Now I know I was new to the 'au-pair' game but I still had a feeling this kind of talk wasn't appropriate. After all, I was just out of school, was a fairly tubby teenager and wore no make-up whatsoever. In fact I still had my favourite teddy bear in my case. However I tried not to be too paranoid. After all, maybe he was just being friendly. Maybe foreign men were different. Maybe I was just overreacting.

We got into Herr Schnizkopff's snazzy Merc and soon we were driving through the magnificent streets of Vienna. Whatever about the vile-looking specimen sitting in the driver's seat, I couldn't help but marvel at the beauty of the city. The buildings were like something from a magnificent painting and conveyed an air of generations of old money and class. I could almost hear the echoes of Strauss. I wanted to don a ball gown, a string of pearls and waltz through the streets to the sound of violins with a tall, dark, handsome Austrian.

However, my little daydream quickly shattered as Herr Schnizkopff suddenly beeped his horn at a woman walking along the street in a very short skirt. 'Very sexy,' he leered as I squirmed uncomfortably in my seat. I said nothing. Did he expect me to agree? To be honest I didn't know what to think. All I knew was that I couldn't wait to get out of the car.

Finally we arrived at the picturesque village of Grinzing, in the suburbs of Vienna. The house was right on the street – an imposing yellow building with pretty flower-adorned window boxes. Under normal circumstances, I would have been delighted at the thought of living in such a pretty palace, but the fact that Herr Tufty lived there, was enough to dampen my mood.

Tufty pulled up outside the house and parked on the street. As he lifted my cases from the boot, the front door opened and a very tall, very thin, almost regal-looking woman with blonde hair opened the front door. Her beauty was reminiscent of Princess Diana and she wore a sad sort of smile. In her arms was a small angelic looking little girl, who looked so excited to see me. Her name was Venetia. Anja was the mother's name.

'Welcome to Vienna', said Anja offering me a hand adorned with knuckle-duster diamonds. Her pregnancy bump was fairly noticeable too. Neat and perfectly round. But her eyes were dull and held an air of disillusionment. I reckoned she couldn't have been more than twenty-eight years old. Tufty introduced us but then had to go back to work. I was never so glad to see somebody leave.

My bedroom was enormous. The four-poster bed was big enough to sleep six and I couldn't believe I was going to have it all to myself. The bathroom, with its shiny ceramic tiles, polished gold taps and huge gleaming mirrors, was worthy of a seven star hotel. I took in my surroundings excitedly. And after dropping my cases on the bed I was ready for the grand tour of the three-storey house.

The house was a showpiece, but most impressive was the basement. It consisted of an enormous oval-shaped swimming pool, a gym, sauna, jacuzzi, and a small juice bar in the corner. Through the glass windows I could see another smaller swimming pool in a stunning landscaped garden. The water glistened under the sun.

I remember thinking that everything would be perfect if Anja had married a gorgeous looking man, instead of Tufty. What a shame that this beautiful house belonged to such an offensive creep.

Because the family had two maids I wasn't

expected to do any heavy duty cleaning, which was great. There were so many rooms in the house that cleaning them all would have been a full time job. The main reason for my being there was to make sure Venetia was dressed, fed and entertained while Anja enjoyed going for various spa treatments and met her equally glamorous mother for lunch.

The first night I didn't sleep too well. I was lonely of course, but the fact that the house was located next to a busy beer garden where tourists sang raucously into the early hours, didn't help. However I soon got used to the noise. But what I never got used to were Tufty's deeply personal comments and the fact that my breasts were under constant scrutiny. No matter how hot the strong Austrian sun became, I refused to take off my black cardigan. Red-faced, with tiny beads of sweat a constant feature on my forehead, I was nevertheless determined to prevent Tufty from getting an eyeful.

I lazed away the days playing with Venetia in the garden, and then during her afternoon nap, I'd do a few laps of the basement pool. Using my imagination, I'd pretend that I was a wealthy woman of leisure and that all of this was mine. It was the only thing that kept me going, especially after Tufty began to play footsie with me at the breakfast table every morning.

On my days off I would get a tram to the city centre. I visited St Stephan's cathedral, Schonnbrunn palace and tasted Sachertorte in the many delightful traditional Austrian cafes. Sometimes I'd go and sit on the banks of the Danube with my feet in the water, which I regret to say wasn't as blue as I had imagined. In fact, disappointingly, it was a nondescript grey.

In the evenings I declined to sit with the family, pretending I was on a strict diet. This bothered Anja and she rang my mother to express concern about my eating habits. However the truth was I couldn't bear to spend a single unnecessary minute in Tufty's company. I didn't have the heart, or indeed the nerve to tell Anja any of this. I needed my job. I had to learn the German language and besides, if I came home to Dublin, what would I do? Work in the local petrol station until school started again? Back to sharing a room with my sister who stole my clothes and regularly shouted obscenities? No way. That just wasn't an option.

But God it was tough. One night I was out dancing with a group of foreign au pairs whom I'd met through the agency. Arriving home I noticed Herr and Frau were sitting watching television. He was drinking whiskey and his eyes were bloodshot. I was wearing a mini that his wife had outgrown. Tufty couldn't take his eyes off my legs as I entered the dining room to wish them good night.

'You are so young and beautiful,' he said, slurring his words. 'My wife used to have great legs too. I remember her in that skirt. She was sexy once. Now she's a mess.'

With that Anja burst into tears and I rushed to my room, feeling ill. I resolved to ignore him completely from then on. However, my resolve crumbled the night Anja was rushed to hospital to deliver her second sprog. The knock came in the middle of the night. At first I thought I must have been dreaming so I tried to return to sleep.

But the knocking persisted and I opened the door groggily to a deeply unpleasant sight. Tufty was at my door dressed in a wine-coloured silk dressing gown. The gown was unfortunately open. And not only was he wearing a pair of ridiculously tight briefs, the smell of stale wine from his breath was vile.

'Give me a kiss,' he hissed as I physically recoiled in horror. My heart began thumping so much I thought it would explode in my chest. The light from the hall flooded my darkened bedroom. I stood in a daze, squinting at him.

'A kiss,' he repeated.

To try and get rid of him, I planted a swift kiss on his cheek. But clearly that wasn't enough.

'Another one,' he said animatedly, pointing to his mouth.

'Oh no!' I answered, horrified. I slammed the door and with a shaking hand, turned the lock. Needless to say I barely slept the rest of the night. The next morning I packed my cases, got a taxi to the sister au-pair agency in the centre of Vienna and in floods of tears I explained my predicament.

So, as you might guess, that particular experience of marriage put me off for life. I vowed at the age of sixteen that I would never marry a rich man believing in happy-ever-after. I'd never be a prisoner like Anja. Fortunately I had been able to pack my bags that night and flee. As a mother of two with no job, and nowhere to go, Anja hadn't had the same choice.

The agency found me another family where both parents worked as farmers. They lived in a small village on the Austro-Hungarian border where I nearly went out of my mind with the heat and the boredom of living somewhere with only 400 inhabitants. The only bit of excitement was going to the local shop with the seven-year-old girl to buy Mars bars. I developed a serious addiction to microwaving them and when I came home in September I was so fat my own mother barely recognised me at Dublin Airport.

I studied hard for my Leaving Cert, determined to be financially independent, and the following year landed in UCD to study arts. My mother said I'd never get a job with an arts degree. I proved her wrong. Straight after college I became a trainee retail manager in a children's clothing shop, and immediately knew my future definitely lay in retail. Moving swiftly through the ranks, I became a department manager and then assistant manager in one of Dublin's best children's clothes shops.

By age twenty-six I had been aggressively head-hunted by a rival company, offering me twice the amount of money for doing fewer hours. Within four years I was manager of my own store. This is where I'm at now. A great job, a fabulous apartment in Dublin 4 and a fantastic company car. I've enough dosh for three foreign holidays a year and I stay in five star hotels instead of kips. I even took a trip of a lifetime last year on a SilverSea cruise ship and think nothing of spending three or four grand during my frequent shopping sprees to London and Paris. Hell, I've even got a personal mobile hairdresser to tend to my tresses after hours!

The only thing that's lacking is a man. I always told myself that when I'd reached the top of the corporate ladder, Mr Right would be waiting. I feel that time is now. So where are you Mister?

Today is January 1st. Last night I spent alone. Of course I hadn't intended spending the evening watching a depressing pre-recorded New Year special. In fact I *had* intended entertaining people in my house. But Catherine couldn't make it because she was in Ennis with friends, Angela had a cold and Grace was feeling depressed. Sandy said she didn't want to leave her mother alone for the New Year, Fiona said she had no way of getting to my house, and Karen said it'd be impossible to get a taxi home. Four people never even bothered replying.

John said he'd come along if nothing else was on, Frank wouldn't commit unless he knew who else was coming, and Simon was skiing in Switzerland. Amy was having a romantic night in with somebody she'd just met the night before, and Robert said he'd drank so much over Christmas that he was detoxing now instead of waiting for New Year's Day. They all had valid points for not turning up to my party but still, that didn't make it any easier on my dented ego. I toasted the New Year alone. Well, alone apart from my teetotal rabbit.

Originally I had thought having a party in my place was a brilliant idea. That way I reckoned, I wouldn't have to go out myself. So instead of going out partying like I usually did, I decided to let the party come to me. Only it never came. No. How very embarrassing. Obviously most people had the exact same idea as me and so we all ended up 'partying' separately. Still, there's always next year . . .

Nevertheless it was great to wake up today without a hangover. Last year I woke with a ferocious thumping in my head, after having been publicly dumped at a New Year's Eve party by Roger, my ex. The whole thing was so ridiculous. First of all, I hadn't really wanted to go to the party, but Roger insisted that we couldn't spend New Year's Eve by ourselves. Apparently he wanted to have 'fun'.

At the party I recognised a few horrible girls from my old school. I made painful small talk as we all stood in the middle of the empty dining room, decorated with silver and white angels. There was nowhere to escape. Luckily though, the place filled up fairly fast. At one stage there must have been about 150 people at the party, but unfortunately there was only one bathroom with a horrendously long queue all night. I was becoming increasingly anxious, standing with my legs crossed, listening to people waffling on about property prices. At a minute to midnight I noticed that the queue had disappeared and made a beeline for the bathroom.

At a minute past midnight I re-emerged. Roger was standing in the middle of the room, the face flying off him.

'Happy New Year,' I whispered, reaching up and giving him a kiss. 'Is everything all right?'

'Is everything all right?' he echoed in a stony voice. 'No it bloody is not *all* right. Where the hell were you?'

'What do you mean?'

'Where were you just now?'

'Me? What are you on about? I just popped into the loo for a second. I was bursting to go.'

'And so you left me standing on my own at midnight? ON MY OWN!' he fumed. 'I can't believe you deserted me. How could you humiliate me like that?'

'Oh grow up Roger, it's no big deal. I'm here now aren't I? Stop making a scene. People will laugh.'

'It's too late. People are already laughing. You made a fool of me in front of my friends. I was the only man in the room who didn't have his girlfriend by his side at midnight.'

Jesus, I couldn't believe he was making such a song and dance about the whole thing. What a child! But Roger just wouldn't let it go. He went on and on about it, making out that I had *deliberately* shown him up in public.

'Listen,' I interjected. 'All the other people here would have been so busy kissing each other at the gong of midnight that they wouldn't have even noticed. Nobody is interested in what you were doing, Roger. Get over it!'

Roger then decided to ignore me for the rest of the evening. He just wouldn't let it go. Things then went from bad to worse but came to a head when he deliberately started chatting up the host's seventeen-year-old sister, who was wearing a ridiculously short skirt, a silly lace garter around her thigh and a set of Playboy bunny ears. At that stage it was four in the morning, balloons had been burst, and all the party poppers had been well and truly popped. It was definitely time to call it a night. But as Roger said he wasn't ready, I decided to go home alone. And basically I've been more or less alone ever since. Oh well . . .

Anyway, no point dwelling on the negative, is there? Now that it's New Year's Day I am making out a set of New Year's resolutions. They will hopefully keep my life on the right track. The rules are as follows:

1) I will not allow my head to be wrecked by men.
2) I will stop hanging out in my local pub.
3) I will treat all my friends the way I'd like to be treated.
4) I will lose a stone and keep it off.
5) I will start my own clothing company.
6) I will buy a second property.
7) I will buy a dog (who doesn't mind rabbits).
8) I will visit Australia.
9) I will learn Spanish.
10) I will be engaged by the end of the year (joke).

I'm quite pleased with what I've written. Everything seems clearer once you put it down on paper. They say if you write things down it really helps you achieve your goals. So this is it. It's the start of a new me. I mean, I know I'm only joking, well *half* joking, about the tenth item on my list but to be honest, although I don't want a husband I wouldn't mind a steady boyfriend at this stage. Or a partner – isn't that the politically correct term for a lover these days?

I pin the list just over my desk so that I'll be able to see it at all times. There's no point hiding it under my bed and finding it this time next year, under three inches of dust. Then, feeling very positive about my future, I boil the kettle to make myself a cup of hot water to help cleanse my system. Health begins in the home, as they say . . . Who are *they* anyway? Those anonymous people with an answer to everything. I'd love to join their club.

The first person who rings me is my mother, reminding me to switch on the TV to watch the annual Vienna New Year's Day concert on RTE. Then my cousin Janine phones, which is quite odd, because she usually never phones.

'Hi Janine, Happy New Year to you,' I say breezily, trying to thaw the coolness that has existed between us since Christmas Day. As usual, the scabby brat put zero thought into my present. Would you believe she gave me a crumby CD for Christmas while I splashed out on a real Gucci bag for her?

'Hi Lara. Good New Year?'

'Yes, brilliant. Quiet enough though, you know. Took it pretty easy.'

'So you didn't go out at all?' She cuts straight to the point.

'No.'

Some things never change. When I was younger and used to snog gorgeous men, my friends would always be delighted for me. Janine, on the other hand used to burst my bubble by interrogating me.

'So when *exactly* did he say he was going to call?' she would bark in that awful high-pitched tone of hers. '*When* are you seeing him again? Where is he taking you? Does he drive? What kind of car? Is it his or his dad's? Didn't I hear he already had a girl-friend?' Janine is a physiotherapist. Therefore I suppose she's used to being direct. Her favourite question is obviously, 'so where does it hurt?'

'No', I admit. 'I didn't go anywhere.' *Not that you happened to ring and invite me to join yourself and Alan, of course . . .*

Alan is Janine's boyfriend. He's an okay guy in very, very small doses, but my cousin bums him up so much that it puts me and everybody else off him. We're always forced to hear what Alan thinks, what Alan does, how much Alan earns, how much his boss loves him, and how every other woman in Dublin was chasing him until Janine finally nabbed him and broke all their hearts. I've only met him once when he came to one of my parties with four cans of Heineken and drank them all himself. I remember thinking that kind of behaviour was strange for somebody who was making so much money. I mean his bonus alone this year was supposed to be 45K. But if someone was that wealthy would they honestly always arrive with one arm longer than the other and only buy their girl-friend sterling silver jewellery?

Janine runs her own physiotherapy clinic and is therefore fairly raking in the dough. Apparently when Alan discovered the size of her income, he was terribly impressed. I don't doubt it. As far as I can remember, Alan became a lot more attentive and stopped flirting with attractive nurses, models, air hostesses and beauty therapists after seeing Janine's bank balance. Nothing would ever come between them again . . .

'I've got some good news.' She speaks to me in the same way I imagine she speaks to a patient in agony with back pain.

'Really?'

'Yes. Oh my God, you'd better take a deep breath. I know you are going to be so, so thrilled for me.'

I wait for my thrill.

'I'm engaged!'

Oh *great*.

'Great!'

'Isn't it? Wait till I tell you. Alan got down on one knee and proposed in front of all his friends. It was mortifying. I didn't know whether to laugh or cry. Everybody was staring at me waiting for my answer. To be honest it was the *last* thing I expected.'

'But didn't you give Alan an ultimatum on Christmas Eve?' I frown.

'What?'

Janine has conveniently forgotten our drunken Christmas night conversation.

'You said you told Alan it was your way or the highway. Remember you said if he didn't produce a ring this year you were breaking it off?'

'Oh, well that was just a joke you know,' Janine sniffs dismissively. 'God Lara, you take everything so seriously,' she adds with a strangled laugh.

'Oh.'

'Yes, well, I'd better go now Lara. I've so many people to ring with the good news. By the way, any men yourself? Did you meet anyone over the holidays?'

'No.'

'Oh well. At least you have my wedding to look forward to.'

'Why? Will there be any eligible men at that?'

'Oh God, no. Don't be ridiculous. Everybody's married now Lara. I mean I can't think of *any* men our age who are still available,' she added with gratuitous brutality. 'But not to worry, there'll be a good few single women there I suppose.'

'Mmm. When is the wedding anyway?'

'July. In Mount Juliet. I couldn't think of a more romantic venue, could you? It will be such a magical day. And you should enjoy it too. It'll be a good chance for the girlies to catch up. You can exchange dating horror stories and stuff. What fun!'

Hmm. I can think of funnier things I'd rather be doing.

'Oh I almost forgot Lara. I've something very important to ask you?'

'What?' I say, feeling my heart drop.

'I was wondering if you would like to be my bridesmaid?'

'Um . . . sure,' I say, my heart hitting the floor. 'No problem at all.'

Fuck! Have I just said that?

'Great. That's really great Lara. In fact I would sincerely like you to be my maid of honour.'

'Yes, well . . . um, I'd be honoured. And congratulations once again Janine. It's what you always wanted.'

'Thank you. I *knew* you'd be the one person in the world who'd be delighted for me. Of course not everyone will be as delighted as yourself. Marrying Alan means that one more bachelor has been well and truly taken off the market. And both you and I know, available men in Dublin are thin on the ground.'

I take a deep breath.

'Of course,' I say mildly as if I haven't quite understood the insult. 'Well goodbye now Janine. Talk to you soon.'

I put down the phone, pick up my pen, go to the list on the wall and furiously scribble out the word 'joke' on my tenth New Year's resolution.

If Janine can get somebody to pop the question, there's hope for us all.

Chapter Two

This old dating game is a nightmare. And I blame Cinderella. No really. She got her man without even trying. None of this texting 'R U Around?' business. Barbie didn't have to search for a man either. Ken arrived in a neatly packaged box. Anyway, my point is that it's not right for girls to grow up believing in happy-ever-after. We're sold this fruitless dream from a very early age. Think about it. Even Beauty's beast turned into a hunk. Now only that could happen in a fairy tale. Personally I don't think my mother should have read me all those silly stories when I was younger. No wonder I grew up disappointed. I mean, where are all the men on white horses now? That's what I'd like to know. Where are the men willing to go to the ends of the earth to rescue us single women?

In my opinion Barbie is the reason why so many women are on diets and spend fortunes on peroxide and Botox. I'm also convinced she should shoulder the blame for breast implants, liposuction and six-inch heels.

After all, Santa left this plastic wonder woman under the tree for millions of impressionable young girls every Christmas. We grew up with her, loved her, dressed her, undressed her, brushed her hair, then tired of her, hated her and threw her away. But instead of forgetting about her, we then grew up and started spending all our money trying to look like her!

But you know, whatever about Barbie, the one I really had a problem with was Ken. Barbie had him by her side for years. He was constantly smiling, never aged, and the really annoying thing is that, like Cinderella, Barbie didn't even have to go out looking for him. No dodgy nightclubs or chat up lines for Barbie. And I'm sure, unlike me, she never had to make her own way home after a drunken night in Buck's. Nor did she ever sit in a kebab shop at four in the morning, with a thumping headache and blisters on her heels thinking 'what the hell am I doing here?'

Barbie never waited anxiously by the phone. No. She always had her man. Like an ad for plastic surgery, he was always quiet, wealthy, well dressed and handsome in a drag queen sort of way. And he was always just there. Helping out with the barbeque, carrying the shopping basket, towing the caravan, cleaning out the swimming pool or whatever. We never saw Ken out getting hammered with the lads, did we? Or glued to the World Cup. No. Never.

But Ken was just a doll. A figment of somebody's imagination. Hell, he didn't even have a line on his face! No wonder Barbie could make him do whatever she liked. But real life isn't like that and real women aren't like Barbie. Women just can't compete with her, although my cousin Janine gives her a good run for her money. Of course Janine isn't a pneumatic peroxide blonde, but she does have a tiny waist and trendy clothes. And she was always neat and tidy and looked after her dolls very well when we were kids. I, on the other hand, was smacked for beheading my Barbie. I was never again trusted with a defenceless doll.

I didn't mind too much though. Not being a huge doll fan, I preferred to immerse myself in a book anyway. But unfortunately for me I genuinely believed in fairy tale endings. Talk about being set up for failure! I'll never forget Cinderella and her bloody shoe. That was the biggest load of codswallop, as far as I'm concerned. Listen, you wouldn't believe the amount of times the heel of my shoe has come off on a night out. And as I stumble towards the taxi, trying not to break my neck, I secretly curse Cinderella whose man scoured the length of the land looking for the careless owner of her bloody glass slipper. Life's just not like that. I want an official apology from all the children's writers out there.

And don't get me started on the frog that turned into a prince. All too often I have kissed a frog that not only didn't transform into a prince the next morning, but woke up with a sore head, smelly breath, a keen erection and no money for a taxi home. Princes indeed! Leave the frogs in the pond, that's what I always say.

Recently I discussed this theory with my best friend Sandy. Sandy is also single, and it suits us to be friends because we're both fussy career women who'd like a date now and again. Of course, if we don't get a man we're not going to sit in and weep about it, but we've both agreed that it would be nice. And besides January is such a boring month to be single. It gets dark at around four and the long lonely night looms ahead. If you're going to be single, it's best to be single in the spring.

Anyway I urgently need a man for this bloody wedding party now. Much and all as I love 'the girls' we're all a bit long in the tooth to be dancing around our handbags together on the dance floor to *New York, New York* as Janine and her smugly attached friends look on with a mixture of pity and glee. Sandy agrees. She says she's going to set me up with somebody lovely. But the thing is, if Sandy knew somebody lovely, she'd be dating him herself, wouldn't she? So, although she's generously offered me a couple of her brother's friends, and some guy in work with a supposedly 'amazing' personality, I'm not getting my hopes up.

Later that evening she pops around to discuss my

wedding dilemma. I tell her my theory about men letting us down.

'It's because they just can't live up to those heroes in our childhood fairytales,' I explain emphatically.

'I completely agree,' she says knocking back the generous glass of wine I've poured. 'Like, take me for example. I always used to think I'd marry a prince.'

'Did you really?'

'Sure. But then my mother showed me a picture of Prince Charles and my dream was well and truly shattered. I guess I realised that unfortunately there weren't enough handsome princes to go around.'

I have to laugh. After a few more glasses of wine, Sandy tells me that when she was younger her favourite childhood story was *Snow White and the Seven Dwarfs*. She reckons that might be the reason why she has always dated shorter men.

'How's that?'

'Well,' she says, lighting a cigarette, 'think about it. All the men in my life were short with huge hang-ups.'

'Elaborate,' I encourage her. Oh I do love women whose dating disasters are worse than my own!

'Well there was Grumpy who refused to let me talk during the football, Greedy who ate me out of house and home, Happy who was overly fond of e tablets . . .'

'Who was that?'

'God, for the life of me I can't remember his

name. To be honest we only went on a couple of dates. Most of the time he didn't even realise I was there. He just basically needed someone to go clubbing with and I would innocently accompany him to all these raves.'

'We all make mistakes,' I agree with a sigh.

'Than there was Dopey – thick as two planks,' Sandy continues animatedly. 'And Speedy . . .'

'What was wrong with him?'

'Ah come on now, do I have to spell that one out?'

'No, I don't suppose so.'

'And how can I forget Droopy?'

'Oh no!'

'Oh *yes*.'

Really I think adults have a lot to answer for when choosing suitable reading material for their young daughters. Men never ride up on white horses shouting 'Rapunzel, Rapunzel, let down your hair'. In fact, the last man who shouted at us was on the street as we walked home from Renards nightclub. Outside Abrekabra he yelled, 'Are yiz all right girls? Fancy some of me kebab?'

Needless to say, we didn't.

Chapter Three

Today I started the fruit 'n' veg diet. It's supposed to be brilliant and you can eat all you want. As long as it's fruit and vegetables. But you're not allowed bananas or avocados for some strange reason which is a pity 'cos I really like them. Oh and you're not allowed nuts either 'cos they're supposed to be really fattening. Somebody actually told me that a packet of peanuts has as many calories as an entire meal. I nearly died when I heard that. I mean, how many times have I scoffed several bowls of peanuts in bars and then gone home thinking I hadn't eaten a thing?

Anyway, today I skipped breakfast completely, and instead of eating a buttered croissant during my coffee break as I usually do, I opted for a big juicy green apple and a bottle of fizzy water. Everything was going great but by the time my lunch break came along I thought I was going to pass out with weakness. However, instead of going out for lunch or eating a calorie-laden sandwich and chocolate, I bravely opted for a boring salad.

The lettuce was limp, the onions stank, the beet-root was bitter, the tomatoes were soggy and the corners of the cheese slices were curling and had little droplets on them. I didn't enjoy my meal one bit but I kept thinking of that bridesmaid's dress I'll have to squeeze into.

God, I'm dreading this wedding. It's going to be awful. If it was anybody else's big day I wouldn't dread it so much, but the fact that Janine will be the snide bride makes it all a bit unbearable. She rang last night with a suggestion. She says she wants to announce the engagement in three months at our joint thirtieth birthday party. I wasn't even thinking of a party this year, but there you go. Janine says the wedding isn't until the middle of the summer but she confided that she wants myself and her two skinny bridesmaid sisters to wear the same fuchsia colour. Apparently she has already gone ahead and instructed her dressmaker to make two size tens, and a size sixteen for me, even though I'm only size fourteen.

'Well just to be on the safe side,' she said inconsiderately as I felt my blood pressure practically hit the roof. 'Don't take it personally or anything. I had the same problem with Cynthia. She insisted she was size eight but I took no notice. You know what teenage girls are like. Always eating chips and chocolate and thinking they can get away with it. I went ahead and ordered a size ten for her anyway. Better safe than sorry, you know? The only size eight I could order with absolute confidence was my own wedding dress, hahaha.'

I bit my lip and said nothing. I didn't trust myself to speak.

'Yeah,' she carried on regardless, 'you know, my weight stabilised a long time ago. I guess I'm just lucky that I'm one of those people who can eat whatever they want and not put on weight. Sometimes I wish I could put a bit of meat on me. Everyone always says that I'm wasting away. I'm almost thinner than Nicole Richie!'

Listening to her babbling on and on, I made a decision. I vowed there and then that not only would I lose weight, but I'd be a svelte size ten for the wedding! Then Janine would be in a right panic. Let's see how she'll be able to sort that one out with her dressmaker!

The minute I got off the phone I rang Sandy and told her what Janine had said.

'What a bitch!'

'I know,' I agreed unhappily.

'How can you be friends with someone like that?'

'I dunno. We're not even friends. We're family. So I'm stuck with her.'

'Lara, she's your cousin, not your sister. And even if she *was* your sister you shouldn't have to take that kind of shit from her. She obviously has very little respect for you.'

'Oh, I don't think she means to insult me. Janine is just incapable of thinking of anybody but herself.

She just wants everything to be perfect for her wedding, and doesn't take other people's feelings into consideration.'

'That's the understatement of the year. She's a little bitch if you ask me. I know what I'd do if she was my cousin. I'd tell her to take her size sixteen fuchsia dress and shove it up her arse.'

I took a deep breath. There was no point getting annoyed. I decided to switch subjects and tell Sandy about my plan to lose weight.

'Good on you girl. I'll try and lose weight with you. I could do with toning down the size of my backside. Anyway it's always easier to lose weight with a friend. So they always say in slimming articles anyway.'

'What else do *they* say?' I asked, ready to jot down a few notes. I just love these clever clogs with all the answers. *They,* whoever they are, should write a book.

'To keep a diet journal.'

'Oh no, I can't be bothered with that. Imagine going around writing everything down. It's too much like hard work.'

'Okay, if you don't mind being a big fuchsia-coloured plum at Janine's wedding, that's up to you. But there's nothing for nothing. Else we'd all be slim, you know?'

She was right. I've got to be strict on myself. The thought of standing out like a ginormous piece of purple fruit is too much.

'I'm sorry Lara, I don't mean to come down on you. But I'm just being cruel to be kind.'

'I know.'

And she *was* being cruel to be kind. Janine, on the other hand, is different. She's just cruel to be cruel.

After lunch (if you could even call it that), I feel completely dissatisfied and my stomach is still grumbling. All I can do is think about food; soft freshly baked bread and full fat cream cheese. And crusty rolls with butter and coleslaw. And I keep thinking about Twixes even though I don't even particularly like them. Weird, huh?

It's Monday afternoon and it's hard to motivate the staff after their weekend. It's so hard to get them interested in anything ever, but especially when it's early in the week. The area manager sends me off on these tedious management courses twice a year to learn different methods on how to motivate staff but it's all a load of bollix really. I mean, all the staff really want to do on Mondays is discuss their mad weekends and their love lives.

It's depressing listening to them, but still I can't help cocking my ear. How come their love lives are so hectic? Where am I going wrong? I mean, am I the only female working in this shop who doesn't get a regular snog? Of course I'm not *supposed* to be listening to gossip or anything, because being an important shop manager, I have to pretend that I'm only interested in soaring sales charts and the new ground breaking collections of children's clothing. But in the canteen, as I sit alone, pretending to read *Irish Retail Today,* I want to find out if Bernie ever took Anto back after he'd shagged her sister. Or if Angie is back talking to the father of her unborn baby, what's happening in *Desperate Housewives,* and who appeared on *The Podge and Rodge* show the previous night.

The girls who work in Baby Bloomers know everything about everything, except trivial things like, say, who the vice president of America is. However they do know about important things, like their rights. Like what time their coffee break, lunch break and 'going home' time is. And you can't ask them to help out their colleagues if their colleagues happen to work in a different section. Because the Union doesn't allow it. Confused? Well, so was I when I first started working in retail. For example, Emma who works in baby wear will not under any circumstances assist Cathy in the 'teenage' section, although the two girls are not only drinking buddies, they're also godmothers to each other's children. Because of the 'rules', even if Emma is in danger of breaking her neck due to all the baby shoes on the floor, Cathy will stand by idly, twiddle her thumbs and eye the shop clock. Baffled? I don't blame you. In the canteen, the girls would rather stare into space than go back down to the shop floor and risk cutting short their lunch break.

I see them sitting in the storeroom pretending to

tidy the shelves and put odd socks back together, when in fact, they're really skulking among the babygros, chatting about their weekend. And I don't get annoyed any more when they come straight back from their lunch break and ask to go to the toilet. Or request a cigarette break straight after their toilet break. What's with all the breaks anyway? No wonder so many of the non-smokers have taken up smoking since the ban. It's a licence to doss.

Sometimes when I tell Sandy about the complicated love lives of my staff she can't believe it.

'You mean they openly discuss their sex life? In front of everyone else?'

'No problem to them. These girls have grown up reading *More!* And *Cosmopolitan*. They have no problem talking about 'positions of the month' or comparing vibrators while enjoying a cup of tea. Ann Summers is their favourite shop.'

'No way!'

'Yes, way. And when they're not discussing sex positions, they're talking about Jordan and Peter Andre, or Sienna and Jude, or the fact that they spotted Stephen Dorff on Grafton Street.'

'I would have thought that women working in a children's clothes shop . . .'

'Would talk about children? Are you mad? They talk about anything but. They talk about how *not* to have children and have lengthy debates on whether having the coil inserted is better than having your tubes tied. And when they're not talking about what a prick Simon Cowell is, they're discussing their next holidays in Gran Canaria, Ibiza, or worrying about STDs. Do you know that most of them go on at least two foreign holidays a year, sometimes three?'

'Are you serious? Jesus, I'm in the wrong job so I am. I'm definitely not doing something right anyway. Everyone thinks the long holidays are so fantastic but I can't afford to lounge around a beach for an entire summer twiddling my thumbs. Does anybody have any idea how woeful our salaries are? I spend the holidays indoors giving grinds to sulky brats in an attempt to make ends meet.'

Poor Sandy. All she ever wanted to be was a national schoolteacher. It was almost like a calling. She just longed to teach children the difference between right and wrong, and help them learn how to add, subtract and spell. When she got her first job teaching five-year-olds in a very disadvantaged area of Dublin, she was over the moon. Tired of being a teacher's assistant, she reckoned this was her chance to shine. However, now Sandy realises what a taxing vocation it is. Sometimes the kids turn up to school wearing odd socks, carrying their schoolbooks and lunch in white plastic bags. Other times they fall asleep during class and have big dark circles under their eyes from lack of sleep. Apparently, at the last annual parent teacher meeting only one parent showed up. Sandy says it's heart-breaking. But then again, she's in it for the long

haul. Say what you like about national school-
teachers, but they certainly aren't in it for the money.

But back to Baby Bloomers. I'm sure you want
to know all about the company, not. But I'll just
fill you in really quickly so it won't be too painful.
Basically we have a sale on at the moment so everything's a bit mental. The shop is full of buggies and
it's very hot and stuffy. Because I'm so thirsty I keep
drinking more and more water, which is, you know,
good. Sandy says I'm to drink eight glasses a day.
Hmm. Is that eight small or large glasses, I wonder?
And what's wrong with old Diet Coke? That tastes
much better than boring water, if you ask me.
Drinking gallons of water is such a chore. And the
problem with drinking this much, is that I'm up
and down to the toilet like a yo yo. The staff must
think I've a bladder infection.

Soon it's 6:00pm and I'm so proud of myself for
getting through the day on so few calories. Where
did I get the discipline at all? I wonder how many
calories are in a portion of beetroot? I must ask
Sandy when I get home. She knows more about
dieting than I do. She should write a diet book and
make a fortune.

But enough about calorie counting. The store is
in an absolute mess. Toys are flung around the floor.
'Everything Reduced' signs have been ripped off
shelves. There's a large round wet stain in the middle
of the carpeted floor. I don't like to think what that
could be. I must get the cleaners to sort it out.

They've just arrived and are putting on their aprons and stuff. But the cleaners clean but won't tidy up. They're unionised too, you see. The only mug here who isn't part of a union, and doesn't seem to have any rights at all, is actually me.

Right, I can't let the cleaners start hoovering while there are toys, clothes, shoes and rattlers on the floor, can I? If one of them trips and sues Baby Bloomers I'll be in big, big trouble. So I roll up my sleeves and for the next twenty minutes start tidying like a madwoman. Sweating like an overfed pig, I keep convincing myself that I must be losing loads of calories. I remember reading somewhere that an hour's gardening burns something like 600 calories. So how many calories would you lose tidying clothes? I must find out. Isn't there some kind of help line you can call?

By the time the cleaners are gone and I've locked up it's well after seven. Good. That means it'll be half past seven by the time I get home. Then I'll only have four hours to kill before bedtime. I won't be going for a post work drink this evening because a) it's January and most pubs will be dead, b) I've nobody to meet anyway and c) there's a hundred empty calories in a glass of wine.

I'll just stop off at the shop on my way home and buy a slimming magazine and calorie-free gum, and maybe a Milky Way for a treat. I think there's only 113 calories in a Milky Way. Must actually check that out, to be sure. Oh my God, I can't believe it's only day one of my diet and already I'm torturing myself. The next six months are going to be hell.

I pop into Spar on Baggot Street and for some reason (habit I suppose), I head straight for the biscuit section. I spend at least ten minutes staring at the different packets of biscuits. I'm not allowed any of them. There's absolutely no point buying a packet and pretending I'll only eat one. That's like going out on a Friday night for just one drink. Eventually I buy myself a big juicy orange, the latest Weight Watchers magazine, a low-fat yogurt and a can of Sprite Zero. I don't even buy that Milky Way I've been dreaming about. Sandy would be proud.

Back in my flat, I head straight for the sitting room, avoiding the kitchen entirely. I read my magazine and play my James Blunt CD loudly to drown out the sound of my stomach grumbling. Flicking through the magazine, I begin to feel more positive. I mean, there are photos of women in here who were obese, and now they fit into tight fitting jeans. If they can do it, so can bloody well I.

I stumble across an interesting article, which tells you to treat yourself when you're losing weight. Apparently this keeps your mind off food. They suggest reading a good book, but unfortunately I've read all the good books on my shelves, and the boring ones, which send me to sleep at the first chapter, hardly classify as a treat. They also suggest a massage but since I live on my own I've nobody to do the honours. I suppose I could give myself an old foot massage but that sounds too much like hard work. Buying a new lipstick is another suggestion. Hmm. I wonder is the late night pharmacy still open?

I read on. Aha. Now *this* is more like it. Here's an interesting tip. *Run a hot bath and fill it with delicious smelling bubble bath*. Well now, even *I* could manage that. And it'd be cheaper than buying a lipstick that I don't need. Besides, I got so much bubble bath from unimaginative relatives for Christmas last year, that even if I had a bath every night from now until the end of the year, I still wouldn't be able to get through it all.

I start peeling off my clothes. I'm half tempted to stand on the scales while waiting for the bath to fill, but refrain. After all the water and fizzy drinks I've consumed today, the scales wouldn't realistically be able to tell my real weight. I'd better leave the weigh-in until the morning.

I pour the coconut-scented oil into the bath and inhale deeply. The smell is divine. It reminds me of the suntan oil I used on my last holiday in Cyprus. Yum. Oh, I would SO love a holiday right now. Unfortunately though, the smell also reminds me of Bounty Bars. Ooooh. I would absolutely ADORE a Bounty. How many calories in a Bounty? More or less than a Mars, I wonder?

I'm about to put my toe into the bath when I

hear the doorbell ring. Jesus, who the hell could it be at this time of night? I wonder could it possibly be Shane, the drop dead gorgeous hunk who lives downstairs? Nah, he's practically married. And he's never once attempted to chat me up. It must be somebody trying to sell scratch cards. Whoever it is though, I don't feel like answering the door with only a towel for modesty.

I won't answer it. I'll just wait till they go away. Yes, that's what I'll do. I head back to the bathroom.

The bell rings again, more persistently this time. Then my mobile rings.

'Hello?' I answer tentatively.

'Lara, it's Janine. What's going on? Would you ever hurry up and press the buzzer? I'm standing outside in the rain and I'm bloody frozen with the cold.'

'Janine?' I utter, astonished. I truly am surprised. What on earth is she doing here? Something must be up. Since Janine met Alan she rarely bothers with me. She must be looking for something. Whatever it is, I'm intrigued.

Of course it wasn't always like this. No. To be honest I used to see quite a lot of Janine when we were younger. When we were both single, she was a regular visitor to my place and always stayed here on a Saturday night to save herself getting a taxi home to Dalkey. But from the moment she met Alan, I was more or less history, thrown on the scrap heap to rust and disintegrate. Janine no longer needed an escort to go to clubs with. Socially I was made redundant.

'Thank God, Alan rescued me from Leggs,' became her favourite saying once she became attached. I couldn't believe what I was hearing. I'd always been under the impression that Janine *loved* clubbing in Leggs!

When we were younger no Saturday night was ever complete without ending up drinking sickly sparkling white wine in a dark Leeson Street basement club where everyone was shit-faced, bleary-eyed and on the brink of collapsing. However Janine used to always insist on going to Leggs because all the doctors drank there. Janine had always had her eye on a medic called Garry. As had I. Unfortunately for both of us though, Garry always had his eye on somebody else. And more often than not had an impossibly long-legged model type hanging out of him.

'Yes. It's Janine, your favourite cousin. Quick, let me in. I've a surprise for you.'

'A surprise!' I'm intrigued. I do love surprises. As long as they're nice of course.

I press the buzzer, quickly put on a robe and slippers and make sure all my slimming magazines are well and truly hidden under the sofa. Sandy told me it was best if I didn't tell *anybody* about my diet. She said that people are sometimes funny when they hear you're trying to shed some weight. In fact she says, some will actively try to sabotage your efforts.

I open the door of my apartment and Janine is standing there holding a huge tin of Quality Street.

'For you!' she beams, thrusting the heavy tin into my arms.

Oh GOD!

'Janine, you shouldn't have.'

'Oh don't thank me. It's nothing. I got so many boxes of sweets for Christmas, you wouldn't even believe it. Patients are always giving me cakes and sweets. I have so many in my kitchen now I don't know what to do with them all. Alan suggested giving them to you.'

'He did?'

'Well, we couldn't think of anybody else. My sisters are constantly watching their weight, and his own sister is a model so naturally she doesn't eat.'

'She doesn't eat? You mean she doesn't eat at all?'

'Well, she eats diet cottage cheese sometimes . . . anyway I don't know what she eats,' Janine begins to look annoyed. 'It's not like I quiz her about it. That would just be rude. Why the sudden interest?' She eyes me suspiciously.

'Oh no interest. I'm just surprised that Alan thought *I* would like the sweets.'

'Well you're the only person we know who would genuinely appreciate them, you know?'

'Why?' I feel myself flush. 'I'm not the type of

person though who'd sit down and eat a whole tin myself. That's ridiculous.'

'Oh, aren't you? Don't be daft Lara Hope. Of *course* you are. I know you better than anyone. We shared a room in boarding school in case you've forgotten. I remember the way you used to hide chocolate under your pillow.'

'That was a long time ago,' I answer huffily.

'Having a healthy appetite isn't something to be ashamed of,' Janine brushes past me and plonks herself down on my sofa. 'Large people are wonderful, especially large women. There are too many sticks in the world. Society needs more jolly people.'

'Like *me*?'

Am I hearing things? Just when I think Janine cannot possibly insult me anymore she always goes and proves me wrong.

'Yeah, people who don't give a stuff about their appearance have to be admired. Women like you should be an inspiration to us all. Hey, any chance of boiling the kettle? I'm just back from my yoga class and I'm dying of the thirst.'

'Would you like a cup of tea?'

'Coffee if you don't mind. Black, no sugar.'

'Right. I won't be a minute.'

Trying not to let her get the better of me, I go into the kitchen, take a few deep breaths, make two black coffees, put a couple of fig rolls on Janine's saucer, and head back into the sitting room. She ignores the biscuits and sips her coffee contemplatively.

'So, any other news?' I ask her.

'Oh God, where do I start? Planning a wedding is such a hassle Lara. *Never* get married. It's just not worth the stress!'

'It'll all be worth it in the end though,' I say encouragingly.

'It'd better be. I want the day to be the best day of my life. And I want to look fabulous for Alan. He deserves it. After all, he could have had *any* woman in the country but he chose me to be his bride and the future mother of his children.'

I bite my lip to refrain from commenting. I then take a seat beside her but after fifteen minutes listening to Janine boast about Alan's job, his amazing salary, the incredible respect his boss has for him, not to mention all the women who failed in their desperate quest to pin him down, I'm exhausted and ready for bed. I glance at my watch, holding it right up to my face for about ten seconds. Fortunately, my very obvious hint pays off.

'Well I'd better not keep you then,' Janine stands up and stretches herself like a cat. Her velvet tracksuit bottoms are practically falling of her tiny backside. I can see her thong. It's pink, the same colour as her tracksuit. I'm impressed. If my bra matches my knickers I think I'm doing really well.

Janine hasn't even seemed to notice the packet

of unopened fig rolls on the coffee table. 'Thanks a million,' she says, 'for your company.'

'No, problem.' I smile.

Obviously she hasn't noticed that I've barely said a word.

'It's good to see you too Janine. And er, thanks for the surprise,' I add, nodding towards the tin of Quality Street.

'What surprise?'

'The . . . you know, sweets.'

Janine looks momentarily confused. 'Oh *them*? They're not your surprise you silly thing.'

'Oh.'

'Noooo. Gosh I can't believe I have completely forgotten to tell you the *real* surprise,' she sits back down again. 'You see, Alan and I have been talking about you . . .'

'So I gather,' I answer dubiously. I bloody well wish they wouldn't.

'. . . and we feel that since we have found love and happiness with each other, it's only fair that we should now help other people.'

'What do you mean?'

'Well, we have decided that we're going to play matchmakers to all the people who are dear to us.'

'Oh no.'

'Oh *yes*. We don't mind. We think it will be fun actually.'

'Fun for you maybe, but not for anyone else. I

appreciate your generous offer Janine but honestly, I neither want nor need help.'

'Oh but you do Lara. I know . . . *we* know what a jungle it is out there. Meeting strangers in pubs and clubs and everyone pretending to have a good time and acting like they're not interested in meeting someone, and . . .'

'Hang on a minute Janine,' I say crossly. 'Not everybody out there is desperately looking for a mate. Maybe yourself and Alan never set out to just have a laugh on a night out but believe me, other people do.'

Janine's thin, tanned face looks mildly offended, and for a few seconds it seems her voice has completely escaped her. Sadly though it boomerangs back.

'Of course,' she says candidly, 'people *do* sometimes go out to have fun, but at the back of their minds I always think they're looking for their soul mate, even if subconsciously.'

'Mmm.'

There's really no point even arguing about something this stupid.

'So anyway, we're inviting you to come along to this charity ball with us on Saturday night. It's going to be a very glamorous affair with lots of eligible men at it. Anyone who is anyone will be there.'

'Oh I dunno . . .' I begin doubtfully. God, there's no *way* I'm going to a black tie affair. I'm too

fat. I've nothing to wear. It's simply out of the
question.

'We won't take no for an answer,' Janine insists.

What's with all this 'we' business anyway. I know
Janine and Alan are getting married and all, but
don't they have minds of their own? Pass me the
puke bucket somebody.

'I'm sorry but . . .'

'The ticket has already been paid for.'

'How much did it cost?'

'A couple of hundred euro but don't you worry
about the cost. It's for charity. We'll look after that.
We just want you to show up and have a good
time.'

I eye her warily. Since when has my personal
enjoyment been of any concern to our Janine?

I'm beginning to smell a rat and it stinks.

'Who are you planning to set me up with?' I ask
her straight out.

'Em . . .'

'Come on Jan, don't play innocent with me.'

'Well, there's this lovely guy. Works with Alan.
Very well paid . . .'

See? I *knew* there had to be a catch. Why does
everyone always think I want to be set up?

'We think you'll like him.'

'*I* don't think I will.'

Janine gives a big dramatic sigh. 'That's always
been your problem Lara. You're too quick to judge
others. Give the guy a chance. If you don't like him,

well then you never have to see him again. You're
not signing a contract or anything.'

Hmm. She has a point. I mean, if he's *that*
awful I can always walk away and get a taxi home.
And it's true that I'll never meet anyone sitting at
home watching re-runs of Sex and the City. Oh,
what the hell, it's just a dance and a meal . . . A
MEAL!

'I suppose it's a three-course meal.'

Janine gives an annoying little laugh and makes
her way to the door. 'Well,' she grins manically, 'for
the price of the tickets it would need to be at *least*
three courses!'

'Mmm, that means I'll have to run about ten
miles to work that off.'

Janine frowns. 'Sure why would you do that?
You don't have to eat everything on your plate, you
know. Leave half of everything. That's what I always
do.'

'But what about the starving children in Africa?'
I protest.

'What about them?' Janine throws her eyes to
the ceiling. 'Do you honestly think that if you leave
food on your plate that the hotel staff will package
it up and post it to the children of Africa? Cop on
Lara. Now, there was something else I wanted to
tell you.'

Oh no! Don't tell me she has any more wise
words for me. Jesus, she's like a meddling old
woman. That's the problem with Janine. She's never

been young. Even at college she was itching to settle down. It was always as if she couldn't wait to fast forward her life to middle age.

'Oh yeah!' she says suddenly, making me start. 'You know that fortune teller we went to years ago?'

'What fortune teller?' God, I've gone to so many in my lifetime that I couldn't possibly remember them all. I only ever believe them if they tell me good things. Like that I'm going to marry somebody fabulous or make a lot of money. But most of them are crap and tell you that you're going to have to choose between a dark-haired man and a fair-haired man, that you're going to travel overseas, that you're a bit psychic yourself, that you'll probably do a course and does the letter M mean anything? I usually only go to them when I'm at the end of a relationship which is going nowhere fast. And more often than not, they tell me that I'm experiencing problems in my love life. And I leave thinking they're brilliant. But they're not brilliant. They're just second-guessing. Because let's face it, if you were completely secure with your man, would you be bothered going to see a psychic about your relationship? Huh?

'That one we went to in the caravan,' she says, exasperated.

'Oh yeah, I remember it now. Jesus, that was a frightening experience. Do you remember we were afraid to leave the car outside in case somebody burned it?'

'I don't remember that part,' says Janine dismissively, 'but I did write everything down so one day we could see if everything came true.'

I shake my head in wonder. Does Janine seriously believe in that psychic rubbish? But I have to admit I'm curious to see what she wrote down. I mean that visit must have been made over five years ago!

'Okay,' she pulls out a grubby piece of paper from her bag. 'Who will I start with? You or me?'

'You,' I say, knowing that's what she wants to hear anyway.

'Grand so. Now brace yourself Lara. You listening? Here's what she said:

'You are very close to your mum and have a relative who died that's always looking out for you. You have a great personality and have lots of friends. You did well in college and work for another woman but the two of you are clashing. I see you moving on within the year, maybe setting up your own business.'

'Go on,' I urge her, leaning forward to listen with interest. So far so good. Janine is indeed very close to her mum, to the point of irritatingly quoting her at every possible opportunity. Our grandfather died about six years ago so that must be the dead relative, and Janine left her old practice about four years ago to set up her own successful clinic. So when you think about it, the old woman was not too far off the mark, except of course, the bit about Janine's 'great personality.' She was completely wrong about that.

'*The man you are dating now is not for you. You both have very different visions for the future. You want one thing and he wants another. He will cause you a great deal of pain.*'

I nod sagely. It was no secret that Janine badly wanted to marry her ex, a successful businessman with a penchant for fast cars and sadly, even faster women. She desperately wanted to tie him down and get his signature on a joint mortgage before his twenty-eighth birthday. He wasn't having any of it however and ran off with a young psychology student who became pregnant a few weeks into the relationship. Janine had sunk into a deep depression at the time and we were all worried she wouldn't pull through. But she did, more determined than ever, and hasn't looked back since. She now guards Alan like a rottweiler, and was so determined to sink her claws into him at the start that she wouldn't even introduce him to any of her friends. We were beginning to think he was a figment of her imagination.

'*The next man you meet and fall in love with will put you on a pedestal. He'll be a professional man, very high up in a reputable company. He'll marry you and father your children. You'll have a boy and a girl and will settle in Dublin. However you will also spend some time abroad, possibly England or America, and you will always work part-time because that's the type of person you are. Your future husband has an A in his name and will be older than you.*'

'Well she was right about the initial A but Alan is only a few weeks older than you,' I point out.

'Yeah, but he's still older,' she says triumphantly. 'You see? That woman was right about everything, even about moving abroad. Remember I went to London to that course in alternative therapy?'

'God yes, I'd actually forgotten that! Wow! I must say I'm impressed. We must go back to her.'

'I dunno where she is though,' Janine admits, still scrutinising the piece of paper. 'Before my friend Ruth got engaged, she wanted me to take her to the caravan. We went out to the site in Clondalkin but the caravan was gone and a massive apartment block had been built on the old site. God knows where she is now. She might not even be alive for all we know. She was fairly old as far as I can remember.'

'Mmm. Yeah she was. Anyway tell me what she said about me. I can't remember at all.'

'Well, isn't a good thing I decided to write everything down then?' she looks at me with a glint in her eye. 'Now are you ready for this?'

'I can hardly wait,' I answer dryly.

'*You are a kind and sensitive soul . . .*' she begins in a sarcastic tone of voice.

I start to laugh. Sensitive soul. That's me alright, haha.

'*. . . you are very ambitious, yet you love people and animals.*'

Well, I *do* love animals, especially rabbits and horses.

'You've been hurt in the past . . .'

Too true. But then again, who hasn't? Janine hasn't said anything to impress me so far.

'. . . and you will get hurt again.'

Cheers for reminding me.

'You will lose a lot of weight.'

'Really?' I perk up. 'When?'

Janine ignores me. She's concentrating on the piece of paper.

'*I see hospitals.*'

'Hospitals? That's not very good, is it?'

'*And doctors. A handsome doctor in a white coat.*'

'Jesus, touch wood I don't end up with a serious illness,' I say reaching out and touching the mahogany TV table. 'I'm not a big fan of hospitals, although I wouldn't mind a George Clooney-type hunk looking after me.'

'*You will meet the man you'll marry shortly before your thirtieth birthday.*'

'Hey, that's only a few months away.'

'*But if you let this opportunity slip then you will remain single forever.*'

'That's harsh, man. I'd better get a move on then,' I say jokingly.

'I know! That's why I had to come around and show you this,' Janine says excitedly. 'I mean who knows? You could meet your future husband at this ball. It might even be Clive?'

'Who's Clive?'

'Alan's colleague.'

'Oh I see. Everything's beginning to make a little more sense now. You wouldn't be, by any chance, trying to set me up with this colleague of Alan's?'

Janine does her very best shocked expression.

'As *if* I would do that to you . . . unless, unless of course you wanted me to Lara . . .'

'. . . well I *wouldn't* want you to. It is extremely unlikely that I will end up marrying any of Alan's colleagues. Accountants aren't really my cup of tea. Give me a break Janine.'

'You should give him a chance Lara,' she counters.

'Oh for God's sake! What else does your piece of paper say?'

'That's it,' she says swiftly putting the paper back in her bag.

'Show it to me.'

'Why? You wouldn't be able to read my writing anyway. The woman spoke very fast so I had to write very fast. I'm sure there was stuff I even missed but I jotted down all the important stuff, so that's the main thing.'

'Show it to me,' I insist.

Reluctantly she fishes the shoddy piece of paper from her bag again and hands it over. I read over what Janine has just read aloud. And then I get to the bit she has conveniently left out concerning my future.

'*I see TV, lights and cameras. I see you on the small screen.*'

And with that I laugh and I'm still chuckling to myself as Janine leaves with a mountain of excuses about how busy she is, and there never being enough time in the day for anything. And as I stand at the door of the apartment block waving her good-bye, I mutter to myself, 'What an unbelievable load of old bollocks!'

Chapter Four

Tuesday.

1. Breakfast – half an orange.
2. Morning break – nothing.
3. Lunch – small tin of spaghetti hoops and one slice of bread without the crusts.
4. Snacks – I small Baby Bell cheese.
5. Evening – 2 jaffa cakes.

I am very, very pleased with myself, considering how many temptations have been thrown my way today. A girl in work had a birthday, resulting in a chocolate fudge cake being passed around, and somebody else brought a large pizza into the canteen at lunchtime. A piping hot pizza with everything on it. Its owner told me to help myself. I declined. Instead I wrapped my slice of chocolate fudge cake in tissue paper and said I'd bring it home.

Later on, I ring Sandy to tell her how little I've eaten today. We discuss the day's diet in great detail. To my dismay I find out she has eaten even less than I have. I feel fairly deflated finding out that she has consumed 211 calories less. Suddenly I think I've no reason to be clapping myself on the back. Dammit. Then we arrange to go power walking on Sandymount Strand.

As we battle against the wind on the sea front, looking out to Howth, we discuss the many, many benefits of not eating.

'All I've eaten today is a salad without any dressing at all and half a kiwi,' Sandy shouts loudly, struggling to be heard over the howling January wind, as we stride along the prom, our cheeks flushed red.

There's hardly a soul around. A few cars pull into the car park, delivering Christmas trees to be recycled. Mmm. I love the smell of Christmas trees. It just kills me to take mine down every January. Usually I wait until the very end of the month to get rid of it, even though that's supposed to be bad luck.

Apart from the odd car rocking from side to side with suspiciously steamed up windows, the area around the prom is virtually deserted. Most people are obviously sitting at home with the heat on full blast. And who could blame them? Only a crazed health freak would brave this outdoor weather. The people in Met Eireann have predicted gale force winds and most of the channel crossings have been cancelled. They've even warned people not to drive unless absolutely necessary.

Suddenly I feel really guilty about the slice of cheese and two chocolate biscuits I had earlier. I mean, if I'm supposed to be on a fruit 'n' veg diet and I can't last two days, what hope is there for me? Don't I possess *any* willpower? I start walking a bit faster. I'm worried now. This charity ball is in five days and I have to lose five whole pounds before then. That's a whole pound a day. How am I going to do that? I'm certainly not going to reach my goal by eating Jaffa Cakes, even if they are under 50 calories each!

'So have you decided what you're going to wear to the ball yet?' Sandy wants to know.

'Well, I have a blue velvet dress with lace sleeves,' I tell her. 'It hides the fat nicely, thank you very much. And it's long, which is good. It means I won't have to show off my legs. Or shave them.'

'Sounds lovely. How come I've never seen it?'

'Well, I suppose I haven't had an occasion to wear it for a while,' I admit. 'The postman hasn't exactly been laden down with invitations. I wore it to my neighbour's wedding last year, and basically I haven't had the chance to wear it since.'

'Will you wear it to Janine's wedding too?

'No. Unfortunately I'll be wearing the hideous fuchsia bridesmaid dress. But I bloody well won't be wearing a size sixteen.'

'That's the spirit. You go girl. So anyway, are you looking forward to this ball thingy?'

'No.'

'Why not?'

'Because I think there's a catch involved. There's *got* to be a catch. I mean think about it. When was the last time Janine selflessly did anything for anyone? Sure, even when she was a teenager she deliberately used to leave me out of everything. And in my twenties, she only used to call if nobody else was available to go out.

'I don't understand why she treats you like that.'

'Well, I suppose she thinks she can. She considers me family. I'll take the abuse. Our mothers are sisters; we lived next door to each other as toddlers until my uncle got a bit of cash. Then they moved to Dalkey so I got a bit of peace until we went to the same boarding school and were forced to share a bedroom for five years. There isn't even a month in our age difference.'

'So you were brought up as sisters? I didn't realise that.'

'Well, almost. Our own sisters are younger than us.'

'When you were younger did yourself and Janine have joint birthday parties and stuff?'

'Yeah, but there was always friction. Like Janine's dress always had to be nicer than mine, and she always got to invite more friends than me, and would throw an absolute tantrum if anybody gave us identical presents.'

'So are you going ahead and having this joint thirtieth now?'

'Well Janine wants a joint party. I'm not too keen on the idea. I'd rather not announce so publicly that I have officially entered my third decade but I suppose it's Janine's big chance to announce her engagement.'

'Why doesn't she just announce it in The Irish Times?'

'Oh no doubt she'll do that too. Our Janine will make sure that everybody in Ireland gets to know about her engagement.'

When I get home after our walk I'm about to collapse with exhaustion. The starvation combined with vigorous exercise has left me feeling completely drained. In fact I almost feel dizzy. I sit down in front of the TV and start flicking the remote control . . . and then I spot the Quality Street. The big shiny tin. I'd actually forgotten it was there. Sugar!

I ignore it. At first I do anyway. But it's hard. The inviting tin just begs to be opened. Maybe I should just hide it so I won't be tempted. My stomach begins to rumble. I look over at the tin again. Well, just one tiny sweet couldn't hurt now, could it?

Like a naughty child, I start peeling off the sellotape. I'll just have one, I tell myself, and then I'll sellotape the lid back on and put the tin away. Of course I will. I have willpower the same as everybody else. I didn't get to be a top retail manager without putting in the effort, did I? I open the lid and stare excitedly at the mass of colour and temptation. Oooh, which one will I choose? Let me see . . . I opt for a green triangle and slowly unwrap the foil paper. Then I sink my teeth into half the triangle and let the chocolate melt in my mouth. After that I eat the second half. Yum. If chocolate is so bad then why does it taste so damn good?

I close the lid and sellotape up the tin. There, that wasn't so bad now, was it? You see, I am disciplined. I do have self-control. I could have eaten more sweets but I had the willpower not to.

Within minutes however I've reopened the box. I stare longingly at the vast choice. If I just have one more . . . I go for the purple one this time. And then I try a strawberry cream. And then a chocolate-covered toffee. Yum. I keep going. After six Quality Streets I reckon I've done the damage. What the hell, I'll have a few more and resume the diet tomorrow.

I suddenly remember the slice of chocolate fudge cake I have wrapped in tissue paper in my bag. I fish it out and eat that too. I feel guilty now but think at this stage I may as well be hung for a sheep. Like a woman on a crazed mission, I stand up from the sofa and make my way to the kitchen. I'm heading straight for the fridge . . .

Chapter Five

If you've a bad day don't beat yourself up over it. So they say. And as *they* always seem to bloody well know everything, I decide to take their advice. The following morning I bring the tin into work and let the staff stuff their pockets. I should have done this yesterday. But not to worry, I decide I'm going to have a no calorie day today. That's right. I'm going to eat nothing at all to see if I can shrink my stomach. The charity ball is in four days. At this stage drastic measures are called for.

Sandy tells me I should go through my photo collection and take out my two fattest photos. She says I'm to put one in my wallet and carry it at all times as a reminder of what I don't want to look like. The second photo is to be pinned to my fridge where I'll see it every time I decide to pig out. Going through my photo collection is an intensely emotional experience, bringing back quite a few painful memories. There's a photo of myself and Janine, aged thirteen, standing on a rock on Spiddal beach. We're both wearing swimsuits and are approximately the same height and size. Yes, we were both tiny slips of things back then. Oh, those were the days! Then there's a picture of me in hospital with my leg in a cast. I broke it playing hockey at the age of fourteen and subsequently had to give up sport for a while. That was around the time my weight started to balloon.

There's a photo of me in a paddleboat with my ex-boyfriend John. I look at the photo with immense sadness. He was the guy who broke my heart. He looks so handsome, tanned and toned. I continue to scrutinise the snapshot. God, I'd been so obsessed with that man. John had become my life. How bloody naïve was I? On closer inspection, his light-blue eyes look pretty hard and ruthless. But maybe that's because I'm looking back in hindsight. If I'd known then what I know now . . .

In the photo my face is round and sunburnt, and I'm wearing a red bandana. I shudder at the memory. It's painful looking through those photos, even now. It would be nice to look at them and feel absolutely nothing at all. I'll never ever forget that holiday. By the end of the week, I was practically having a nervous breakdown, my self-esteem was in tatters and I genuinely thought that nobody would ever love such a crap person as Lara Hope.

I met John in my late twenties, about a week after I had signed for the mortgage of my new apartment. John had just been kicked out of his place by his ex-girlfriend. He'd also lost his job. When I met him in a club he was practically cross-eyed from too much booze. Handsome but hammered, very, very hammered. His dark hair was dishevelled and he looked like he hadn't shaved in at least three days. He was propped up at the bar and so was I. He was there out of choice. I wasn't.

Janine was with some guy as usual. I, of course, was left to amuse myself while Janine showed off on the dance floor.

John and I got talking. Nothing too unusual about that. When a pair of inebriated people are sitting at a bar counter at 3:00am, some kind of nonsensical conversation often follows. I offered him a drink. He accepted. Then after a while he started blabbering on about his ex-girlfriend. Once he started he couldn't stop. I should have taken that as a sign. A very clear sign spelling EXIT. I should have just shaken his hand at the end of the night and wished him luck. But with my self-esteem at an all time low, the truth was I was so pleased to be talking to such a handsome man that I just wanted to stretch the night out for as long as possible.

John was a couple of years younger than me but that didn't put me off. In fact I was fairly flattered that somebody so young and attractive would want to spend time with me.

However, during our conversation he kept repeating himself, his eyes were becoming glazed, and at one stage I wondered if he even knew where he was. About an hour after meeting John, it dawned on me that Janine had already left the club, without even telling me. I was stranded. All alone. Therefore when the nightclub lights were turned on, and everybody was being turfed out, it seemed only polite to invite John back to mine for a coffee.

He seemed very impressed with my apartment. Sobering up somewhat over coffee, he kept asking me whether the place was mine. I told him it was.

'It must be worth a fortune,' he murmured appreciatively.

We went to bed shortly afterwards and crashed out fully clothed. Nothing happened the first night. Everything happened the second. And by the third night, John had moved in. Nobody thought I was acting rationally, least of all me. But I didn't care. Why shouldn't I grasp love with both arms? What I did with my life was nobody else's business. After all, I'd been playing solitaire for too long. Now I was part of a couple. I was one half of 'we' instead of lonely old 'me'.

John didn't have any money to speak of, but he was looking for work as an actor/TV presenter. He didn't really care what he did as long as it was something in the media. He couldn't take an ordinary office job because he wasn't an ordinary guy. He had the looks, he kept telling me. And I agreed. As far as I was concerned he was definitely the best looking man in town. Women stared openly in the street and other men felt threatened. In a way, I suppose, I hoped that some of his attractiveness would rub off on me.

I didn't mind being the breadwinner for a while, as John went to one audition after another. Life was tough as a struggling actor, and he would complain bitterly about Ireland being a goldfish bowl, the cruel casting couch, and the fact that there weren't enough decent parts to go around.

'They're all looking for Colin Farrell, you know?' he used to moan. 'But Colin Farrell is just one person. He had to start somewhere too, didn't he? All I need is just one break. Just one miserable fucking break.'

When he wasn't wallowing in the depths of self-pity, John was the most romantic person I'd ever met. He used to leave little love poems on my pillow along with a single red rose. He would sing silly songs to me in the bath and was great at doing the small things like putting out the rubbish and feeding Twiddle, my pet rabbit.

My friend Sandy didn't particularly like him and said as much, but at the time I presumed she was just jealous and chose to ignore her. She'd come around eventually, I'd tell myself. My sister Carly called him an IT boy and said he was the male equivalent of a lady who lunched. Only all the lunches were on me.

I didn't mind. After all, his social welfare allowance didn't exactly pay for dinners at Roly's Bistro. But the way I looked at it, I was making good money, and if the tables had been reversed, I reckoned John would have done the same for me.

Oh yes. I was in denial. Big time.

I worked harder and harder and spent a lot of time travelling abroad with work, checking out new children's wear all over the world. I didn't mind John staying in my flat when I was away. After all, it was his home now too. And anyway I felt the place was more secure with John there. And my rabbit would have company.

Sometimes when I'd come home and find empty wine bottles and beer cans strewn across the living room floor, John would explain that the lads from the acting school had come along to practise their lines. When I found my tub of expensive moisturiser empty in the bathroom, John explained that he needed to look after his skin a bit more carefully, as looks were everything in acting these days.

But when I found a shocking pink lacy bra and matching thong under the cushions of my sofa, I finally had to seek the truth. John lamely tried to explain that he was auditioning for the part of the ugly sister in a Cinderella pantomime. I threw him out, just like his last girlfriend had thrown him out months earlier. Three days later he moved into another girl's apartment. Probably the owner of the cheap-looking underwear. I saw them shopping in Tescos a few weeks later. She was fat, forty-ish and was wheeling a trolley full of food. He had one hand gratefully placed on her bum.

I've moved on somewhat. The emotional scars have almost faded but I find it impossible to erase the past completely. Also I'm a hoarder. I don't like to throw out anything. I keep birthday cards, airline stubs, old postcards, certificates and photos . . .

But now it's a new year. And hopefully a new me. So I take out the photos of myself and John on that holiday in Cyprus. It's the first time I've ever been able to look at them without feeling a searing pain stab at my heart. He looks like a male model in them. I, on the other hand, look like a fan who has asked a reluctant film star if he wouldn't mind stepping into the photo. The body language is all wrong. He has his arms folded, but mine seem to be at a loss, dangling by my side. I'm wearing a one-piece swimsuit with a sarong. I had fooled myself into thinking that the sarong would hide everything. It didn't.

I get a scissors and with a newfound sense of determination I cut John's head right out of the photo. It feels liberating. I throw the cutting in the bin. It feels strange doing this. Imagine, next week John will be in a dump somewhere among eggshells, cigarette butts and discarded beer cans where he belongs. The ugly fat photo of me, I pin to the fridge. All I can see is my big flabby arms, tree trunk legs and double chin.

I hate it so much. However this photo will be a constant reminder of who I once was. A reminder of where I once was and where I never want to go again . . .

Once that is done, I feel somewhat exhilarated. I now have the strength to fish out my gruelling exercise video. With steely determination I brush off the dust from the top and stick it in the video recorder. I hate this video. It's absolute hell. The hour-long session always makes me sweat like a pig and leaves me exhausted and gasping for breath. But it's about to become my best friend. I'm going to make myself love it.

The woman in the video is Australian, with a tiny waist, firm bronzed thighs and a stomach like an ironing board. She smiles all the way through the video, without perspiring and makes silly jokes about the weather. I glare back, huffing and puffing and wondering when the hour of torture is going to end. Eventually it does and I collapse on the ground, red-faced and shattered. Why oh why am I putting myself through this?

Up and finally showered and dressed, I take myself into town. Today I walk with a cap pulled down on my head in the hope that I won't bump into anybody I know. I'm having a particularly bad hair day and don't feel like stopping to have a chat with anybody. Anyway it's a nice sunny morning and getting the bus or driving into town would only defeat the purpose of my mission. I intend wandering around the shops all day killing time. If I can keep my mind off food, I'll be doing well. The sales are on but that doesn't make much difference. I have the money but I don't want to spend it buying size sixteen clothes. Sure what would be the point? In a few weeks, when I'm nice and slim, I'd only be giving them away to charity.

After a couple hours in Arnotts, looking wistfully at Miss Sixty jeans, tight-fitting Diesel tops, but refusing to even attempt to try any of them on, I make my way up to the cinema in Parnell Street. I'm going to watch a decent flick with a large cardboard cup of Diet Coke. No popcorn, no Revels or pick 'n' mix for me. Just Diet Coke and an extra large portion of willpower.

Chapter Six

The ballroom banquet is fit for a king. My plate isn't big enough so the man in the white apron behind the counter suggests I use the entire tray to pile the food high. This is a great idea, I think. I start with bread rolls and soup. Then I have roast potatoes and mashed potato smothered in butter. I also enjoy the buttered carrots, coleslaw, different types of cheese, spaghetti strips, pizza slices, quiche slices, more fresh bread rolls, chestnut stuffing, chocolate roulade, chocolate éclairs, meringues heaped with cream, ooooh ... are you sure I can have anything I want? 'Oh yes', the waiter insists. 'You are on the fantasy island of food.'

'But won't I put on weight?'

'No dear, you have paid thousands of dollars to be in this special place. You are one of the privileged few. Everybody here is wealthy and thin. We have film stars, supermodels, singing divas . . .'

'And nobody ever gets fat?'

'No. This is Hollywood's best kept secret. The more you eat here the thinner you get.'

'*I see. How wonderful! Gosh, I should definitely come here more often. Why on earth didn't anybody ever think of this before? It's a great idea. I don't even feel full.*'

'*Well then, help yourself to another slice of sugar-coated cherry log with fresh cream followed by a saucer of petits fours.*'

'*Okay, I don't mind if I do.*'

I wake up in a sweat. Oh my God. I'm going completely mad, aren't I? Instinctively I run my hand over my stomach. It has shrunk. At least I think it has. I'm almost sure it feels flatter than yesterday morning. Thank God for that anyway . . .

Yesterday was a killer. I only had 791 calories, worked out to that horrific fitness video with that annoying, smiling woman whose make-up remains intact no matter how many press-ups she does. I walked in and out of town and jumped up and down on the spot two hundred times before going to bed.

Getting to sleep was difficult as my stomach was in pain. And I'd drunk so much bloody water that I had to keep getting out of bed to go to the loo. But the kitchen remained very much a no-go zone and that, believe me, took all the will in the world. But what the hell was that dream all about? Is that normal for dieters? Isn't there some kind of dream expert I could phone?

I'm back in work today and feel fairly disciplined, having only had a black coffee for breakfast. The funny thing is, I don't even feel very hungry now. All that stuff about your stomach shrinking when you starve must be true. At lunchtime I refuse to go anywhere near the canteen. Well, it makes sense, doesn't it? I mean if you were an ex-alcoholic, you wouldn't hang around bars, would you? And if you were a non-smoker, you wouldn't choose to stand outside the pub with smokers blowing clouds in your face. So sitting in the canteen staring at everybody eating and inhaling all the various enticing smells would be nothing short of madness. Instead I decide to go to Stephen's Green for a brisk walk.

I text one of my friends, Karen, who works in a record company just around the corner from me, hoping she's free. I haven't seen Karen in ages and she's always a good laugh. She texts back telling me she's having lunch with colleagues in Bang Café and that I'm welcome to join them. I lie about having a few errands to do first, adding that I'll join them for a cup of coffee in about twenty minutes. God, I'm trying to avoid food. There's no way I can go to a restaurant where I can't vouch for every calorie on my plate.

I do a quick round of the Green and then make my way down Baggot Street. Karen and her two friends are sitting near the window of the restaurant. Karen works in music PR, so obviously the two boys have something to do with the music industry. They look kind of funky and cool as if they could be musicians themselves. God, maybe they're even famous! Suddenly I feel a bit over-dressed in my cream suit.

Everyone looks up when I walk into the restaurant. I suppose they just look at everybody out of vague interest but I feel terribly self-conscious. It's awful being stared at. Sometimes I think it must be great to live in one of those countries where women are covered head to toe in those blanket yokes, with just a slit for the eyes. Not that I agree with them in principle or anything. After all, it must be a nightmare wearing all that black clothing in soaring temperatures in the deserts, but it would be great for fat days or bad hair days, if you know what I mean.

Karen's two colleagues are like chalk and cheddar. Dermot is small and skinny with bright red hair and an angry red spot in the middle of his eyebrows to match. Brian, on the other hand, is tall, dark, handsome and like something straight from a Mills and Boon book cover. Without the flowing locks obviously. He's wearing ripped jeans and a black t-shirt. I'm pleasantly surprised to see such a good-looking chap in this city of ours. Lately Dublin has been experiencing something of a drought when it comes to men. I wonder why Karen hasn't mentioned Brian before. She sometimes comes out man hunting with me, but why does she bother when men like Brian hang around her office?

Quickly I do a ring check. No, no rings. On either of them. Good. Not that I particularly care whether

Dermot is married. I tell the boys I work in a children's clothes shop and they both look politely interested. They tell me one of their bands has just hit the number one spot in Greece. The name of the band doesn't ring any bells but I don't let on.

'Oh yes I love their music,' I beam enthusiastically.

'But this is their first single,' explains Dermot, looking slightly confused.

'Oh yes I know,' I laugh, feeling quite foolish. 'But it's so great. I reckon all their music must be fantastic.'

'Well, their number one spot is partly thanks to us,' Karen tells me triumphantly. 'We have been breaking our bloody necks trying to get the feckers publicity and international radio airplay. Not that they're grateful or anything. But anyway now they're at number one in Greece and number four in the home charts, it'll be a bit easier to get them coverage.'

'Congratulations then. No wonder you guys look like you're having fun.'

Apparently their boss is so thrilled he let them go on an early lunch. Hence the celebrations. Hence the bottle of wine . . .

They offer me a glass. It looks so tempting but I shouldn't . . . not while I'm working . . . I should really have something to eat instead . . . or stick to black coffee . . . or . . . oh go on then . . .

A glass and a half later I'm rushing back up

Baggot Street with a big smile on my face and a skip in my step. Oh it *is* good to be alive, isn't it? The sun is shining and everybody is rushing back to their offices. God, how *bor*ing. I think it's such a shame that so many people spend their lives cooped up in offices spending most of their time working with people they can't stand. I just want to sing or something!

I can't wait to chat to Karen later and get the low-down on Brian. I mean, he *is* a bit of a hunk and hunks in Dublin are practically non-existent. I wonder if he's single. I hope Karen doesn't fancy him. If she does, she might not want me to get together with him. Mmm, better be careful what I say to her. I'd better not praise him too much. Some women can be funny when it comes to men. They might not fancy a man at all, but as soon as anybody else says they find him attractive, they suddenly start finding him irresistible too. My sister is a bit like that. If you point out anybody good-looking in a club, the next minute she's got her tongue down their throat. Carly has a bit of a reputation so I don't go out clubbing with her any more. When we were younger we used to hang around together 'cos it was handy for getting taxis home and stuff seeing as we shared the same house. And when nobody else was going out Carly was always available. But now that neither of us lives at home, we rarely socialise together. We've nothing in common any more except that we've the same mum and dad.

I don't know Karen all that well really. Not as well as I know Sandy or Janine anyway. I met her when we were both doing a PR course a few years ago. Funnily enough after the course, which was gruelling, I decided against a career in PR altogether. I reckoned it wouldn't be a lot of fun hassling obnoxious journalists for a living, or trying to get newspaper coverage for free on behalf of some angry client, so I stuck at retailing. Still, the PR course was good experience, even though the classes were held in a freezing cold room and always on a Tuesday and Thursday (oh how I missed the late night shopping!).

I learned a lot about getting publicity for my store however and Baby Bloomers even paid for the classes. Karen and I have remained friends ever since. In fact, looking back, she was the only normal girl in our class, as well as being terribly glamorous and fun. The other students had been extremely pushy, very weird or unbearably competitive. And as for the men? Well, there had only been three men in the class for a start, and two thirds of them batted for the other team. In fact, the only hetero tried to jump us all at the Christmas party and then out of sheer embarrassment perhaps, never showed up for class again.

Back in the shop I'm feeling quite light headed. The wine must have gone straight to my head. I'm smiling at all the customers and they stare back blankly. Obviously Baby Bloomers isn't your average corner shop and we get thousands through the doors here every day. Therefore a smile from a manager is treated with the utmost suspicion.

Normally screaming children get on my nerves after lunch. Today though, I look around and think how adorable they all are. There's a tubby little kid with a shock of yellow hair trying to climb into one of the playpens. Oops! I'd better not let him do that in case he falls and his folks sue us. I run over and scoop him up into my arms. He starts to yell and tries to scratch my face. Now I'm beginning to think he's not so nice after all. His mother comes rushing over and scoops him from my arms. Phew!

For a minute there, I thought I might be stuck with him. I'm serious. You wouldn't *believe* the amount of mothers and fathers who just dump their kids in the shop to play with the toys while they go off to do their grocery shopping. Like, haven't they heard of crèches?

Ok, now let's see. What am I going to do first? Some of the new spring collection has started coming in. It needs to be priced and displayed, but the sales stuff needs to be reduced further. If it doesn't shift within the next few days we'll be stuck with it for another year and the stockroom is overflowing as it is. Then again . . . oh God, my head's feeling a bit woozy now . . . I think I'll just sit down at an empty check out desk . . . God, it's very hot in here . . . very, very hot . . .

'Excuse me, do you stock baby shoes?'

'Oh yes we . . . just over there . . . behind the . . .'

The walls are closing in on me. It's just so so hot. I think I'll just . . .

Oh, *hello* handsome man. Who are you? What the hell are we doing on the floor? And why is everyone looking at us?

Yes, I *am*, believe it or not, lying on the floor with a baby blanket over me and a soft yellow duck supporting my head. And with me on the floor is a tall, exquisitely good-looking man with wavy light-brown hair, high cheekbones and startling green eyes. I rub my own eyes. I feel like I've been asleep for hours. What is going on? Did I go to sleep here on the shop floor? How completely embarrassing! What was I thinking? I know I was tired but . . . come *on*, that's no excuse. I lift my head in confusion. And then I feel the pain searing through my head. Ouch! Jesus, I feel like I've been stabbed.

'Put your head back down. You're going to be all right. Let's just put you in the recovery position now,' says George Clooney (well, his twin brother anyway). This is just like a scene in ER. Who does that guy think he is? A doctor?

'Is she okay?' asks somebody. I recognise that voice. It's Anna from the babywear department. The colour has drained from her face and she looks terrified. What on earth is the matter?

'Yeah, don't worry, I'm a doctor,' says the hunk.

A doctor? Somebody called a doctor? Well, I'll be damned. What did they go and do that for?

'Was I asleep?' I ask.

'You passed out,' the doctor says with a slight smile, touching my forehead. 'You'll be fine though.'

'Do we need to call an ambulance?' somebody else asks.

'No, I think she'll be fine. Who's in charge here anyway?'

'I am,' I say.

'Now don't you say anything else. Just relax,' the doctor says, the warm palm of his hand remaining firmly on my forehead.

This is a dream I think. It's all grand though. I'm going to wake up any minute now, go to work and laugh while I tell the staff about my dream later over coffee. It's better than the food dream anyway. What is it with all these dreams anyway? I've really got to go and see a dream doctor.

'Lara?'

Oh. It's Angela, the assistant manager. She's kneeling on the floor now beside me. A crowd has gathered. I'd wish they'd all bloody well go away. Everybody is making a big fuss over nothing. I want to wake up now. If only I wasn't so so tired. If only my head didn't hurt so much . . .

'Oh, hi Angela.'

Her face is frowning. 'I think we're losing her again.'

'Angela, give me a slap. I want to wake up. Want to . . .'

An ice pack on my forehead brings me around again.

'You're going to be fine Lara,' says Angela when I come around completely. 'Will I tell the doctor to go?'

Tell the doctor to go? Will she what? Over my dead body, I think. There's no bloody way she's telling him to go anywhere! Haven't I waited all my life to be swept off my feet by a handsome medic? Well, actually I haven't. Not really. Janine has though. Or at least she waited around until she gave up and settled for the 'I'm-so-hot-I-might-set-fire-to-myself' Alan.' But nevertheless I'm not letting this fine-looking specimen run off until I at least find something out about him. Suddenly I remember what the fortune teller said. She said something about doctors, didn't she? Maybe it's a sign?

'I'm feeling a bit weak,' I murmur. And I'm not lying. I do feel terrible. My head feels like somebody is kicking it with a football boot.

'You got a nasty bang to the back of your head, didn't you?' the doctor speaks in a low soothing voice.

'Yes, I suppose I did.'

Did I? How odd!

'But you didn't cut it though.'

'No, well, that's good. Thank God for that.'

'Can somebody get a glass of water for Lara?' the doctor asks.

How does he know my name? Does he know me? Do I know him? Why did I faint? Was it the glass of wine I had earlier? Can he smell alcohol on my breath? Does he think I'm an alcoholic?

'Oh thank you,' I sit up and slowly sip the water.

The crowd has dispersed now. It's obvious I'm not going to die or anything. How boring for them. The water is very welcome. Just what the doctor ordered. Literally.

I'm finished my glass now. What a pity. It means I've to go back to work now. So much to be done . . .

'Well thanks very much for everything,' I tell the doctor. Our eyes meet and I can't seem to be able to look away. He has such a magnificent face. Really incredible. Can't believe he's Irish. He looks Italian or something. 'I, er, really appreciate all your help.'

'Can I give you a lift home or anything?'

'A lift? Oh no, no, the shop doesn't actually close until six. Thanks very much all the same though.'

'Hey, you're not working any more today,' the doctor says firmly.

'But . . . but there's so much to be done. We're very busy . . .'

'But nothing. You're in no fit state to do anything except go to bed. Anyway I've cleared it with your boss.'

My boss? Ohmigod, don't tell me Mr Magee was

in the store today? Oh Christ, why didn't anybody tell me that the area manager was calling? He normally phones in advance when he's coming. This is a bloody disaster. Did he see me lying on the floor?

'Where is he?'

'Who?'

'My boss.'

The doctor looks worried. He helps me to my feet.

'What day is it today Lara?'

I look at him in amazement. He thinks I've got concussion, doesn't he?

'Wednesday.'

'And who is your boss?'

'You mean the area manager? His name's Mr Magee.'

Now it's the doctor's turn to look confused.

'But . . . but the woman that was here a second ago . . .?'

He looks around as if to call her back.

'Angela? Oh no, I'm *her* boss.'

'I hope I didn't insult you back there,' says Dave (that's the doctor's name!) as he drives his shiny black BMW out of the Brown Thomas car park with me sitting in the passenger seat. 'It's just that you look very young to be managing your own store.'

'Thank you.' What a *nice* man! So many men

these days don't give any compliments at all. They feel by giving you a compliment, their own status diminishes or something. So silly. Compliments are free and always gratefully accepted. If I were a man I would tell every woman I met she was great.

'So did Angela call you? Are you a GP?'

Dave laughs. 'No, I actually work in Tallaght Hospital. But today's my day off. I was just in town doing a bit of shopping. I was actually standing quite near you when you collapsed.'

'Oh.'

'So you're going to Ballsbridge then?'

'Yes, please. Are you sure you don't mind driving me home?'

'No, not at all.'

'You're not going too much out of your way, are you?'

'No, actually. We're neighbours. I live in Sandymount.'

'Oh!'

'Yes, so I'm sure we'll bump into each other again'

Well we will if you ask for my number!

Suddenly a thought strikes me. What was a guy like Dave doing in Baby Bloomers? After all, it's not a shop where single lads usually hang out, is it? There's no ring on any of his fingers, but sure that means nothing these days. Maybe he doesn't wear a ring. Or maybe he's not married but has a partner. A partner who has kids. His kids.

'Er . . . Dave?' I feel weird calling him Dave. After all, we've only just met. But I can't keep calling him 'Doctor'. And he doesn't even look like a doctor. He's not wearing a stethoscope around his neck or anything. And he's wearing jeans and trainers. No white coat.

'Yep?'

'Are you sure I'm not taking you out of your way? Did you need to pick something up in town?'

'Oh no, I can do that later. I was just looking for a baby seat. You know, for the car.'

For the *car*? I presume he means for the *baby*.

'Right,' I say, feeling a bit disappointed. So who's the lucky kid that gets him to be their daddy? And more so, who's the lucky mum? Not that it's any of my business though. I mean, it's not like I even know the guy. He's just some stranger doing me a huge favour, that's all. I have no claim on him whatsoever.

We pull up outside my apartment block, which, although I say it myself, is very impressive. There's a big pond just outside my apartment with a cute little fountain and benches around it for people to sit on. Mind you, in the four years that I've lived here, I've never actually seen anybody sit on the bench. But one of these days I intend to do just that. One day, when it's nice and sunny, I'll bring my pals around and we can spend all day laughing and chatting and drinking champagne like the cast of *Friends*.

Here we are now. I'm almost sorry, but kind of glad at the same time that I'm home from work. I'm beginning to feel a little light-headed again.

'Are you okay?'

'Oh, yes,' I raise a hand to my head. It's quite clammy. 'I'm fine. It's just that . . .'

'You're as white as a sheet.'

'Oh . . . I . . .'

'Lara?'

Mmm. I like the way he says my name. He's got a really nice voice. I just wish I didn't feel so, so . . .

'Lara? Hang on a minute. Don't move. I'll come around and open your door for you.'

He hops out of the car and runs around to the other side. He opens the passenger door and I step unsteadily onto the tarmacadam. The last of the afternoon sun is shining. But it's weak. A bit like me.

Dave grips my elbow. 'You'll be fine. Would you like me to see you in the door? Perhaps I could make you a cup of tea?'

Yeeha!

'Oh, that'd be great,' I whisper appreciatively, acting quite the helpless damsel in distress. God, this 'confused woman' thing really brings out the best in men, doesn't it? I must remember to play it more often.

Dave carries my handbag up the steps to my apartment. Aw. What an absolute gentleman. As I put the key in the door I'm so glad that I gave the place a good spring-clean yesterday. Ever since I found out that vigorous house work burns approximately 300 calories an hour, I've been on my hands and knees.

'Is this your place?' Dave takes in his surroundings appreciatively. 'It's very nice.'

'It is, isn't it?' I say delightedly. My apartment is my pride and joy, my little haven.

I just love when other people love it. God knows I worked hard enough to pay for it. In fact I'm still paying for it. And will be for the next twenty-five years. I'll be old and grey and my place will still officially belong to the bank!

'Now, you go into the sitting room,' Dave orders. 'And sit down. I'll make you a pot of tea.'

Great, I think. What a domesticated man. Making tea for strange women who faint. Not only is he kind and thoughtful, he's also caring, helps the sick get better, is charming, gives compliments, is exceptionally good-looking and . . .

'Do you take milk Lara?' Dave calls from the kitchen.

'Yes, please. There's fresh milk in the fridge.'

'Got it,' he calls cheerfully.

I put my head back on the mound of cushions, close my eyes and relax. But as I do so, I suddenly remember something. Oh Jesus! The fat photo! Oh no. Oh God no! This cannot be happening to me. It just can't.

But it is. At this very moment the man of my dreams is in my tiny kitchen. And a photo of my backside in all its cellulite glory is pinned to the front of the goddam fridge!

Chapter Seven

'Listen, I'm sure he didn't even notice,' says Sandy kindly, as she tries to calm me down. 'Anyway, the photo's not *that* bad,' she adds unconvincingly. 'Hey, who put all the food in the fridge?'

'He did,' I answer mournfully. 'And he gave me a big lecture about not eating and said that no wonder I'd made myself ill.'

'You mean to say he went to the supermarket and bought all this stuff for you?'
Sandy looks gobsmacked.

'Yeah, what a guy, eh?'

'Wow! Talk about the perfect man! Do you have his number?'

'No.'

'Does he have yours?'

'Nope.'

'God, you big eejit you. Why not?'

'Um . . . I dunno. He didn't ask for mine. He's got kids 'n' stuff so there you go. He's probably married. And if he is I certainly don't need that kind of baggage.'

'Did you ask him?'

'Whether he was married? No, of course not. What do you think I am? We weren't on a date, you know.'

Sandy shrugs resolutely. 'So now you'll be left wondering the rest of your life.'

'Well so be it. There's nothing I can do about it now.'

She gives a big exaggerated sigh and shakes her head.

'Another one bites the dust,' she sniffs.

'That's it,' I say, wishing she'd just drop it. I'm getting a bit irritated now because she is undeniably making a point.

'So, are you looking forward to going to the ball?'

'What do you think? You know damn well I'm not.'

'Well you could have brought Doctor Love along. Now *that* would have been fun.'

'Don't call him that.'

'Ok, then you could have brought *Dave* along,' she teases.

But I'm in no mood for jokes. Actually I am still a bit sick with myself over the fact that Dave saw the photo of me looking my worst ever. The suit that I was wearing today was extremely expensive and well-cut, but the frightening photo on my fridge leaves nothing to the imagination. Sandy's to blame for it all. It was her suggestion to post a fat photo to the fridge. Because of her brilliant suggestion, I'll never ever hear from him again.

'Listen he probably didn't even notice it,' she repeats.

'You don't think he noticed? He's not blind you know. And he didn't ask *Thunder Thighs* here for her phone number now, did he?' I say bluntly. 'And don't go on about there being more fish in the sea because I'll never again meet such a good-looking fish. All I ever seem to meet these days is the pond life.'

'Right. Come on.'

'Come on what?'

'Put on your coat. We're going out,' says Sandy.

'Out where?'

'Out anywhere. I don't care. I will not let you sit here and wallow over some guy you've just met. You look like you've just been served divorce papers. Come on, you only met him for like, five minutes. And besides, I'll bet you'll see him again. He knows where you live and he knows where you work. You also know where he works. Perfect.'

'Perfect? Why? Do you expect me to stalk him at work? Have you ever been out to Tallaght hospital? It's flipping enormous. That place is like a small town. There's no way I'm going out there hoping to bump into him. Anyway, he'd think I was mental if he spotted me!'

'No he wouldn't. Anyway, he lives around the corner from you for God's sake, not in flipping Germany. What are the chances of you two bumping into each other? Excellent, if you ask me.

He probably does his shopping in Tesco in the Merrion Centre.'

'No Sandy, the chances are not excellent. I'm just going to try and forget about him. I'll probably never see him again.'

'God, it's not like you to be so pessimistic . . . hey!' she suddenly yells, causing me to flinch.

'Hey, what? What are you shouting for?'

'I just remembered something. Do you remember Janine said something about you meeting a doctor? Didn't that old fortune teller in the caravan say something about a doctor?'

'Ah, you don't believe that old crap though, do you? I mean everybody goes to the doctor at some stage in their lives. So what? The same woman also said I was going to be on TV, didn't she? I doubt Ryan Tubridy is losing too much sleep over that prediction.'

Sandy laughs. Mind you, she might have a point about Dave you know. I mean, maybe he was too shy to ask for my number. Or maybe he was afraid of taking advantage of me when I was clearly so vulnerable. It's unlikely . . . but possible. Maybe, due to some miraculous reason, he didn't notice the 'fat' photo on the fridge, or thought the photo was of someone else. It doesn't really look like me. Not anymore. I've dropped a good few pounds since then and my face was very red on that particular day, due to the blistering Cyprus sun.

'So where will we go then?' I stand up and stretch

my arms over my head, suddenly feeling more positive and energised. Dave made me take some kind of sugary energy drink before he left. He actually stood over me while I forced it down my throat. It had tasted absolutely vile and all the time I was panicking, wondering how many calories were in the damn concoction. I couldn't exactly ask Dave, as he'd already given me somewhat of a bollicking about having nothing stocked in my fridge. Apart from the milk, you see, all I had were two bottles of wine, a can of Guinness, and a tub of eye cream. Yes eye-cream. I can explain. I once read that you should put eye cream in the fridge to keep it cool. It helps prevent wrinkles apparently. But, as you can imagine, Dave was not overly impressed by my explanation. When he came back from the shops, he made me promise to eat a banana sandwich within the hour. I promised I would (with my fingers firmly crossed behind my back). Banana sandwich indeed.

'Maybe we shouldn't go into town, if you're supposed to be off sick,' Sandy advises. You don't want anyone from work to spot you. How about we just go to the local pub?'

'No way,' I shake my head adamantly. 'My New Year's resolution is not to put a foot in there until next Christmas at the very least.'

'How about The Queen's in Dalkey then?'

'Um, yeah, fine. I like that pub actually. It's not bad for talent spotting. And you can sit outside.'

'Not really in January though.'

'No, I suppose not. You're right.'

We take the lower road out to Dalkey. Sandy drives slowly while I look wistfully out the window towards the sea. Howth is barely visible, and the waves are particularly high this evening as the tide is fully in. I'd say we're in for more storms judging by the blackness of the clouds. Hopefully not though. The wind has been so bad the past couple of nights I haven't been able to sleep properly for fear of the roof taking off.

Soon we're in The Queen's. It's a gorgeous, cosy but spacious pub with a really nice atmosphere and wooden floors. U2 sometimes come in here, I believe, but there's no sign of them today. Bono and the gang must be off on tour or something. There aren't many people here at all actually, but it's early I suppose. Most people are still at work, watching the small handle of the clock inch slowly towards the number five.

Sandy orders a glass of dry white wine and I have a tomato juice (no calories and lots of vitamin C). Although I would seriously love an alcoholic drink, there's no way I would risk it after this afternoon's fiasco. Could you imagine if I fainted in here too?

'So any news yourself?' I ask Sandy, suddenly realising that I've spent the last two hours talking solidly about myself.

'Oh dear,' Sandy sighs, 'well this week has been tough to say the least. 'The roll call, for a start.'

'The roll call?'

'Yeah, the attendance sheet. Every morning I call out the children's names and they have to answer "present" if they're there.'

'I see.'

I wait for her to continue.

'Sounds very uncomplicated, doesn't it? Well not this week. I called Jimmy Murphy's name out three times and the little fella wouldn't answer even though he was sitting right under my nose.'

'What was wrong?'

'That's what I asked him. He said his mum told him he was to be called Jim O'Toole from now on. O'Toole is the name of his mum's new boyfriend. Apparently he moved into their flat over the Christmas holidays.'

'Oh the poor little thing. God that's terrible.'

'Yeah, these poor kids don't really have a chance with their mothers swapping father figures on a regular basis. It's an ongoing problem.'

'No wonder they're so confused.'

'I know,' says Sandy with a sigh. 'Teaching youngsters is a tough game and getting tougher all the time. You need to be so strong.'

'But what can you do about it?'

'Not a damn thing, I'm afraid. My hands are completely tied.'

The phone rings suddenly.

'I'll just take this,' I say apologetically. 'Excuse me a sec.'

'Hello? Oh hi Karen, how are you? No, no I'm fine, thanks for asking.'

'You looked a little off when leaving the restaurant,' she says, sounding concerned.

'I did? Well, would you believe, I had a blackout when I got back to work. I collapsed and a gorgeous doctor came to my rescue, resuscitated me and drove me home in his BMW convertible. No, I'm not joking, I swear to God. Yes, so I suppose my faith in humanity has been restored. He was like a knight in shining armour. Well hopefully I will see him again. Say a little prayer for me.'

'Listen, considering you were swept off your feet once already today you might not have much interest in my little proposal.'

'Which is?' I ask with interest.

'Well one of the lads today thought you were absolutely gorgeous and was wondering could he have your number?'

He did? He was? God, well, this is great news. I'm gobsmacked. Karen's colleague was a complete ride. Now, what are the chances of two such amazing looking guys taking a shine to me in the same afternoon? Things really do seem to be looking up. About time too! My weight loss plan is slowly but surely beginning to yield results.

'Oh, well I'm extremely flattered. At a loss for words in fact,' I laugh.

'I gave him your number. I hope you don't mind. He says he'd like to call you over the next couple of days and ask you out for dinner or something?'

Dinner? Oh God, I'm still on a bloody diet!

'Well coffee might be better,' I suggest. 'Dinner might be a bit too formal for a first date if you know what I mean.'

'Yeah, I do know what I mean. Well when he calls, suggest coffee instead. Or a drink. Just be sure to let me know how it all goes with Dermot, won't you? Text me as soon as he calls, right?'

'I will,' I say excitedly. 'Talk to you soon Karen.'

I press the off button. Phew! Now let me digest this great piece of news. God it's almost too much to take in. Two hunks within the space of two hours? Sure you couldn't *make* it up. Hang on though . . . hang on . . .

Panicking somewhat I phone Karen back.

'Karen?'

'Yeah?'

'Did you say *Dermot*?'

'I did.'

'Which one was Dermot? Not the ginger . . .'

'The one with the strawberry-blonde hair. He's a lovely chap. He said he felt a certain chemistry between you at Bang's restaurant.'

'He did?'

Oh God!

Chapter Eight

Okay, so the blue dress isn't *too* bad. And it kind of suits my blue mood. But I don't have a coat to match, which is annoying. It's frigging freezing out there. I can already see frost building up on the bonnets of the cars parked outside. I wonder what I should do. I mean, I can't exactly wear my black waterproof bomber jacket with a blue crushed velvet dress, can I? I take a critical look at myself in the full-length mirror. I think my thighs might have shrunk. Seriously. They *definitely* don't look as chunky as they did a few days ago. And although I know I've only lost two miserable pounds this week, I've been walking a lot so I feel fitter. And the dress has long sleeves to keep my upper arms well hidden. Very important that.

I twist around to try and get a better look at my arse, convincing myself that maybe the night won't turn out to be so bad after all. Perhaps Janine and Alan *are* in fact inviting me along out of kindness. People must be given the benefit of the doubt. I've got to stop being constantly suspicious.

A bottle of champagne is chilling in the fridge. Janine and Alan were supposed to be here at seven thirty and I was going to offer them a glass each. But it's now a quarter to eight. I may as well have a glass myself while I'm waiting around. I need something to settle my nerves anyway. It's been so long since I've gone to a formal event.

I attend the annual retail awards every year, which are dull beyond belief. But that's just a work related torturous event that nobody ever enjoys. If I could possibly get out of going every year I would. Nights like those aren't supposed to be fun.

Formal events in general are a bit naff. They remind me of my debs when I had to invite my second cousin and make him swear he wasn't related to me. It's just the whole black tie thing that gets to me. It brings back such awful memories. If I were a man, I suppose it'd be different. I'd just stick on my dickie bow and be off. But as a woman these things are a flipping nightmare. Surrounded by all these skinny things in clingy sparkling dresses competing with each other. And for some reason there are *always* more women than men at charity balls too. Like at the school discos years ago when the dance floors were full of girls dancing around their handbags.

Mmm. This champagne is lovely. I take another sip. Yes, it's going down an absolute treat. I got this particular bottle as part of a Christmas hamper from Baby Bloomers head office in the UK. So generous of them . . . I dim the lights, turn on a bit of classical music and relax on the sofa with my crystal flute. I have decided not to let myself get worked up about Janine and Alan being late. They'll arrive when they arrive. No need to panic.

The sitting room looks great with the lights turned low. I could quite happily stay here all night and not go out at all. The reason the place looks so good is because I've been hoovering, polishing and dusting all evening. Yes. I'll be damned if I'll give that Alan any more chances to pass remarks about me. He obviously thinks I'm some sort of loser who spends all my free time stuffing myself with sweets and chocolates. The cheek of him! He probably even thinks I throw the empty wrappers on the floor when I'm finished too.

Okay, right, it's now five minutes to eight and there's still no sign of them. I'm beginning to feel a bit edgy now. I don't want to ring Janine's mobile all the same, in case she thinks I'm panicking. I've finished my glass of champagne, but it has only left me wanting more. If I could possibly have another glass, it won't do any harm, will it? And there will still be enough for Janine and Alan when they arrive.

At seven minutes past eight I drain the last drop from glass number two. As I do so the doorbell goes. About bloody time . . .

I stand up and press the buzzer to let in the tiresome two.

'We're not coming in,' I hear Janine's voice telling

me impatiently. 'We don't have time. Put your coat on quickly Lara. We're waiting outside in the car with the engine running.'

God, that is so typical of Janine. She never considers anybody but herself. I can't bear to be rushed. I take a look out the window and to my dismay I notice that it has just started to rain. Oh no! My hair always goes horribly frizzy when it gets wet and I've just spent a fortune getting it blow-dried!

I look wistfully at the bottle of champagne just begging to be drunk. By the time I get back later on tonight all the fizz will have gone out of it. What a waste! Quickly I pick up the bottle and take another few gulps. Sure what harm can it do? Anyway, I've already had a low-fat vanilla yoghurt to line my stomach so I should be all right. I stick on my bomber jacket (who cares if it clashes with my dress?) and grab my umbrella.

As I slip into the back seat of Alan's Saab, I catch him looking impatiently at his watch. Jesus, you'd swear it was *my* fault we're running late!

'Hi guys,' I say cheerfully. 'How are you both? Janine, you look stunning as always.'

'Thanks,' she mutters and doesn't return the compliment.

We then sit in silence until we get to Jury's. Although arriving at the hotel in record time, we seem to spend at least ten minutes looking for a car park space close to the front entrance. Eventually we find one but it's nowhere near the front door of the hotel.

At last we make our entrance. As soon as we arrive into the lobby, I feel we're being scrutinised by everybody else. It's like a bloody fashion show in here! I've left my bomber jacket in the cloak-room at Janine's insistence and now I feel almost naked and certainly very awkward.

Before long we're joined by Alan's friends and we all make chit chat about nothing, before somebody starts ringing a loud bell and telling us in a very bois-terous manner to make our way into the ballroom.

At the table, there seems to be some confusion about seating arrangements. Our table is for ten, which is nice and intimate I think at first. The good thing about round tables is that you get to talk to everybody, whereas at those long tables you never get to mingle with people sitting at the other end.

I take a good look around at the others at our table. There are four couples as well as myself, and a very tall, thin man with wiry dark hair and glasses. That's Clive. Obviously. Janine tells me I'm to sit beside him. I take my seat and immediately Janine sits on my right. Clive is on my left.

'But surely I should sit beside Alan?' I suggest.

'Why?'

'Well it's usually boy/girl/boy/girl, isn't it?'

'Oh don't be making a big fuss Lara,' Janine bris-tles. 'Anyway, Alan says I should sit beside you 'cos he can never think of anything to say to you.'

Right. Insult number one of the evening. That didn't take long. I can tell the night is going to drag.

Clive gives my hand a cold limp shake. He has the smallest, darkest eyes I have ever seen, and they peer in a most intrusive questioning way.

'What's your name?' he asks me.

'Lara.'

'Right. And you're Janine's cousin?'

'Yes.'

'I see.'

'And you're Clive, aren't you?'

'Yes.'

'Nice to meet you Clive. Where are you from?' I make a forced stab at continuing on the conversation.

'Leitrim.'

'Oh, that's nice.'

''Tis, I suppose.'

We sit there awkwardly until I reach for the little menu card on the table and pretend to be absolutely fascinated with it. Clive does the same. I feel all eyes at the table on us. We are obviously being set up. The only two singletons. What fun, not.

Like myself, Clive doesn't know anybody else at the table. But he looks like he couldn't care less. He makes no effort to integrate.

'Where did you get your dress Janine?' one girl asks in a most affected southside accent.

'It's Christian Dior,' she beams. 'I had it flown in from London especially.'

Everybody looks suitably impressed. Except Clive of course. He looks like he wouldn't notice if Janine had worn a bikini.

'So how are you two getting along?' Janine whispers in my ear half way through the melon starter.

'Fine.'

'He's *very* nice, isn't he?' she intones in a ridiculously false voice.

'Well, he's quiet. Very quiet.'

'Maybe he's shy. Alan says he keeps his cards very close to his chest.'

'Mmm.'

This is all too weird. I'm still trying to figure out why I'm even here. This is couple hell as far as I'm concerned. Everybody in the entire room seems to be paired off, except for one table full of cackling girls behind us. They're knocking back wine at an alarming rate, desperation written all over their made-up faces. I hate to think I'm part of their club. Suddenly it's not so much fun being single anymore.

'Apparently he's first into the office in the morning and last to leave at night,' Janine says out of the side of her painted-red mouth. 'They all reckon he's got his eye on the boss's job. In fact, Alan says one of these days he's going to bring his sleeping bag into the office to save himself the bother of going home at all, hahaha.'

I fail to see the hilarity in her little joke. Nor do I feel the slightest bit comfortable whispering about somebody when they are sitting right beside me and clearly within earshot. It's so rude.

After our plates are cleared, Janine wants to sneak out to the car park for a cigarette without Alan knowing. Alan hates her smoking so she has promised to give up completely before the wedding. She pretends to go to the Ladies, and the next minute we're standing outside shivering with the cold as the relentless wind prevents Janine from lighting a match.

'So,' she says, through chattering teeth after she finally manages to light up. 'What do you think?'

'Think? Think about what?'

'Clive, silly.'

'Well I haven't really had a chance to talk to him so far as *you've* been so busy chewing my ear all night.'

'He's very attractive,' Janine says. 'If I wasn't attached to Alan, I'd definitely go for him myself.'

'No you wouldn't.'

'I would too.'

'Don't give me that shit. Cut it out Janine. Something's going on here and you'd better tell me what.'

'Nothing's going on,' Janine puffs obstinately on her cigarette.

'Seriously, you'd better come clean. I mean it. What's going on? Why was I brought here tonight?'

'Well . . .'

'Go on.'

Janine refuses to meet my eye, 'Well . . .'

'One more piddly excuse and I'm gone.'

'Okay, it was all Alan's idea. He thought Clive and yourself would make a great couple. And I said I'd try and help you get together. I was only trying to help out.'

'Were you now?' I answer frostily. 'Tell me the truth Janine. Why on earth is Clive's love life any concern of yours and Alan's? It doesn't add up. Haven't you got other things to talk about?'

'I told you before . . .'

'Don't feed me any more rubbish about yourself and Alan wanting to spread the love. Be honest.'

Janine's lip quivers and suddenly she looks ready to cry. But I'm not backing down now. I'm determined to get to the bottom of this if it kills me.

'Listen Janine, if you don't tell me what's going on, like I said, I'm going straight over to the taxi rank there and going home,' I threaten.

'Lara, please *don't* do that! There's no need to be so dramatic.'

'So tell me then.'

'Fine.'

Janine stares at the ground looking like a kid who's just been caught with her hand in the cookie jar.

'Right,' she repeats herself, 'but promise you won't tell Alan I told you anything?'

'Promise.'

'Well Clive, you see, is up from the country and

he has no life except for his job. I mean, he doesn't play golf, he doesn't drink, he doesn't seem to have any hobbies and basically all he does is sit in front of his computer working.'

'So? It that's what floats his boat . . .'

'But you don't *understand* Lara. All he does is show up the rest of the lads in work. If Alan leaves the office before 7:00pm these days, it looks really bad because Clive will always sit there until at least 10 or 11pm.'

'Well they should let Clive do whatever he wants. Just 'cos he's sitting at his desk doesn't mean he's working hard, you know. Sure he might be playing online poker for all anybody knows.'

'*I* know that. And *Alan* knows that. But Mr Welsh, their boss, seems to think that Clive is the greatest invention since grated cheese. That fellow has only been in the office a wet weekend and already rumour has it that he's being tipped for the next big promotion. Alan, on the other hand, has been working for the company *way* longer. He *deserves* the promotion. We *need* the money for our wedding Lara.'

I'm gobsmacked. I really am. What is this all in aid of? The 'Save Janine and Alan's marriage' fund? I can't believe what I'm hearing! That pair are so selfish. They both have designer clothes, stay in five-star hotels, eat out in expensive restaurants at least twice a week and have a house worth almost three times as much as my little apartment! They conveniently ignore me for most of the year and now they want me to help them out by dating the office geek?

'Really Janine, I don't see what any of this has to do with me. Do you expect *me* to ask Clive not to go for the promotion? Or should I tell him that he needs to start leaving work early? Perhaps I should suggest that he takes up a sport? Come off it Janine. I don't even know the guy.'

'But if he had a girlfriend . . .' Janine continues in a whiny voice, '. . . if he was involved with someone, then he wouldn't *want* to spend so much time in the office.'

Aha. Now this is all beginning to make sense. My scheming cousin and her fiancé have obviously put a lot of thought into this hair-brained idea. Of *course* they don't want anybody to fall in love with anybody else. They just want a girl to distract Alan's main office rival so that he doesn't get promoted. Did you ever hear the likes of it?

'But why me?' I ask feeling hurt now.

'Well, because you're the only single girl we know,' Janine answers bluntly, taking a long drag of her cigarette. 'So,' she adds in a much softer tone of voice, 'do you think . . . do you think you might . . .?'

'No,' I snap. 'The answer is definitely no. I am not attracted to him, and as far as I'm aware the feeling is definitely mutual. In fact I think I would get more excited having a conversation with the parking meter over there.'

'Right, if that's the way you feel.'

'Yes. It *is* how I feel.'

Janine is visibly furious. We head back into the hotel, walking in stony silence towards the ball-room. As we do so, I spot a couple of guys chatting by the bar area. One of them is extraordinarily familiar. He's also very handsome, with short sandy hair and a twinkle in his eye. He swings around as we walk past. Janine storms ahead but somehow I catch his eye and he gives me a wink.

'Jesus!' I exclaim as I catch up with Janine and pinch her arm with unnecessary force.

'What?'

'Did you see that guy back there?'

'No, why?'

'That was Garry Clarke.'

'Garry Clarke?' she whispers back, the colour visibly draining from her face. 'Where?'

'Back there at the bar. I think he must have recognised us.'

'Oh my God. Are you sure?'

'Well it definitely looked like him.'

'I don't believe it. I haven't seen Garry since Leggs all those years ago. Is he as handsome as ever?'

'More handsome. He still has all his hair and he isn't sporting a beer belly like most Irish men his age.'

'Damn, I almost wish he was. It'd make me feel a lot better. Do you think he definitely saw us?'

'Without a doubt.'

'Do you think he remembers us?' she pats her hair self-consciously. 'Do I look okay?'

'Would you get away out of that?' I laugh. 'You're practically married missus. *I'm* the one who should be getting excited about seeing him again.'

'But you can't be flirting with him.'

'Why not?'

'Because that wouldn't be fair Lara. *I* was the one who always had a crush on him. You know that.'

I can't figure out whether Janine is being serious or not. She certainly looks like she is.

'Come on,' I take her arm. 'The others will be wondering where we are.'

And as I lead her into the ballroom, I make a mental note to return to the bar as quickly as possible.

Chapter Nine

We've been gone so long we've managed to miss our main course, which you know, is quite good. Alan however, looks positively livid as he spots Janine and myself making our way to the table.

'They've taken away your plates,' he fumes as we sit down. I can almost see smoke bellowing from his ears.

'Not to worry,' Janine coos, and leans over to give him a kiss.

He suddenly recoils in horror. 'Have you been smoking?'

Now it's Janine's turn to look mortified.

'Lara went out for one and I just took a quick puff of her cigarette,' she lies blatantly.

I decide not to get involved and turn my attentions to Clive.

'Did you have the salmon or the beef?' I ask, trying to drum up some sort of conversation.

'The beef.'

'Oh. Oh, right.'

Clive then takes off his glasses and starts polishing

them carefully with his napkin. I genuinely cannot think of anything else to say so I give up. Maybe Alan was right. Maybe I'm not such a good conversationalist after all. Words have eluded me. I can hardly discuss what I ate because I didn't have anything to eat at all. Not that I'm too worried. It means I can have a little dessert now without feeling guilty.

The tension between Janine and Alan is mounting. Sitting beside them and listening to their bickering just makes me glad to be single. A would-be bride is supposed to glow, but all Janine does is glower. Maybe I shouldn't have told her about Garry being here. But she probably would have bumped into him later so it's best that she won't be caught off guard.

I can't believe how cute he still is. I mean I know so many men who were gorgeous in their teens and twenties and now look like my dad on a very bad day. Personally I think it'd be good to meet your future husband when he's in his thirties. If he still has all his hair then, the chances are he'll keep it. You can't tell if a guy in his early twenties will get to hang on to his hair or not. It's way too much of a risk.

Now that I think about it, I do hope Janine wasn't serious when she told me to stay away from Garry. That wouldn't really be fair, would it? After all, she's getting married now so she has no right to tell me to stay away from other men just because she *used* to fancy them.

Clive has finally finished wiping his glasses with his napkin. I'm about to make one last attempt to start up a conversation with him again when he puts his glasses back on his face and proceeds to blow his nose with the same napkin. Right, I've had enough. That's it. Finito. I'm off to the bar.

I wander out towards the bar area trying to see where Garry is. Then spotting him out of the corner of my eye chatting to a group of guys, I deliberately go to the other end of the counter. There are so many 'penguins' at the bar that I don't know how I'm going to push my way in to be served. I'm beginning to feel a bit uncomfortable. I'm sure I can feel Garry staring. I don't like to look but instinct tells me he's looking over in my direction. I wonder if he recognises me. Maybe he just thinks I'm vaguely familiar. After all, you don't necessarily remember all the people you used to meet in Leeson Street clubs at four in the morning!

I'm beginning to get annoyed now. The barman has served at least four other people since I've been standing here and hasn't even seemed to notice little old me. Suddenly I hear a voice in my ear. 'What are you having?'

Garry is at my side. Oh my God, I can't believe it! I try to play it cool but my smile naturally breaks into a grin. I'm so delighted with myself.

'Oh thank you,' I say gratefully. 'I'll have a red wine please.'

Garry is served immediately.

'Janine, isn't it?'

'No, Lara is my name. I can't believe you can't remember,' I say jokingly.

'Of course. Janine is your little sister, isn't she?'

'Cousin. And we're the same age.'

'Didn't I see her earlier on with you?'

'You must have.'

'Well, you both look stunning tonight.'

'Thanks.'

Huh! A double compliment only ever has half the effect.

'So, I know this is a very annoying question but what are you up to now?'

'I work in Baby Bloomers.'

He's obviously never heard of it. He raises an eyebrow.

'It's a baby clothes shop. Um . . . I'm the manager.'

'Oh really?'

'Yes.'

We stand there awkwardly. I'm desperately trying to think of something else to say. Should I tell him about our latest range of prams? I think not.

He looks down at my left hand.

'You not married?'

I shake my head.

'Why not?'

'Nobody ever asked.'

'Haha. Good answer,' he laughs.

'*Janine* is engaged though,' I'm more than happy to inform him.

I search his face quickly for a reaction. But I get none. I can't read him at all.

'Oh, so who's the lucky man?' he says casually.

'His name is Alan. They've been going out for a couple of years now.'

'I meant you,' he says, looking deep into my eyes, as I feel myself flush. 'Who are you here with tonight?'

I'm completely taken by surprise. My cheeks are burning. It's probably the red wine. At least I *hope* it's the red wine. In the distance I see Clive. He's wandering around and looks like he's looking for someone. Oh Jesus, he's probably *is* looking for someone. He's probably looking for me! Okay, he's spotted me now. Shit. He's making a beeline in my direction.

'Would you ever excuse me a minute?' I tell Garry hurriedly. 'I er, seem to have something in my eye.'

I rush off in the direction of the Ladies. My legs can't get me in there fast enough. I know I'm panicking but I really don't want Clive annoying me any more tonight, or worse, trying to make a claim on me.

God this is desperate. I'll never forgive Janine for forcing that awful fellow on me. Does she honestly think I'm that stuck for a man? My head swimming with doubt, I take a sharp left at the Ladies and collide with a very tall raven-haired girl in a black satin dress. The contents of my wine glass spill all down my front.

I apologise profusely, even though it's not my fault. She gives this great big dramatic sigh and then storms off. I look in the mirror at my ruined dress. Fuck. The night is so over for me now. There's no way I can ignore this stain. I look like a stabbing victim. Resolutely, I sit in front of the Ladies mirror for what seems like an age. God what a really shit end to an even shittier night. I need to go out now and get my coat. However I don't really want to have to leave with this big stain all over my dress. Jesus, I'm so stressed. I wish I could have a fag now. Damn the bloody smoking ban anyway.

'Oh my God, you poor poor thing!'

A very slim girl with poker straight blonde hair, interrupts my internal monologue. She has perfect bone structure and a fabulous fake tan. She takes a seat beside me in front of the mirror and stares at my chest with the big red stain on it. The sympathetic look on her face makes me want to burst into tears. I look like a mess, especially beside her. My hair has gone completely frizzy, thanks to having stood out in the rain earlier with Janine, and my eyes are slightly bloodshot. The red wine seems to have blackened my teeth also. Yuck. Maybe I've drunk too much. I mean, I don't feel that drunk but I wouldn't mind going home now. I'm beginning to feel a bit depressed.

'Yeah, it's a bummer, isn't it?' I acknowledge the pretty girl's sympathy. I kind of wish she'd just go away though and leave me alone.

'Can I do anything to help?'

'No,' I mutter vaguely. 'Thanks anyway though.'

'Are you sure?'

'Well . . .'

'Go on. If there's anything I can do to help.'

Who is this? My guardian angel?

'Em, well I wonder . . . I *do* need to get my coat.'

'Have you got your cloakroom ticket with you? I can get it, no problem.'

'Are you sure?' I ask gratefully rooting in my bag.

'Of course. It's the least I can do.'

'Thanks so much.'

'If you don't want to go home I could lend you my wrap? Then you probably wouldn't notice the stain.'

I think about it for a second but then shake my head. I kind of want to go home now anyway. The party's over. At least for me and my dress it is. It's very nice of her to offer though. After all she doesn't know me from Adam. It's terribly reassuring when strangers help you out. It doesn't happen very often. People these days usually wonder what you can do for them, not the other way around.

I hand her my cloakroom ticket. She disappears. I hope she doesn't run off home with my good bomber jacket! Then I fish out my brush in an attempt to do something with my frizzy hair. I wish I had dead-straight hair like that girl. I wish I had her figure too. I'll bet *she* isn't stuck here with

somebody like Clive. I'm sure she's got this complete
hunk . . .

'Here you go.'

She's back. That was quick.

'Thanks a million.'

'Do you need anything else? Will I ring a taxi
for you or anything?'

'Ah no, there's a taxi rank just outside. I'll be
grand.'

'Are you here with somebody? They might be
worrying about you.'

I think of Janine and Alan. And I think of Clive.

'I'm sure they won't,' I say adamantly.

'I'll see you to the door anyway,' the girl offers.

My God! Who is this chick? Does she fancy me
or what?

To my complete surprise, as we emerge from the
Ladies, I see Garry waiting outside the door. What
is he like? Has he been outside all this time?

'Lara?'

My new 'guardian angel' turns to me in surprise.
'Do you two know each other?'

We both nod. Garry looks slightly uncomfortable. 'Are you the girl who spilt wine all over your
dress?'

I nod, mortified.

'And Kelly here came to your rescue?' he said,
ruffling her hair. 'It's a small world isn't it?'

Funny, that's exactly what I'm thinking right now.
Small? It's a bloody cardboard box.

'I'm just going to see the poor girl out,' Kelly says, maybe a little too enthusiastically for my liking. 'You go back to the bar. I won't be long.'

'It's alright Kelly, *I'll* see her out,' Garry offers. This is all too much. I can't stand it.

'Listen, I'll see myself out,' I insist. 'I've taken up enough of both your time already. Thanks for all your help. I really appreciate it.'

I shake both of their hands formally and then walk very, very quickly towards the door. I have never ever wanted a night to end so fast in all my life.

Chapter Ten

When I wake, I've some bloody head on me. I'm still wearing the crushed-blue velvet dress, which is now in fact crushed blue and burgundy thanks to the accident with the wine glass. No dry cleaner is going to able to do anything with this thing. I groan and roll over hitting my head off something. Jesus, I've even brought my handbag to bed. How did I do that?

Somehow I must have managed to take off my shoes and tights before I clambered into bed, but my earrings and necklace are still on me as is my make-up. I feel grubby and awfully sticky. I am so, so dehydrated. How come I never remember to leave a pint of water by the bed like they tell you in magazines? What time it is now anyway? The sun is streaming in through a crack in the curtains, urging me to get up and not waste my day feeling sorry for myself.

I really should go for a walk or something. Or at least go out and buy the Sunday papers and get a bit of fresh air. On second thoughts I don't think

I'll bother. I don't feel like doing anything. No. My head is cracking, like somebody is using it to practice their golf swing with it. I feel like shit.

Last night's memories come floating back to me in dribs and drabs. Janine and Alan. Clive. Garry. Kelly . . . Ah yes I remember now. Me leaving the hotel all alone like a complete moron and having some kind of discussion with the taxi driver about all men being bastards. I vaguely remember him agreeing but I wouldn't bet on it.

What a nasty night that was! An involuntary shudder creeps along my spine as I think about it. All that crap and I'm still not even a step closer to finding a man for this goddamn wedding. However, the way I feel this morning I don't particularly even care. I just don't want to go. I wonder how I can find a way out? Suppose I conveniently twist my foot? Nah, too obvious. And I can't blame a crisis like a death in my family because you know, Janine *is* family.

Maybe I could just emigrate to Australia or something. Then again that'd be kind of extreme. God, I think I'll just have to continue my pathetic journey of trying to find a man. And what a never-ending journey that is. The only light at the end of the tunnel seems to be an oncoming train flashing at me to get out of the way.

I honestly didn't think it would be this difficult. I don't get it. I mean, what's wrong with me? How can I hold down a fantastically well-paid job, own my own apartment, drive my own car and *still* not attract one single man? Why isn't there a course you can do with a graduation day at the end of it, where you go on stage to collect your man (instead of your diploma) as your folks clap proudly?

Right. Enough, Lara. Get up and do something with your day. Live for today and all that.

Reluctantly I haul myself out of bed, and force myself to get on the scales, which are conveniently placed beside my bed. The results are neither good nor bad. I haven't put on any weight since last night but haven't lost any either. But sure what did I expect? A miracle? This losing weight business is so fecking long and boring. I need to do more exercise. Starving isn't enough.

I take a good look at myself in the full-length mirror and sadly examine my orange peel thighs. No amount of 'miracle' cream is going to dissolve those dimples dearest, I tell myself bluntly. I turn around and strain my neck to get a good look at my arse. It's heading dangerously south towards the back of my knees. There's no point kidding myself any longer. If I don't tackle my weight now, soon I'll be a middle-aged frump.

Refusing to let myself get all miserable and rush to the fridge for some 'ah-what's-the point?' temporary comfort, I decide to look at things practically. Exercise burns calories so that should be the way forward. Simple. Now, should I go for a run? Oh God, maybe I should, but I hate running. I hate

going along the road with my boobs jogging along
in front of me, and perverts stuck in traffic staring
as I huff and puff getting more and more red-faced
in process. And walking everywhere takes far too
long. Mmm. And then it hits me. *I* know what I
should do. I'll book myself into a luxury day spa
and detoxify. That way I can lose weight by just
doing nothing. Perfect. What a good idea. Why
didn't I think of it before? I'll just lie back and let
somebody else do all the hard work. I don't mind
paying for the pleasure. No. I've never minded
paying. Just as long as I don't have to suffer or
exert myself unnecessarily.

It wouldn't be the first time money exchanged
hands in hope of my losing a few inches either. No.
I, Lara Hope, am a slimming salesman's dream. It
all started about a decade ago when my mum paid
for a course of toning tables for me. I thought it
was a great idea at the time. You'd just sit on a
table, it would vibrate underneath you, and apparently the weight would just miraculously drop off.
Only it didn't. And I felt so guilty about all the
money that my mum had doshed out that I started
dieting. Lettuce and tomato and only the odd fun
size Mars bar for a treat. Okay, I know you're
thinking that if I'd been serious, I would have just
cut out chocolate altogether. But I don't believe in
complete self-denial. In fact I lost quite a few pounds
on that diet but sadly put it all back on again.

Then, a few years later, Mum and I were at this

Health and Beauty exhibition in the RDS. Part of the exhibition was a fashion show so we both sat there with our glasses of white wine watching these skinny models parade up and down wearing hardly any clothes. Once the show had finished we then went for a wander and stopped at a stall where a woman was selling this bottled stuff, which she claimed made you lose weight as you slept. We both thought this was absolutely fantastic. Especially me. Mum purchased a bottle for herself and one for me as a present.

I was so delighted until the woman of course had to go and ruin the moment by giving us the terms and conditions. Apparently, for the best results, we weren't allowed to eat anything after six o' clock in the evening. Oh, and alcohol intake was strongly not recommended. We both stared at her blankly, glasses of wine in hand. No alcohol? What kind of a boring diet was that? Needless to say we felt very disappointed. After all, one teeny weeny glass of wine never did anybody any harm. And besides, didn't they say red wine was good for the heart? Good old *they*. You've just got to love them.

Anyway, that old bottle of diet stuff is still lurking somewhere in the back of my fridge. I'm sure that any day now it will be able to walk out of my kitchen all by itself.

My eternal search for a quick weight loss solution didn't stop there of course. No. A couple of years ago, while trawling the Internet, I came across this amazing site, which claimed to help you lose a stone in six weeks. Now, *that's* more like it, I thought excitedly. Log on and lose lard. How fantastic! Why hadn't anyone ever thought of it before?

To register all you had to do was tap in your credit card details. Easy peasy. Even *I* could do that. I happily tapped in my details and lo and behold, within minutes an email popped into my In box informing me that the transaction had been successful. I was delighted.

Then I got another email with hundreds of low fat recipes and exercise tips. What was that all about? I wondered. After all, I certainly didn't have the time to be out buying complicated ingredients, nor did I have the inclination to buy an enormous exercise ball to roll around on. I felt I'd been robbed. Yet again, I'd been sucked into the multi-billion pound diet industry. This time I wanted my money back.

I vowed that from then on I was just going to stick to a sensible diet. Every Monday morning I would start with the best intentions. But by every Monday afternoon I'd just cave in. There was always some excuse. I'd always convince myself I needed energy in a job like mine, or that I would wait until my holidays, or that I really needed a personal trainer or something.

I get dressed slowly. Sunday is a day for going

slowly though, especially if you've been out drinking the night before. With a great deal of sadness, I dump my blue crushed-velvet dress in the bin. I'll never be able to get that red wine stain out anyway, and when I eventually lose weight it will be way too big for me anyway. Then I switch on my phone to see if anybody has been in contact.

WER DA FUCK R U?

It was sent this morning at 1:14am. By Janine. Oh well, it's a bit late to be answering that now, I think with a chuckle. She can sod off. Who does she think she is? Janine must have been furious with me for running off like that. But then again, what did she expect? Imagine trying to set me up with a geek like Clive! Honestly, the nerve!

No more messages. Right. I decide I am going to do something healthy with my day. I am absolutely determined not to spend it reading all the Sunday papers because they all just tell you the same thing and it's depressing. I fish out a copy of the Yellow Pages from under the bed. Feeling very optimistic now, I start to leaf through the directory. I intend spending the entire day in a luxury spa. And I won't even feel guilty about pampering myself. It's my little reward to cheer me up after the absolutely shit weekend I've had so far.

Right. I've found one that looks all right. Great. And it's not too far from Dublin either. With any luck I'll be there by lunchtime. Not that I'll be having any lunch of course. God, no! I discover that this place has a website so I'll be able to give it a once over on the computer. Oh I can't wait to treat myself.

Logging on, I have to admit this spa really looks impressive. It's near a river. *Perfect for long leisurely walks*, the website states. Well I won't be going for any long walk today. Sure if a walk was all I wanted I could stay at home and walk around the block!

I want to know about the treatments that make you lose weight. And make your skin glow. And take years off you. They're the things *I* want to know about.

I ring in advance to let them know I'm coming. I book a facial, a detox wrap, a body scrub and a forty-five minute session in a flotation tank, which is apparently the equivalent of getting about eight hours sleep. Bliss!

Sandy rings to ask me how my night was. She offers to call round. I say she can't as I'm on my way to a spa.

'Oh that sounds nice. Maybe I'll come with you. Is it expensive?'

I read out the prices. She decides to give it a miss this time around.

'My credit card is so maxed,' she sighs, making me feel a bit guilty. 'But you have a great time anyway. Are you going to have a seaweed wrap?'

'Not this time. I don't really like seaweed. When I was small I got my legs caught in some seaweed on the beach in the West of Ireland. It scared the life out of me. I think being wrapped up in the stuff would bring back some unpleasant memories. I'm going for the chocolate mud wrap whatever that is.'

'Well, I'll call over later to see the healthy new you. By the way, how was last night?'

'Don't ask. I'll tell you later when I've had my day of pampering and relaxation. I'm too trauma-tised to think about it now.'

'So you didn't meet the man of your dreams?'

'No but I did get plenty of material for future nightmares.'

'That doesn't sound too good.'

'No. Oh well . . . talk to you later then.'

Fifteen minutes later I'm on the road, listening to some shock jock on the radio. I can't understand why the traffic is so bad on a Sunday. I mean don't city people ever relax? I don't get it. People are always moaning about the traffic in Dublin so why do they insist on getting into their cars on their days off?

I relax a lot more once I'm out of Dublin. I change radio stations. A bit of soothing music should put me in the mood for my day at the spa. Already I feel a lot mellower. I should really do this more often. After all, a few years ago I wouldn't have had the money to do anything. Even going to the cinema was a big treat back then. As a student, there was so much time and so little money. Now there's money but hardly any time.

Of course I do happen to have one of the most

demanding jobs around. Anybody working in
retailing becomes a slave to the industry. It's just
as well I love my job. Okay, maybe I wouldn't
go *that* far but I do enjoy it anyway and I love
the responsibility of running my own store. I'd
hate to, say, work in a post office or something,
with people coming in and looking for 48 cent
stamps.

At the moment we're getting in the spring/summer
collections and the clothes are so adorable.
Especially for little girls. I'd love to have a little
girl. I love kids when they don't belong to other
people. It'd be so exciting going shopping for baby
stuff. I get a massive discount on all the clothes of
course, being the manager. But it's not much use
since I've no sprogs of my own. Don't tell anyone
this, but I actually do have a stash of baby clothes
hidden on the top of my wardrobe. Just in case.
Sometimes the clothes and toys are just so cute I
buy them for the hell of it, but obviously I draw
the line when it comes to purchasing things like
prams, playpens and pushchairs. A childless woman
has to know her limits.

I'm nearly there now thank God. I've a map lying
on the seat beside me but I don't want to read it
unless it's absolutely necessary. Reading maps just
does my head in! So far I've been doing alright
following the signs.

Suddenly my phone beeps. I wonder who that is.
People don't usually text me on Sunday afternoons

because, you know, it's cheap to call people at weekends. I reach down for the phone to check. Who knows, maybe it's a secret admirer? No such luck however. It's another message from Janine. Fuck. I don't know if I want to read this or not. Maybe I should wait until after the spa. Then again, I don't want to read the text from Janine later. That will only undo the good of having all those treatments. I read it. And read it. And read it again. And then I actually stop the car to read it because I can't quite believe my eyes.

GOT GARRY'S NUMBER!!!

My first reaction is of course one of complete shock. Then I feel a little ill, for a number of reasons. First of all Janine is getting married so she shouldn't really be getting *any* man's number. And secondly I'm extremely annoyed that she had the sheer chutzpah to send me that text. As if she's trying to make me jealous and make me sorry that I left early. And thirdly, to think that Garry was only talking to me because he wanted an introduction to Janine! Fourthly I'm thinking what a complete and utter bastard he is and, fifthly I'm feeling sorry for his lovely, lovely innocent girlfriend, Kelly, who was so unbelievably nice to me. And sixthly . . . sixthly . . . Oh God, I take a few deep breaths, and try my best to calm down.

She's a bitch to send me that. It's way below the belt. I'm not going to text her back, that's for sure.

Jesus, surely I deserve at least one full day without that interfering bag of bones gloating over me. What have I ever done to her?

Once I've recovered somewhat, I turn on the engine again and continue driving in the direction of the spa resort. I will not, absolutely not, let Janine ruin my lovely afternoon. I switch off my phone. There. I should really have done that before I set out.

Okay. Here we are. Long sweeping drive. Oak trees. Peace and tranquility. Oh, and there's the river. It's as pretty as a postcard. Mind you, I don't see many people walking along it. And it has just begun to rain. I grab my bag out of the boot and make a run for it.

At the reception, a girl called Danielle with an Australian accent gets me to sign in, and explains in detail what treatments are on offer. She sound just like someone from *Neighbours*. Then I get a tour, which is all very interesting. Everything looks terribly therapeutic except for the bunch of stones underneath a few inches of water. Apparently if you walk on these you soon feel the healing effect. I try not to laugh as Danielle explains this with an earnest face. Honest to God, if I'd wanted to walk on stones I would have headed for Killiney Beach! After the little tour, Grainne from Galway fetches me a nice oatmeal-coloured bathrobe and matching slippers, and Hilde from Hungary leads me into the treatment room for my detox. Once inside, I de-robe and stand awkwardly in my bathing suit as she slaps some warm mud on the white plastic sheet covering the small hospital size bed. Then she motions at me to take off the swimsuit. I'm mortified at the thought of stripping in front of a stranger, but then I remind myself that Hilde from Hungary must see naked people all the time. She gets me to sit on the bed and my bum sinks into the squishy warm mud. It feels weird. Then I lie back and Hilde paints the rest of me with some kind of brush. Then she wraps me up. My arms are by my side and I feel like an Egyptian Mummy. Then once I'm all wrapped, she presses a button and I feel all this warm water bubbling underneath me. Oh *I* get it now. This is a waterbed. What fun! I wish I had one of these at home. This is definitely a lot more pleasant than say running on the spot in a gym or doing a hundred nasty press ups. I wonder how much weight I'll have lost once it's all over.

Before Hilde leaves the room, she lights a white candle in the corner of the room, and turns on some kind of whale music that I'm sure I've heard a million times in supermarkets. Then thankfully she turns out the lights. She tells me to relax for the next half an hour. Good. That sounds alright to me.

So anyway there I am trying to relax as the mud hardens and attacks the cellulite on my thighs (or so I like to believe). I try to think of a peaceful scenario to help me relax but soon all I can think about is that bloody text from Janine. Trust her to ruin my day. I just don't get it. What on earth was she trying to prove? And how the hell did she get his number off him? God knows she certainly tried hard enough to catch Garry's eye back when we were all students, and failed miserably. But now that she's getting married, and he has a steady girl-friend, it doesn't make any sense for them to flirt. And whatever about a bit of innocent flirting, it certainly shouldn't have ended in the swapping of numbers!

Maybe, just maybe, Garry is one of those awful men who just wants what he can't have. That would explain his eagerness to chat up Janine. If he knows he can't get her now, maybe that's encouraging him all the more. What a sad bastard. A lot of men can be funny like that though. When they know they can have you they don't want you. But by God if somebody else wants to make an honest woman of you, they'll do their best to sabotage it.

Anyway who cares about Garry? He's not worth a second's thought. I had a lucky escape there, as far as I'm concerned. I mean thank *God* it wasn't me he was trying to woo. But then wait a minute . . . why am I so bothered about it all? Why am I lying here spending a fortune trying to relax and thinking about that eejit? You'd think being a doctor and all, that Garry would be caring and honourable. Well, it just goes to show that you can't trust *any* men. I bet Dave wouldn't be like that. Lovely Dave who saved my life when I just happened to collapse in the shop. Whoever has him is the luckiest girl in the world. I am so, so jealous. *He* wouldn't dream of chatting up a woman who was about to get married. No. I mean, he didn't even ask for *my* number and I would have gladly given it to him.

I'm beginning to feel a bit hot now. And dehydrated. I suppose I had quite a bit to drink last night and the effects were bound to hit sooner or later. I wonder how long I've been lying here. At least 10 minutes I'd say. Maybe longer. How am I going to stick it for another 20 minutes? I wonder am I getting any thinner? Suddenly I want to scratch my forehead. It feels itchy. Or maybe I just think it's itchy. You know when you can't scratch something you just want to do it so badly. I can't stand it. Another five minutes pass. If I can't scratch my forehead now I think I'm going to die. I try to free my arm. It's not that easy. I tug and tug and finally I manage to yank it out through the plastic. Mud flies everywhere, spattering the walls. Uh oh! Hilde from Hungary isn't going to be one bit pleased about this. I give my head another good scratch as well as the tip of my nose, which has also become a bit itchy. Then I end up giving my entire head a good old scratch and hope that my mud wrap won't last for too much longer. Hilde, Hilde, where are you?

Jesus, that old whale music isn't doing anything to relax me either. It's a bit of a farce to be honest with you. I mean I'd much rather they played some decent pop tunes. I close my eyes. If I fall asleep the time might go faster. I stare at the white ceiling and try to think of nothing, but the more I try to think of nothing, the more I start thinking about Garry pursuing Janine after I'd gone home. What a scoundrel. That poor, poor girlfriend of his. He doesn't deserve her at all.

'Did you enjoy that?' says Hilde in her thick Hungarian accent as she turns on the light. Phew! Thank God she is back.

If she notices the mud spattered room she says nothing. She turns on the shower, blows out the candle and places a soft fluffy white towel on the floor for my use.

Then she unwraps me. The relief is enormous. I don't think I'll be rushing back to do this treatment, I can tell you. I think part of my brain was detoxed as well as my fat cells. I go to sit up but I feel uncontrollably dizzy. I can't move. The room darkens.

'Is everything alright?' Hilde looks mildly alarmed.

'I feel weak,' I mutter. 'Er, my head.'

Oh God, please don't let me faint again, I silently pray. It was one thing passing out on a shop floor fully clothed, but collapsing here in front of Hilde, still naked and spattered in mud, would be quite another thing.

'I need sugar,' I say weakly. 'Could I get a cup of tea with lots of sugar in it?'

'Certainly,' says Hilde, looking a bit worried. She wraps me in a bathrobe and guides me to a chair. 'Would you like some biscuits too?'

'Yes please.' Feck the diet. I have honestly never felt so drained in my entire life!

Hilde is back almost immediately and I take the cup of tea from her as though my life depends on it. I don't even particularly like tea but at this very minute I'm glad of the sugary taste. Within seconds I'm feeling a lot better, and more than ready to shower off all the muck I'm covered in. Hilde leaves me alone to wash. It takes ages to scrub myself clean. God, pigs must be really, really healthy, I think. They get these daily beauty treatments for free! I take a look in the mirror. I still have mud all over my face from where I was scratching it earlier. I also still have my big belly. The mud has gone but my tummy is still very much hanging out. What's that all about? When Hilde comes back in I ask her how much weight I should have lost. She gives me a vague unsatisfactory answer about the treatments taking time to see a definitive change. Then she goes on to recommend getting a course of mud treatments to optimise results. She also urges me to buy some special oils at the reception desk before I leave. She can feck off, I think to myself. I wonder what kind of commission she's on?

'What time is it?' I ask.

'Nearly three o' clock.' Hilde informs me.

'Thank you. And *thank* you for the biscuits,' I add, although I only ate one of them. Sure, the whole point of coming down here was to lose weight, not to put it on. Okay, if it's only three now and my flotation tank appointment isn't until four, which means I've an hour to kill. I can go for a swim, sauna, a stint in the steam room and Jacuzzi or else I can indulge in all four. What a decision, eh? I should spend *every* Sunday down here.

My skin is still quite red and blotchy from the heat of the mud wrap and, as there are still streaks of mud on my face, I think I'd better go into the steam room. It will soften the skin on my face and hopefully then the mud will be easier to get off.

I spot the steam room straight away. Opening the door, a cloud of steam hits my face. I close it quickly again so as to keep the heat in and not annoy the other people in the steam room. Mind you, I don't seem to see anybody else here. It's difficult. My eyes need to adjust. God it's hot. It's also very quiet. Good. That means I can steam away in peace. Bliss.

'Hello,' says a deep male voice, making me jump.

Jesus, where did that come from? I'd better be careful about where I'm going to sit. I don't want to land on anybody's lap.

'Hello,' I answer sort of apologetically and seat myself in a slippery corner.

'How are you?'

'Fine, thanks.'

Jesus, would he ever feck off? I hate people who chat away to you when you're in a steam room or a sauna. He'd better not start asking me where I'm from or whether I'm staying in the hotel. I just don't fancy idle chitchat at the moment.

'Well, this is a pleasant surprise I have to say.'

Oh my God. Who is this freak? And why is he talking to me like this? If it wasn't so bloody hot in here there'd be a chill running down my spine. Suppose your man is a complete pervert? Suppose he sits in this steam room all day waiting to pounce on unsuspecting females in their swimsuits? But why is he picking on me? All I wanted was a relaxing afternoon. I'd better say nothing. It's probably the best thing to do. If I say nothing maybe he'll shut up. If he insists on talking then I'll leave and have a dip in the pool. I won't look at him anyway. That way he won't be encouraged.

'I can't believe it's you.'

Jesus! I think I recognise that voice. I stare straight ahead trying to focus. My eyes become accustomed to the steam. But surely . . . surely he couldn't be who I think it . . . ohmiGod . . .

'Dave?'

'Yes.' He's laughing.

But I'm not. I feel sick. How can this be happening? There are about four million people living in this country but the only person in this steam room is Doctor Dave. Fuck it anyway! He's already seen my fat photo but now he's getting to see the real thing. I can't believe it. What are the chances? I feel faint. I really do and this time I'm not blaming the chocolate mud wrap.

Dave is as gorgeous as I remember him. Sitting opposite him almost naked I am completely intimidated. I rack my brains for something interesting or witty to say but all I can come up with is . . .

'So what are you doing here?'

'Hey I was about to ask you the same question. This isn't your neck of the woods. Are you here on a weekend break?'

'No, I wish! I just checked into the spa for the afternoon. I was out at a ball last night and when I woke up this morning I decided to treat myself. How about yourself?'

'I'm here with the kids.'

Right. My heart takes a sudden nosedive along with my imaginary slap in the face. Oooh that hurt. So did the punch in the stomach. Kids. Right. How many? One? Two? Five? Where are they?

'Oh, where are they?' I try to sound breezy and bright, although I actually feel queasy and shite.

'Out in the play area with their mothers.'

'Mothers?'

Jesus, how many wives does this guy have? Do all his exes meet up with their kids for some family Sunday fun? Is he going to invite me to join in? I feel hot. But I can't stand up. I don't want to give him a view of my thighs if I can help it. He's already seen enough. If I walk towards the door he'll get a good glimpse of my arse. I wish he'd just leave now and leave the exit clear. This is awful. What on earth did I do to deserve this? What about my day of relaxation? Huh.

'Yesterday the mums got to use the spa and I looked after the kids. Now it's my turn.'

'So today it's Daddy's turn?' I echo faintly, thinking how surreal this whole conversation is.

'Exactly,' he laughs, as I try my best to ignore the fact that he is so attractive with no clothes on.

'It's getting hot in here,' Dave says suddenly.

Indeed!

'Do you want to come for a swim?'

'I think I'll wait here a while,' I say, willing him to leave the steam room as quickly as possible.

'Well, perhaps you'll join me in a few minutes then?'

'Sure.'

He stands up to reveal a perfectly toned bronzed stomach, broad shoulders and strong lean legs. If he wasn't a doctor, I would have said he was a world class soccer player. Wow. I wonder how much longer I can bear sitting in the steam room. This is torture. I desperately need some fresh air but there's no way in hell I'm leaving here until the coast is clear. If I jump into that pool all the water will splash out. And besides, I don't want Dave feeling sorry for me. I don't want him giggling later in the bar with all his skinny wives. I don't want them to . . . to . . . Jesus, I have to get out of here. I don't care anymore what

Dave thinks. Sure he's a family man. Who cares? And he's a doctor. He's seen loads of bodies. Of all sizes. And anyway I've only ever seen him once before. And despite this unbelievably strange coincidence, I'll probably never see him again. I need to cop on and stop making an eejit out of myself. After all this is *my* Sunday treat too.

Right. I'm on my feet now. Just about anyway. God I'm dizzy. So, so dizzy. My head feels very light. As if it's not there at all. The walls of the steam room are closing in on me. Panicking, I take a step forward. I just need to get out of here. I need some fresh air. It's so, so . . . so hot. I stumble forward into blackness.

Chapter Eleven

'Can somebody please call a doctor?'

The concerned woman's voice sounds a million miles away. My head feels like it is being crushed by a crane.

'She's hit her head. It's cut. We need an ambulance.'

I wonder what's going on? All these people are talking about falls and cuts and ambulances. Somebody must have injured themselves but all I want to do is go back to sleep.

'Don't let her go back to sleep. It's really important. Can you fetch me her bathrobe?'

A man's voice. I know that voice. It's Doctor Dave's voice. What is he doing here? Oh God, am I still in the spa? I try to lift my head but the pain is excruciating.

Doctor Dave's face is right beside mine. I experience a frisson of excitement as I spot him kneeling on the floor. His deep, green eyes are anxious.

'The ambulance will be here in a while,' he says

in a soft, gentle voice. 'You got yourself a nasty
bang to the side of your head.'

He touches my skin and I wince. How did this
happen? I've only fainted twice in my life. Doctor
Dave has been there to save me. Twice. He is my
saviour and I think I'm in love with him. I've always
believed in love at first sight anyway. It just never
happened to me . . . before now.

'Will you come with me in the ambulance?' I ask
him, suddenly terrified of being alone.

'Sure I will.'

'I won't get to use the flotation tank now I
suppose.'

'I suppose not,' says Dave with a smile. 'But I'm
sure you'll be back down again.'

'Yes.'

One of the spa employees wraps me in a robe,
and herself and Dave help me to my feet. My head
is killing me. Dazed, I'm led into the foyer and out
the door into the waiting ambulance. One of the
assistants has put my clothes in a bag. I want to
settle up for my day in the spa but they won't hear
of it. They're just concerned about my health. And
who can blame them? I suppose it doesn't look too
good for business for one of their clients to be leaving
in an ambulance!

At the hospital I have to fill out a form. Being here
with a doctor however means I don't have to wait
ages to be seen, which is handy. My head is soon
bandaged and I'm given painkillers. I'm asked about

my medical history, and once they're confident that I'm not going to pass out again, I'm told I'm free to go home. We get a taxi back to the spa and Dave says he's going to drive me home in my car.

'But what about your car?' I ask, concerned.

He assures me not to worry. Somebody else is going to bring his car home.

'Your wife?' I ask.

'Partner,' he says staring straight ahead and choosing not to divulge too much information. 'She's back in the hotel with her sister.'

We drive home. I'm in the passenger seat of my own car and Dave is at the wheel. He tells me he's worried about me. This isn't too surprising. After all, I've only met him twice. Both times I've collapsed. He asks me whether I'm eating properly. I assure him that I am. He doesn't believe me. We pull in at a café on the way into Dublin. Dave makes me eat a cream bun. He asks me why I've been dieting. I break down and confess to him all about Janine's wedding and the bridesmaid's dress I'm terrified I'm not going to be able to fit into. As I'm speaking the tears spill from my eyes. I try to fight them but it's no good. Dave reaches forward and wipes them away with the back of his hand. The touch of his skin on mine is electrifying. I want him to scoop me up in his arms and hug me. I want those strong arms of his to protect me. I don't want him to just walk away like the last time and leave me on my own again.

'I don't know why such a beautiful girl like you is starving herself,' Dave looks at me tenderly. 'There's no need for it. You look perfect the way you are.'

He's lying. He's got to be. I'm not beautiful. I'm not even attractive. At the ball last night, not even Clive was remotely interested. Nobody chatted me up, except Garry. And he only did it just to get Janine's number. No wonder my confidence is at an all time low. Can I remember my last boyfriend? Hell, I can't even remember my last date!

'Thank you,' I sniff. 'You're very kind.'

'I'm not being kind, I'm being honest,' says Dave in a voice that's tugging dangerously at my heart strings. If this guy was single he'd be my ideal man. Why is he taken and how on earth has he suddenly become involved in my life again? I believe in fate. And the fact that I've met Dave twice when I've been at my most vulnerable must be a sign. Of course it is. It's just too much of a coincidence to mean nothing at all, isn't it?

I wonder why he isn't married. Why doesn't he marry the mother of his kids? Maybe she trapped him. Maybe he doesn't love her at all but is sticking around for the sake of his children? That might be the reason of course. Dave is one of the kindest men I've ever met. He wouldn't abandon his own flesh and blood. No. He's not a cad like Garry who, not content with having one lovely girlfriend, hits on people like me as well as my cousin Janine, despite the fact that she's engaged. With men like Garry roaming the streets, it's little wonder that most Irish women despair of meeting Mr Right.

'I've been working pretty hard lately,' I confide in the attentive doctor. 'Working as a retail manager involves a lot of hours.'

'As does working as a doctor,' Dave agrees. 'Where did we both go wrong?'

'Dunno. It's a bit too late to switch careers now. Anyway I love my job. I couldn't work in an office staring at a clock and pushing my pen around the desk pretending to be busy.'

'Me neither,' Dave laughs.

'Sometimes I think how much easier my life would be if I was a librarian or something.'

'You don't look like a librarian though.'

'What do librarians look like?'

Dave shrugs and we both laugh.

'Come on,' he says. 'Let's get back on the road.'

By the time we reach Dublin I've definitely relaxed. I think I've also finally convinced Dave that I don't have an eating disorder, nor do I make a habit of collapsing in public in a desperate attempt to be scooped up by handsome doctors. In fact I've relaxed so much, I end up explaining my reasons for not leaving the steam room earlier.

'But you don't have cellulite,' Dave says, looking genuinely baffled that any woman would go to such extremes to hide her backside from public view.

I don't know if he's just being considerate but he

has definitely succeeded in cheering me up. By the time I'm dropped home we're joking and laughing and I just keeping thinking what a great end this is to an otherwise disastrous weekend. I don't invite him in for coffee because I'm sure Dave has had more than enough of me for one day. However I'm kind of sad to be saying goodbye.

Dave says he'll hail a taxi on the street. I want to drive him home. It's the least I can do but he won't hear of it. I wonder why. Does he not want me to see where he lives? I already know he has a family so what else would he be trying to hide? Does he not want me to know anything about him? He certainly knows a lot about me. Too much probably. He knows that I'm single, he knows where I work, that I'm going to be bridesmaid to Janine, and that I'm desperately self-conscious about my weight. He knows that I live alone and have a 'fat' photo on my fridge and that I've 'orange peel' thighs.

Dave, on the other hand, is something of a closed book. I know he works as a doctor in Tallaght. I know he has a partner and a child. But that's all. And maybe it's just as well. Maybe that's all I need to know. Dave is taken. He is unavailable. He and Me will never be We. So what is the point in torturing myself and pretending that it could be different? It's best that I forget about him now before I get in too deep. I know what it's like to get burned. God knows I've had my heart thrown on the ground and stamped on before. And instead of learning from the experience I just went out and did it again. And again. And again. But for the last while I haven't let anyone get close.

Oh, I know I've promised myself to get somebody for the wedding. But I can do that without getting emotionally involved, can't I? I'm a retail manager after all. I make a crust from making business decisions. So why do I always fuck up when it comes to personal decisions?

'Thank you so much Dave,' I shake his hand.

He clasps it in his, leans forward and kisses my cheek very softly, his lips just barely brushing my skin. I feel a slight tingle running along my spine.

'Next time I see you I don't want you fainting on me now, do you hear?'

I laugh, with more than just a tinge of regret that there probably will never be a next time.

'Are you sure you'll be okay?'

'Shouldn't *I* be the one that should be asking *you* that?' he smiles.

We stand looking at each other awkwardly, like two teenagers on a first date.

'Lara?' he says, not looking quite so confident suddenly.

I raise an eyebrow. Why is he staring? I'm being paranoid now. I don't have a screed of make up on. My hair has dried naturally on my head, and I have a bandage on the side of my face. I've probably never looked this frightening in my entire life, and yet here I am in the courtyard of my apartment block with one of the most desirable men I've ever met.

'Lara' he repeats himself and to my astonishment, his face turns slightly pink. 'What are the chances of you giving me your number?'

Chapter Twelve

'He what?' Sandy is staring at me, her eyes and mouth wide open.

'You heard me. He asked me for my number and I gave it to him. No big deal.'

'No big deal?' Sandy screeches. 'Yes it is a big deal, a *great* big deal' she adds hysterically. 'I would never have thought you were the type of girl to embark on an affair with a married man.'

'Who said anything about an affair? He's not even married anyway,' I add, somewhat taken aback by her accusation. 'He just asked me for my phone number. He's probably worried about me.'

'Worried my foot! You said he's living with somebody. Suppose he asks you for a drink? Will you go?'

'I don't know,' I say, staring at my fingers, suddenly not wanting to look my best friend straight in the eye.

'"I don't know" means yes,' accused Sandy.

'No it doesn't. It means I honestly don't know. Anyway I don't know why you're doing a song and dance about it. A drink would just be that – a drink.'

'Yeah, and then he'd ask you for dinner. And then dinner would just be dinner – is that what you're going to tell me next?'

'Oh Sandy, just drop it,' I plead. 'We're reading far too much into all of this. I'm sorry I opened my bloody mouth now. He probably won't even bother phoning. And anyway I'm not even thinking about him at the moment.'

Now, this of course, is a complete lie. Since the second I said goodbye to Doctor Dave yesterday evening, I haven't been able to think of anything else. I keep remembering the way he looked at me with those caring green eyes of his, and how my skin felt when he touched it with the back of his hand.

I remember his sculpted body, and the way it looked as he got up to leave the steam room. And most of all I remember the feeling of his lips on my cheek when we finally parted company.

All day today in work, I kept thinking about him and didn't even get angry when I found half the Baby Bloomers staff sitting on cardboard boxes up in the stockroom having a good old chinwag about their weekend. Nor did I lose my cool when Annie, our goods inwards manager, rang in sick after lunch knowing that at least six different deliveries were due before five o' clock. I just simply took it all in my stride, counted every delivery as it came in, and signed everything off myself.

Everything has changed all of a sudden and it's scary. I've even abandoned my diet, sort of. At least I'm not writing everything down like a maniac anyway, although I'm still watching what I eat. I want to look nice for Dave when I see him again. *If* I ever see him again.

'I don't know what the fuss is about,' I say, anxious for Sandy to drop the subject. 'Just because he asked for my number doesn't mean he's going to call. Maybe he's just being polite, you know? Anyway, from now on I've decided to go on lots of dates with lots of people, just like they do in America. That's far healthier than focussing on just one individual. I hate the way there's pressure in this country to become 'an item' after a date or two. It's awful.'

'I agree wholeheartedly.'

At least we're agreeing on something now!

'I need to broaden my horizons and go out with all sorts of people. Then I'll know exactly what I'm looking for.'

'Good on you – that's the spirit,' says Sandy looking at her watch. 'Come on now, get ready, the classes start in 15 minutes.'

In case I didn't tell you, we're off to an aqua aerobics class tonight. Sandy suggested it ages ago and I was more than happy to sign up. Aerobics under water doesn't sound too difficult and it's much more appealing than the thought of huffing and puffing with a load of people on rubber mats sticking their smelly feet in your face.

I must admit though, I'm slightly anxious about getting into my swimsuit and splashing up and down in the water along with so many strangers. But then again I remind myself that dishy Dave asked for my number after seeing me undressed so I can't be that bad.

At the swimming pool I notice with delight that Sandy and myself are almost the slimmest people here. The other women are absolutely enormous. At first I'm relieved but then I start to worry. If aqua aerobics is supposed to make you lose weight, then why are all these women so big, eh?

We all jump in and the shock of the cold water hits me. Then we're given these long blue squidgey things to play around with. They're to keep you afloat I presume. Personally I think it's all a bit ridiculous. I mean, the instructor herself doesn't even look terribly fit and when her old Take That tape snaps in the rickety old cassette player half way through a song I haven't heard since I was in school, I begin to have serious doubts.

Afterwards in the changing room, as I try to get dressed in the shivering cold, I vow not to return for a repeat. I think I should get a treadmill to run in the privacy of my own home. Much more pleasant.

I check my messages to see if anyone – alright then, *Dave* – has called. But the only message is from my mum wanting to know if I can look after Granny on Saturday night as herself and Dad are entering a bridge competition.

As soon as I start to text back my answer the phone rings. It's a private number. Oh God. Normally I don't like to answer private numbers as they're usually from people I don't want to talk to. But this time I'm going to answer it because I've a feeling it's . . . oh my heart . . .

'Hello?'

'Hey!'

'Hey.' I repeat. Who the hell is this? It doesn't sound like Dave.

'Guess who?'

'Er . . . I've no idea I'm afraid. Who are you?'

'Dermot.'

Dermot? Oh yes, the guy I met with Karen. The redhead. Of *course*. It's always guys like that who ring, isn't it? So typical!

'Oh hi Dermot, I remember you now. How are you?'

'Good. Good, I'm really looking forward to meeting you again.'

'Likewise.' Er, not.

'How do you fancy dinner?'

'Well I'm working late tomorrow so how about a drink instead?'

A drink is a much, much safer option I reckon, although it is pretty decent of him to offer dinner.

'Sounds good. Then again, anywhere with you would be good,' he says with a chuckle.

'Thanks.'

Oh Jesus!

'So when do you want to pick me up?'

'Pick you up?' Dermot suddenly sounds put out. 'But I don't drive. I was hoping that perhaps you could pick *me* up?'

Gosh! I inhale deeply. There's no flies on this guy, is there?

'How about we just meet somewhere in town?' I suggest, trying to come to some kind of compromise.

'Well *you* seem to be like a girl in the know. Why don't you name a place?'

God, I hate it when men do that. They ring you up to ask you out and then let you do all the hard work, like suggesting where to go.

'How about The Westbury?' I suggest.

'Ok. What time?'

'Eight?'

'Perfect.'

Uh oh. Maybe I should have suggested some-where quieter. I don't want to bump into anybody I know in The Westbury Hotel. Imagine if I bumped into someone like Doctor Dave again!

'See you then,' Dermot says and hangs up before I have a chance to change my mind.

'Who was that?' Sandy quizzes me as she dries her feet on a blue and yellow towel and then empties half a tub of talcum powder over her toes.

'Oh nobody.'

'Nobody? Don't give me that,' Sandy looks annoyed. 'You were arranging a date. I heard you. Was that Dave?'

'Dave? No, I bloody wish! No it was a guy called Dermot.'

'Dermot? What's going on here Lara? I'm supposed to be your best friend and you're going around arranging all these dates with men without telling me!'

'I am not arranging loads of dates,' I say indignantly. 'I'm meeting just one guy. One miserable member of the male sex. I don't even fancy him. That's hardly ground- breaking news Sandy!'

'Well, it's more news than I have. At least you've something to look forward to now.'

'Believe me Sandy, if you had met Dermot, you'd agree that he's nothing to get remotely excited about.'

'A date's a date though.'

I'm not sure I share her enthusiasm. A date can also be hard work. It'd be a lot less hassle to sit at home with a video and a bottle of wine all by myself. I don't know if I fancy sitting with a stranger being quizzed for the night about what kind of music I'm into, and how many siblings I have.

As we're getting into Sandy's car with damp hair – only one hairdryer in the changing rooms was working – the phone rings again. Private number. What does Dermot want now? Don't tell me he's changed his mind already?

'Hello?'

'Lara?'

I freeze. It's Dave.

'Oh hi.'

'How are you?'

'Listen, can you ring me back say in about 20 minutes?' I ask him cagily.

'Yeah sure.'

'Thanks.'

I switch the phone off.

'That was him, wasn't it?' demands Sandy.

'Who?'

'Dave.'

'Eh, yes. That was Dave.'

Sandy starts the car, shaking her head at the same time.

'It'll all end in tears,' she says quietly. 'Believe me, it'll end in tears.'

I don't answer her back. I don't want to know. I can handle this.

Chapter Thirteen

I recognise Dermot immediately. His 'strawberry blonde' head stands out like a flame. He is seated alone at a table near the bar. He looks thinner than I remember and is wearing a black suit and a shocking pink shirt.

'How are you?' he asks, tugging nervously at his fingers.

'Oh I'm fine,' I smile broadly, attempting to put him at his ease. Bless him.

He doesn't seem to have a drink in front of him.

'Has nobody been around to take your order?' I enquire.

'Oh, yeah someone came around,' said Dermot looking a bit flustered. 'But I told them to come back as soon as you arrived.'

'Oh,' I sit down opposite him. 'Oh okay.'

I look at the drinks menu, wondering what I'm going to order. I wouldn't mind going for one of the cocktails. There's a good choice here. And besides I've had a tough day at work. A treat would be nice. 'What are *you* having?' I ask

Dermot. Maybe we could get a cocktail each or something.

'I'll have a pint of Carlsberg please,' he says like lightening, before standing up. 'I'm just off to the little boys' room. Back in a moment.'

He skips off. The lounge boy is straight over to take an order.

'I'll have a Cosmopolitan and a Carlsberg for my, er, friend.'

The lounge boy scribbles down the order, disappears off and is back in less than five minutes with the drinks. Dermot is nowhere to be found. I produce my credit card. As soon as I hand it over, Dermot returns. He plonks himself down in front of me and picks up his Carlsberg gratefully.

'Thanks doll, I'm dying of the thirst.'

'No problem.'

'So tell me all about yourself,' says Dermot in a voice that seems to indicate that he doesn't want to hear anything at all.

I'm not sure where to begin. Will I start with the day I was born or simply skip a few years on to my schooldays? It's hard to know.

'Well my parents are both from the West of Ireland . . .' I begin, but falter as I notice Dermot's light grey eyes immediately glaze over and he suppresses a yawn.

' . . . but we moved to Dublin when I was five,' I add hurriedly worrying that I'm not really being great company.

'So where are you working now?' he asks.

I'm a tad confused. Doesn't he know where I work? I'm sure I told him the day I met him in the restaurant with Karen.

'In Baby Bloomers.' I tell him. 'It's a baby clothing . . .'

'Oh yes, I remember. So is that fun?' he adds, glancing surreptitiously at his watch.

I take a sip of my Cosmopolitan. 'Well it's work, you know?'

'Good pay?'

'Not bad.'

'And have you your own pile of bricks?' he wants to know. Jesus, maybe I should have just brought along my CV. This date is anything but relaxing.

'I have a place in Ballsbridge,' I tell him, with a hint of pride.

He seems to perk up. 'Oh! Is it yours or do you rent?'

'It's mine.'

'Cool.'

I take another sip of my drink. I'm beginning to feel slightly bored now.

'Do you live there alone?' he suddenly asks, giving his head a contemplative scratch. 'Or with a gang of girls?'

'With my rabbit.'

'Oh God, I hate rabbits.'

'Why?' I ask coolly.

'I just hate them. Stupid creatures.'

I don't answer. It's not worth it. I notice he has nearly finished his drink, and I have nearly finished mine. I give an exaggerated yawn myself, almost to make a point.

'Don't be fading on me now,' says Dermot leaning forward and ruffling the top of my head.

'I won't,' I say uncomfortably. I hope he doesn't think we're going to make a night of it. To be honest I wouldn't mind going home now. I glance down at our empty glasses.

'Do you fancy another drink?' Dermot says after a long awkward pause.

'Oh okay then,' I say. I shouldn't be so quick to rush off. Everyone deserves a chance.

'Or would you prefer getting a bite to eat somewhere else?' Dermot stands up before I have time to answer, and puts on his coat – a grey woollen thing – that I'm sure must have belonged to his grandfather, or somebody's grandfather in another lifetime.

'Em . . .'

'I know a great place,' he says. 'It's not too far.'

I follow him down the stairs and out the door.

We walk and walk and walk. It starts to rain. My hair gets damp. We walk some more. Dermot stops to light a cigarette. He doesn't offer me one but then again I shouldn't complain. I'm trying to cut down anyway. We walk a bit more and on the way we stop and read a few menus. My stomach is beginning to rumble now. And my feet are getting soaked.

'Should we order a taxi?' I suggest eventually, feeling the back of my left shoe dig mercilessly into my heel.

'Oh no, we don't have much further to go now,' Dermot says cheerfully as we trip through Temple Bar. He doesn't seem to notice the rain, which is getting heavier by the minute. After walking a bit more I check the back of my heel where it's hurting like mad. A blister has formed. It looks like it's about to burst. I don't know how much further my feet can carry me.

I tell Dermot I need to pop into a pharmacist to get a plaster. He gives a kind of impatient sigh. 'Okay, I'll just pop into the take away here to sit down and wait for you so.'

I hobble into the chemist to buy my plasters. I stick one on my swollen heel and then limp from the shop. Dermot is nowhere to be seen, and then I remember that he's popped into the take away. I peer in the window. Oh yes, there he is. He seems to be sitting with two other men. Their heads are bent together. Over kebabs. I cannot believe my eyes.

My temperature rises as I walk into the take away. It's a bleak place with neon lights, overflowing bins and old coffee stains on the tables.

'Dermot?'

He looks up.

'Oh hi Lara,' he says nonchalantly, as if he's just met me. He bites into his kebab, some

mayonnaise dribbling down his chin as he does
so. 'Oh, this is Murphs and Aido from college.
Haven't seen them for ages. I just saw them
through the window.'

'Alright?' one of his college pals says, his mouth
full of chips. I'm not sure which one is Murphs and
which is Aido and I don't care either. I just want
to go home.

'Have a seat,' says Dermot, failing to notice my
frustration. 'Do you want to go up and get yourself a kebab or chips or something?'

'I'm fine,' I say icily. 'I'm actually going home.'

'Oh. Are you getting the bus? If you hang on I'll
walk you to the stop.'

'I've done enough walking for tonight, I think.
Anyway I've a very early start tomorrow so I'll be
getting a taxi. Don't worry, I can see myself to the
rank. Enjoy the rest of your night.'

'Night,' say the lads, barely looking up. They
look like they've been drinking and this greasy
looking food is simply soakage. I'm sure they don't
realise myself and Dermot are on a date. Sure I can
hardly believe it myself.

'Hang on,' Dermot leaps up and follows me as
I make my way out the door. 'Are you okay?' he
asks, half his kebab still in his hand.

'I just want to go home,' I say forcing a smile.
I'd love to clock him over his strawberry red head,
but he's not worth it.

'I am not letting you stand at a taxi rank on

your own,' says Dermot, blocking my exit. 'I mean it, what kind of monster would that make me?'

He actually looks genuinely apologetic. Maybe I'm overreacting. I mean, I know I'm drenched, with a blister about to burst on my heel, but it's not Dermot's fault that it's spilling rain and that I'm wearing high heels.

'I'm sorry,' I relent. 'I'm just a bit tired, that's all. Maybe I can hail a taxi on the street?'

'I'll hail one for you. It's the least I can do,' says Dermot jovially, popping the last of the kebab in his mouth.

Sure enough, he's able to hail a cab immediately and I jump into the back. I'm about to tell the driver my address when Dermot opens the passenger door and hops in.

I open my mouth in surprise, but before anything comes out, I hear Dermot telling the driver, 'Drumcondra and then Ballsbridge please.'

I'm gobsmacked. I really am. Drumcondra is nowhere *near* Ballsbridge! It's on the other side of town, in fact. The driver puts his foot down and we speed away in the wrong direction. I barely say a word, and besides, the driver has Radio One on at full blast.

At Drumcondra, Dermot gives specific directions to his house. And then, as soon as the car stops, he hops out. 'I'll be in touch Lara!' he smiles and blows me a kiss.

The driver turns the car around. Then he turns off the radio.

'Ballsbridge?'

'Yes, please.'

'Was that your boyfriend?' he asks.

'No. No it certainly was not.'

'Thank God for that.'

'We were on a date though.'

'Really? Where did he take you?'

'Well, nowhere actually,' I admit, thinking I sound like a bit of a fool. The driver must think I'm desperate for a man or something.

'I hope you don't mind me asking, but did he give you any money for the fare?'

'Er, no. It doesn't matter though.'

'Right. I hope you're not seeing him again, are you?'

'No.'

'Good. He's an ugly bastard, excuse the language miss.'

'Oh don't worry, I agree with you,' I say giggling.

This gives the taxi driver the green light. It's full steam ahead for the entire journey home.

'Ugly scabby bastard. You're too good for him, do you know that? The tide wouldn't take that fella out. His own coat wouldn't wear him. If I had a penny for every cheap bollocks who sat in my car, I'd have retired long ago. Who does he think he is?'

'I don't know,' I say laughing.

'I could write a book about men like him.'

'Oh so could I,' I say having cheered up a bit now. 'Believe me I could write ten of them!'

Chapter Fourteen

It nearly kills me to get out of bed. I feel weak. The first thing I did this morning was pat my stomach to see if it felt smaller. It did. Just a little bit. The fact that I had nothing to eat last night seems to have paid off enormously in the shrinkage stakes. The memory of Dermot stuffing his face with the kebab still makes me shudder, but at least he succeeded in putting me off food for the rest of the night. I didn't even feel remotely hungry when I got home.

I dreamt about Dave last night. Yes, he and I were getting married on some remote Caribbean Island. It was so fantastic. Janine was my brides-maid. I was very thin and she wasn't so thin. It was a glorious dream but now the dream is over I've to haul myself out of my bed and go to work.

Just before I hop into my car, I quickly check my text messages.

Enjoyed last nite. Dermy. X

Ugh. The *cheek* of him. How dare he send me a text like that! It certainly doesn't warrant a response anyway, I think, as I promptly delete it. Good riddance.

I get into work early, which is good. It means I can relax, have a strong cup of coffee and check my emails before staff and customers alike invade the store. But as soon as I sit down, the shop buzzer goes.

'Hello?' I answer.

'Delivery.'

Delivery? Hey it's a bit early for deliveries. The goods inwards manager won't be in for at least a half an hour! So much for a bit of peace.

'You'll have to go around to the goods inwards entrance,' I inform the deliveryman. 'How many boxes?'

'Boxes? I've a bunch of flowers here for a Miss Hope.'

Flowers? Now, there's a surprise. I can't remember the last time somebody sent me flowers. Excitedly I make my way to the shop floor to start the electronic shutters. As soon as I sign for the floral bunch, I tear open the accompanying card.

Hope you're keeping well. Dave.

My heart soars. Oh my God, this is the sweetest thing anybody has done for me in such a long time. I skip back to the small staff kitchen and search for a vase. I can't find any so I use a couple of empty Fanta bottles instead. I stand there admiring the glorious riot of vibrant colours for at least five minutes. I feel special and wanted and the horrible memories of last night's so-called date, seem a million years away. I'd love to text Dave and thank him but I don't have his number. Sugar!

Various staff members admire the flowers throughout the day. I'm sure they are as surprised as I am to see them in the staff kitchen. Even Tommy in the stockroom reckons they must have cost a good few bob. He's been trying his best to find out who they're from. I won't tell him. The less this lot know about my personal life, the better. Of course I know they secretly think I'm celibate, and to be honest they're right, at the moment anyway. But with any luck I won't be for much longer. I have a feeling that romance is in the air. Even my horoscope in *The Star* says so.

Sandy rings me at lunchtime to tell me she has a crisis on her hands. She says it's too important to discuss over the phone so we must meet for a glass of wine after work. Fair enough. Then, to my complete surprise, Karen rings to ask how the date went.

I wonder is she taking the mick?

'Did Dermot not tell you?' I ask her curiously.

'No, he said he didn't want to jinx the relationship too much by talking about it in the early stages.'

In the early stages? Give me a break! Oh God I have to force myself not to laugh out loud.

'Listen Karen,' I say in a hushed voice. 'I'm in the canteen at work so I can't really talk now. But

I'm meeting Sandy later for a drink so maybe you could join us?'

'Okay, great. Dying to hear how your night went. Dermot's being very coy about it all. I don't blame him. He's actually had a bit of a rough time with some of the women he's been out with recently.'

'Has he now? God love him. Anyway, I'll be more than happy to fill you in pet. Meet you later. How does The Bailey at 6:30pm sound? You can sit outside and smoke your brains out.'

'Perfect, see you then.'

I finish up my low-cal tomato and pepper soup. It's absolutely vile. Next time I buy soup it's going to be of the full calorie creamy kind.

I go out onto the shop floor just as Fergus, our security guard, is stopping Elly, our resident shoplifter, from leaving the store. We all know Elly. She has been our number one shoplifter since we first opened our doors. Of course she knows she's barred but that still doesn't stop her from trying to come in almost every second week trying to rob baby clothes. Once she even tried wheeling a pram out of the shop. She just stuck her baby into it and started pushing it towards the door. We called the police that time. Not because we wanted poor Elly to be thrown in jail or anything, but because we felt she needed some serious help. She got a warning but took no notice. She has five children under the age of six, and a serious drink problem.

This time the police are not called. Instead I have

a little chat with Elly upstairs in my office. I tell
her that she should know by now that she's barred
from the shop and I urge her to contact Alcoholics
Anonymous. I'm not sure if she's listening as she
has this faraway look in her eyes, but then her thin,
haggard face crumples and she bursts into tears. As
she does so, her baby stops smiling and reaches his
tiny hands towards my face as if pleading with me
for help. My heart is torn apart. I can't bear this.
Overcome with pity I fetch a bag in the corner of
my office full of slightly imperfect goods and clothes
from the store that I've been meaning to donate to
charity. I know that Fergus will kill me for doing
this as I shake the contents out of the bag and they
fall to the ground and scatter everywhere and Elly
helps herself.

The reason he will want to kill me of course is
because he'll think I'm encouraging her. He'll accuse
me of playing God. But the way I look at it, Elly
is a charity case. She needs this stuff more than
anyone, at least her children do. As she leaves the
shop with her bag stuffed of goodies for her babies,
I feel strangely satisfied and ignore Fergus's accusing
stare. I've done my good deed for the day.

Betty from babywear then tells me there's
someone on the phone. Taking a deep breath I go
to the customer service desk.

'Good afternoon, Baby Bloomers?'

'Good afternoon.'

'Can I help you?'

'I have dinner booked for us tonight if you're free.'

'Dave?'

'Of course. Who else could it be?'

I feel my heart somersault. Why is he ringing me at work?

'Dave, oh . . . it's good to hear from you. Things are a bit hectic here at work.'

'I gathered that.'

'We had a bit of an incident with a shoplifter. I was busy trying to sort that out.'

'There's always drama going on in that store of yours. I never thought children's clothes shops were so exciting.'

'Well, there's never a dull moment, that's for sure. Listen Dave, about tonight . . .'

'I can pick you up any time you want,' Dave offers.

Oh what a lovely change from Dermot! I'm so tempted to accept but unfortunately I have already promised to meet two of my best friends tonight. I can't let them down, especially not Sandy. She sounded fairly stressed earlier on.

'I'm afraid I'm not free tonight Dave,' I tell him. 'How about the weekend?' I suggest hopefully.

'Weekends aren't good for me I'm afraid.'

I don't like the sound of that. Weekends are usually not good for married men. Or men with partners. Or kids. Or commitments. Maybe Sandy is right. Maybe I should stay away. I'm certainly not a Tuesday or Wednesday girl, thank you very much. Sexy and all as he is, he can sod off if he thinks I'm that desperate.

'I'm sorry,' I say crisply. 'But I've already made plans for later.'

'Well, that's a pity. I guess I'd better cancel so.'

'Yes, it *is* a pity,' I say with a more than a hint of regret. To be quite honest, I would much prefer a night with Doctor Dave than an evening trading trivial gossip with Sandy and Karen, but I can't backtrack now. 'Maybe next week,' I add, not wishing to cut my ties just yet.

'Okay, I'll be in touch. Just give me your mobile, will you?'

I call out my number, then say goodbye and get back to work. Thankfully the rest of the day flies by and I don't have a second to regret my firm decision, much less change my mind.

Sandy is in an awful state when I meet her outside The Bailey. There's no sign of Karen yet so she takes this opportunity to spill the beans on what's going on in her life.

'Well, there's this lovely little girl called Amy in my class,' she begins. 'Amy is one of my favourites but she came into class yesterday morning with a cut on the side of her face. I asked her what was wrong,' she says, pausing for effect, 'but the poor kid said she just fell.'

'Oh.'

'Yes. And then last night, her father rang the head nun about the cut.'

'Really?' I ask frowning. 'Why did he do that?'

Sandy takes a long drag of her cigarette. She looks pale and drawn.

'He said that I hit her.'

'No way!' I say, horrified.

'I'm serious. And Sr. Whyte called me into her office today to discuss the matter. Apparently Amy's father says he wants to meet me in person.'

'My God! He sounds like a nut. I hope you're not going to meet him alone.'

'Of course not. But I have to meet him tomorrow in the school along with Sr. Whyte and a social worker. The father has said he won't press charges until after the meeting.'

'Jesus. He's not going to call the police, is he?'

'I think *he* was the one who hit her, Lara.'

'And he's blaming you? What an absolute brute.'

'I'm sick with worry. I can't eat anything.'

I'm more than a little jealous about that. Immediately though I feel guilty. One of my best friends is going through a crisis and I'm envious of her dramatic weight loss! What kind of a monster does that make me?

'Anyway enough about me,' says Sandy suddenly. 'I'm going to try and take my mind off things. That's why I wanted to meet you. I hope you don't mind. I just couldn't bear to be alone thinking about it all.'

'No.'

'And sure what else would we be doing anyway?'

'Exactly.'

What else? Well, meeting Dave maybe, I think to myself. Of course I don't say this. Instead I tell her that Karen will be joining us. Sandy seems to be quite pleased about this. She met Karen once at a party of mine and they both hit it off, despite being quite different personalities.

Sandy is a down-to-earth, dark-haired teacher who shops in Dunnes Stores, Penney's and Lidl, watches all the soaps, and goes to bed without taking off her make-up. Karen, on the other hand, is a tall willowy blonde whose work regularly takes her to London and New York, jokingly moans about never having enough downtime, and spends a fortune on expensive cosmetics and creams. The only thing all three of us have in common is our singleton status.

I'm dying to tell the girls about Dave but I can't. Sandy has already made her disapproval clear, and I don't think Karen would understand either.

We spot Karen coming along the street, dressed in a well-cut black suit, her glossy fair hair framing her face and her shoulder weighed down by her leather laptop case. She looks fantastic. A few businessmen enjoying pints at the table next to us, turn their heads in open appreciation as Karen sashays towards us. She doesn't even notice.

'Hi girls,' she smiles and gives us both a kiss.

'God, I'm gasping for a glass of wine. It's been a mental day at work.'

Once served, she sips from her glass appreciatively.

'God I need this,' she grins. 'So what's the craic? Tell me all about your night with Dermot,' she urges me. 'I'm dying to get the gory details. He's been singing your praises all day. You must have made quite an impression.'

There isn't a hint of sarcasm in her face or her voice so she's obviously not joking.

'Poor Dermot,' she elaborates. 'He's had a rough time with women recently.'

'Oh?'

'Yes. Apparently the last woman he went out with was only interested in his money.'

'Really?' I say with interest. 'Why? *Has* he money?'

'Well he has his own house. He's doing it up at the moment. Painting the walls and that.'

'How do you know his last girlfriend was after his money?' Sandy asks curiously.

'Well she was always pushing him to take her out for dinner and take her shopping and things.'

'Poor mite,' I stifle a smile. 'And this time around he doesn't want to get stung again?'

'No, I guess not. Now I know he's not the best looking man in the world . . .'

'. . . nor does he have the best personality,' I can't help adding.

Karen gives me a funny look. 'Did you two not hit it off?'

I decide to come clean about our date. I can't sit here for the evening listening to Karen go on about what a great chap Dermot is. So I start my story and by the time I reach the part about the kebabs, herself and Sandy just stare at me open-mouthed.

'Good God,' Karen exclaims. I'm absolutely gob-smacked. However, now that I think about it, he did say that you were far less maintenance than his exes.'

'Well to put it bluntly, I had a lucky escape. I don't exactly see a future between us, do you?'

Karen shakes her head with regret. 'Poor Dermot,' she says again.

I don't get it. What's all this 'poor Dermot' business? He has his own house, right? And he has a good job earning decent money. Granted, he doesn't have a car, but that seems to be his own choice. In fact, there doesn't seem to be anything remotely *poor* about him, except for the treatment of the women he dates. Suddenly I think of Dave and how he tried to persuade me to join him for dinner tonight. Please God, he'll ask me out again soon. Hopefully I haven't blown it.

'Why do you feel so sorry for Dermot anyway?' I ask Karen.

'Well,' she looks from Sandy to me, toying with the stem of her glass. 'I feel bad for him because he fancied me and I didn't fancy him back. I wanted to get him off my case. So after he expressed interest in taking you out, I thought it would be the perfect solution.'

I'm stunned. Honestly, I'm lost for words. Does she realise what she's saying? That's the kind of thing Janine would come out with, but I certainly don't expect my close friends to behave the same way. Karen is supposed to be an ally! I look at Sandy but she just raises an eyebrow and then looks away. I feel extremely hurt.

Do other women really see me as somebody who is quite content with leftovers? Do they think I should be grateful? So it seems. I have come to the worrying conclusion that girls, no matter how nice they are, will never ever set another one up with a very good catch. I reckon I'm on this ridiculous man hunt alone.

Then suddenly I remember the other guy who was sitting in the restaurant with Karen and Dermot the other day. He was fairly cute as far as I remember. In fact he looked a bit like Pierce Brosnan when he was younger. Smooth and charming. And he spoke well. Probably loaded too. Why didn't she set me up with him, eh?

'What was the other guy's name? The guy in the restaurant? Good-looking fellow?'

Karen frowns for a moment as if she can't quite remember. 'Oh him?' she then shrugs. 'He's Brian.'

'Oh yes, that's right. Now *he* was cute.'

'Indeed,' she says, with a sudden coy look in her eye.

'Is he taken?'

'No, but he will be soon, if I've anything to do with it.'

'Oh I see. Are you two . . . have you two . . .?' I try putting the jigsaw puzzle pieces together.

'Um not yet,' she says almost bashfully. 'You see, it's very awkward. Dermot and him have their desks right beside each other. Brian knows Dermot has the hots for me. He's always been quite open about it. In fact he confides in Brian.'

'So if you go out with Brian things will be awkward in the office?' Sandy says, getting all excited all of a sudden, as if she's listening to the plot of an unfolding soap.

I kind of feel ill. I can't believe I've been so blatantly used. Karen obviously fancies Brian and wanted me to cop off with the boring friend as an excuse for us all to hang out together.

Karen nods. 'It would make things very difficult,' she admits.

'You could have an affair?' I suggest. 'You know, keep it hush-hush.'

Karen doesn't seem to think much of that particular idea.

'I don't want it to be hush-hush,' she sniffs. 'Why would I want that?'

I can't say I'm surprised.

'So has he actually asked you out then?' Sandy enquires.

'Well, not *straight* out. As I said, it's very awkward.'

Sandy and I exchange glances. I wonder if she's thinking what I'm thinking. I mean, everybody knows that if a man really wants to ask a woman out, he'll usually move mountains to do so. Men are incredibly competitive by nature. If other men happen to show interest in their 'bird' it usually only increases their determination to score her.

Karen seems determined not to dwell on the negative however, and swiftly changes subjects.

'It's a pity things didn't work out with yourself and Dermot,' she says with a sigh. 'He's a handy person to know. He does a lot of music PR. He could have got you free cds, free tickets to gigs, free back stage passes, free . . .'

'. . . well a free drink would have been *most* welcome,' I can't help interrupting.

I don't want to talk about Dermot any more. In fact the quicker I can erase last night from my memory the better. I'm sick of being set up with the 'ugly friend'. From now on I want to date the guys a bit further up the ladder of good looks. Second best isn't good enough.

Karen goes on a bit about work. She is the type of person who can happily talk about herself for hours. It annoys some people but doesn't bother me usually. Sometimes my mind wanders and I don't even listen. Other people might notice, but not Karen. She is so busy being fascinated by her own life she doesn't notice if other people nod off in her company. Her job sounds pretty stressful

though, all the same. She seems to spend all day
on the phone pleading with journalists for free
publicity for this and that. She says you wouldn't
believe how rude some of the media are. Apparently
most will turn up to the opening of an envelope if
there's free booze going. But more often than not
they show up, get completely smashed, and then
they never bother writing anything about the event
at all.

She says the social diarists are the worst. The
first thing they do at launches is demand to see the
guest list. She says they usually skim through it with
a sneer and then complain that there's nobody on
the list worth writing about. And even if there *is*
somebody worth writing about, the diarist will only
be looking for dirt.

'It's so cut throat,' moans Karen. 'On one hand
you have the band managers demanding unreason-
able coverage for their protégés, and then on the
other hand you have the journalists, acting the
bollocks and refusing to take your calls when they
see your number flashing.'

'So it's not as glamorous as it seems,' Sandy muses
quietly. Maybe she's thinking her own teaching job
isn't so stressful after all. I know that sometimes
I'm guilty of thinking my life in retail is boring and
unrewarding but at least I don't have to schmooze
with alcohol-crazed journalists on a regular basis,
hoping against hope that they'll mention some event
I'm promoting. God, to think I thought Karen's life

was simply a string of non-stop parties and getting her photo taken for society photos!

'Too right it isn't,' Karen sighs. 'There's very little glamour involved. Like for example, at the moment we're trying to launch this guy who has the most incredible voice I have ever heard. Usually I don't rave about our own acts, but this guy writes his own stuff and is incredibly talented.'

'So what's the problem then?' I ask.

'He's not good-looking, he has a wife and two kids, is faithful, doesn't take drugs, doesn't smash his guitar on stage or throw dvd players out of hotel windows. Big problem as far as the media is concerned, do you know what I mean? Nobody wants to interview him. It's so unfair.'

Suddenly my phone starts vibrating in my pocket, letting me know about an incoming text. I excuse myself to go to the Ladies. Even before I check my messages I've an idea of who it is. And I'm right. Dave just happens to be in town. Or so he's telling me. Is there any way we could meet for a quick drink? I feel a shiver of excitement run through my entire body. Oh God yes!

'Wer R U?' I quickly text him back, my fingers not being able to punch in the words quickly enough.

'Conrad Hotel. Meet in 15?'

'OK,' I text back immediately, before casually walking back out to the others as if nothing has changed.

'Anyone for more wine?' Karen offers as soon as

I sit down. She looks from me to Sandy hopefully.

Sandy answers first. 'I'm afraid I'll have to pass,' she says regretfully. 'Sr. Whyte won't take it too kindly if I show up for school tomorrow stinking of drink. But I'm well on for a session this weekend if anybody else is.'

'Sounds good,' I agree.

'Do you want to stay on and have another with me?' Karen looks at me hopefully.

'Um, I'd better not,' I say making a show of looking at my watch. 'We've got some big deliveries coming in from the UK tomorrow. Brand new stock for the spring,' I add, knowing that I probably sound like the dullest person in the world.

'Pity. But, you're probably being sensible. It's a school night and I don't want to get into the habit of drinking during the week. Well not *every* night anyway,' she laughs. 'So where will we grab a taxi?'

Sugar. I definitely didn't see that one coming. How the hell am I going to get a taxi home to Ballsbridge when I'm supposed to be meeting Dave over in the Conrad?

'I think I might walk,' I say. 'You know, get a bit of fresh air.'

Both Sandy and Karen look at me like I've suddenly grown horns or something. I can feel myself redden.

'But what about your blister?' Karen asks, frowning.

'Yeah,' Sandy chimes in. 'You said your feet were

still killing you after Dermot walked you around Dublin last night in your high heels.'

'Oh yeah, I forgot,' I say lamely. 'Come on then, let's go and hail a cab.'

Reluctantly I follow my two pals as they head towards Dawson Street where taxis are lined up and waiting for business. Karen and Sandy are yapping on about a new brand of fake tan that apparently lasts for up to a week without streaking, while I can't help worrying about being late for Dave. I hope I look reasonably okay. I hadn't had much to eat today, which is good. And if I stay out late tonight, then I won't have time to have dinner. Yippee!

'You're very quiet Lara,' Karen comments as we clamber inside the taxi. 'Everything okay?'

'Oh yeah, everything's dandy. I'm just tired that's all. Last night was pretty draining.'

'Oh yeah, I forgot that you ended up walking round town with Dermot,' she says with an irritating giggle. 'Poor Dermot.'

I take a deep controlled breath. If she says 'Poor Dermot' one more time I think I'll hit her. What about poor me?

Chapter Fifteen

Dave looks better every time I see him. Like a film star, with high cheek bones and gorgeous wavy dark blonde hair. He turns around and then stands up wearing a broad smile. I approach him nervously.

I explain why I'm late. In one breath I start babbling on about having to get a taxi home and then having to come back into town again in the same taxi.

When Dave silences me with a light kiss on the lips, I visibly relax. It feels like it's the most natural gesture in the world. His hand rests on the small of my back as he kisses me again. It's good to see him. No, it's more than that. It's amazing. I'm in heaven. And to think I spent last night hoofing around town with that eejit Dermot!

Dave motions me to sit down. I obey, unable to take my eyes off him. I can't believe that he and I are finally alone after all this time. He asks me what I'd like to drink. I go for something from the cocktail menu. Something I've never tasted before. I want to come across as savvy and sophisticated.

This is special. I can't ruin the moment by ordering a beer.

He decides to have the same as me. I take this as a positive sign. We are bonding. Or at least he's giving a good impression of wanting to bond with me. I'm definitely on a high.

'Thanks for meeting me,' Dave smiles as the lounge girl delivers our cocktails. She smiles as he presses a hefty tip into the palm of her hand. 'It means a lot to me. I just hope I wasn't dragging you away from a night with the girls.'

'Of course you weren't,' I lie.

'The truth is, I couldn't wait to see you.'

His eyes never leave mine. I'm smitten. 'I understand. In fact I feel exactly the same way,' I say nervously, hoping my voice doesn't crack. With every minute I'm falling harder for him. It's like a drug. I wish I was in control, but I'm not and there's nothing I can do about it. Fighting the attraction would only be futile. Anyway, I'm not doing any harm. I'm just meeting him for a drink. Just an innocent drink. Where's the big deal in that?

'I was looking forward to seeing you too,' I say coyly. 'It's nice to meet you when I'm not on the point of collapsing. It's been very embarrassing for me really. I don't have a point of falling at strange men's feet. Honest!'

'I believe you,' Dave replies with a very disbelieving smile.

I sip my cocktail slowly, letting it take me to

another world. I'm so relaxed now. This is good. It just feels right. It's like I've known Dave forever.

'How's work?' I ask, simply because I can't think of anything else to say.

'Same as ever. Still as short of beds. It's frustrating, you know? Treating people on trollies on corridors.'

'I can imagine,' I nod sympathetically. 'The health system is a bit of a disgrace. I mean, what are our taxes paying for?'

'I often ask myself that same question,' Dave muses. 'Certainly it's not like the doctors are being overpaid.'

'Aren't they?'

'No.'

I sip some more. I don't think Dave wants to get into a lengthy debate about our atrocious health system. He must get that *all* the time. I try to think of something witty to say but can't. It's a bit surreal sitting here with Dave. I'm still trying not to pinch myself.

Suddenly he reaches out and clasps my hand. His fingers intertwine with mine. I feel a tinge of unease mixed with excitement. He seems very keen but even this slight physical contact makes me feel nervous suddenly. I mean, where do I stand? What about Dave's partner and family? He hasn't mentioned them and I certainly don't like to be the one to bring up the subject. I don't want to jinx this special moment but I can't just close my eyes, wish away Dave's past and hope that everything will work out in the end. God, I feel like a school-girl on a first date. I mustn't let things get too inti-mate. Not yet anyway.

'So?' I take my hand away in order to push a few stray hairs from my eyes. 'Why don't you tell me a bit about yourself? Or a lot if you like.'

He looks surprised at the sudden request.

'There's not much to tell,' he says. 'I'm thirty-two years old, a born and bred Dub and I work way too hard but I still couldn't imagine doing anything else.'

'Ditto,' I reply, raising my glass.

'Tell me about your family,' I say, the alcohol mixture in my hand giving me more courage than expected. I want to know everything about him. I *have* to know. I refuse to enter a relationship shrouded in secrecy.

He takes a deep breath. 'Well my parents are still alive. My mother's a teacher and she is always at me to settle down. My dad has worked in insur-ance all his life. They're a sound pair. Both of them scrimped and saved to send me to medical school. I owe them a lot.'

I wait for him to continue. 'I have two older sisters and they're both married,' he continues.

'But not you?' I probe.

'Sorry?'

'You're not married?'

'No.'

'But you said you had a partner,' I add, hoping against hope that his response won't hurt me. I don't want to talk about his partner but I'd rather know the truth now, and avoid being hurt later.

'Well, we're having problems,' he says with a sigh. 'Big problems. Huge.'

Suddenly his big brown eyes look troubled.

'How many kids do you have?' I ask.

I want to know everything now. I need to know exactly what I'm letting myself in for.

'We have a son,' he says softly, his eyes lighting up. 'He's almost a year old. He's the best thing that's ever happened to me. It's weird but I can't even really remember my life before he came into the world. Before that I was a boring worka-holic.'

'And not anymore?'

'I'm slowing down. I've decided life is for living and that when I'm on my deathbed I don't want to look on my life and realise that I've spent it all in hospitals.'

'I know what you mean.'

'Gerri and I found out we were expecting just six weeks into the relationship. It was an awful shock. For both of us. But we got through it.'

'Oh, what age is er, Gerri?' I ask uneasily. I don't think I like the way he said 'we were expecting'. Surely as a doctor, he should know better than anybody that men don't get pregnant. Men don't have morning sickness, expand rapidly and lose their figures. So what's with this 'we' business? I don't buy it.

'She's thirty-four. Two years older than me. She already has a little girl from another relationship.'

'So the baby wasn't exactly an accident?'

'On no, it *was*,' Dave stresses as if it hasn't occurred to him that it might not be. 'Very much so. Gerri had forgotten to take her pill.'

I bite my tongue to prevent me from saying anything else. You don't have to be a genius to work that one out. Thirty-four year old women don't happen to 'forget' to take their pill. Especially when they already have a child. This Gerri one was obviously out to trap Dave. She caught him. If she hadn't got pregnant they might not have stayed together at all. A six-week-relationship is hardly serious. Didn't Dave's mother ever warn him about women like Gerri?

'So are you two living together?'

It pains me to ask all these questions. I would rather not know of course. I'd love to change subjects but I feel I have no choice. What's the point in burying my head in the sand, only to take it out when the tide is in and find myself drowning?

'We live in the same house, yes,' he says, looking me straight in the eye. 'But we don't share a bedroom. In fact I can't even remember the last time we made love.'

He takes my hand again and this time I don't retract it. I am overcome with desire for this sexy stranger. I want him to take me upstairs to one of the luxurious hotel bedrooms and have frantic, passionate sex with him. But of course I don't suggest anything of the sort, and when he offers me another cocktail I simply nod my head, thankful that he isn't rushing off home to the house he shares with Gerri.

We keep drinking until closing time. Dave's phone rings a couple of times but he doesn't answer it. I wonder if it's Gerri wondering where he is. Then again, why would she be? They're both living separate lives so she probably wouldn't even care. For all I know, she could be out on a date herself.

'So why are you still living together?' I ask Dave as we eventually head down the stairs and out on to the street.

I know I should drop the subject. Honestly, the last thing I want to do is continue to quiz Dave about Gerri and make him feel awkward but I can't help it. Surely it would be easier for both of them if they lived apart. I mean, I can't even imagine sharing my living space with any of my exes. And what happens if Dave suggests I go home with him? Would it be okay? Would we all have breakfast together in the morning? Would Gerri set an extra place at the table for me?

I wonder has Dave ever brought home anybody else before, and then shudder at the thought of it. I can't bear to think about him physically being with anyone.

Outside the Westbury, Dave puts his coat around my shoulders and pulls me close to him. The weather is fairly nippy so I cling to the warmth of his body. Everything feels right now. I trust Dave. He has been very honest with me. Many men would have avoided questions about previous relationships and maybe tried to gloss over the fact that they had kids. Not Dave. He's like an open book. If only all men were that straightforward.

'Want to go somewhere else?' he suggests, whispering so close to my ear that I can feel his warm breath.

'Well, it's tempting, but . . .'

I have to remember the rules. No nookie on the first night. It's important not to blow this. No matter how nice a guy is, he probably won't respect you if you sleep with him immediately.

'You're right,' he says before I even get the chance to turn him down. 'We've both got early starts in the morning.'

'And there's always the weekend,' I add, squeezing him tightly, not wanting to let go.

He doesn't answer. He just strokes my hair and plants a soft kiss on the top of my head.

In the taxi home, we sit in the back quietly holding hands as the driver tells us story after story.

'There was this one time right? This girl got into the back of the cab with her two pals, are you listening?'

'Yes,' we speak in unison.

'Anyway, one girl gets out and then the other gets out and then there's only one girl left, you know?'

We wait for the story to continue. Dave's other hand is now stroking my thigh and it takes all my concentration to listen to the taxi driver's story.

'I ask her where she's going an' she doesn't answer, so I look around and there she is passed out on the back seat. So I start shouting at her but it's no good. She's not budging.'

'Why didn't you just give her a good shake?' I enquire.

'A good shake? Sure I'd be bleeding arrested for doing that. She could take me to the cleaners for putting a hand on her. Oh God love, you're not allowed touch a female passenger, you know what I mean? Anyway, I'd no intention of driving around all night with that lassie asleep in the back so I took her to the nearest police station but you won't believe this . . .'

'What?' I ask, pretending that the suspense is killing me.

'There was no female garda on duty and the male garda refused to touch her either. He had to ring an off duty female officer to come in and wake her up.'

'I'll bet she wasn't too happy,' I say, thinking of some poor woman trying to get a night's kip and being called in for that.

'She wasn't. She was furious. I'm telling you

she gave that one a good slap when she got her hands on her. You never saw anyone wake up so fast.'

'You must see it all in this game,' says Dave.

'I could write a book about it, I'm telling you. If I had the time I would definitely write a book. You wouldn't believe what I've seen. The night shifts are the worst. The amount of people that get into the car and won't tell you where they're going.'

'How do you mean?'

'They just get into the back and say nothing. I ask them where they're going and they go "I'll tell you when we get there"?'

'Are you serious?'

'I'm telling you, you wouldn't believe half that goes on. Now, are you both getting out here?'

Dave and I look at each other. It's obvious that we don't want to say goodbye. I'm about to speak when Dave says, 'will you just give us a minute?' to the driver.

We walk to the steps of my apartment. Dave cups my chin with his hands, leans down and kisses me softly on the lips. I respond back a little more forcefully and soon we're kissing passionately.

'Will I tell the taxi driver to go on?' Dave whispers hoarsely.

I desperately want to say yes. I look over at the taxi driver, who is tapping his fingers impatiently on his wheel. I'd say he's planning on putting the two of us in that book of his right now.

'No,' I say, fighting the temptation. 'You'd better go.'

'Okay.'

I wish he wouldn't agree so readily.

'What do I owe you for the taxi?' I open my purse.

'Don't be ridiculous,' he snaps it shut. 'I'll talk to you tomorrow Babes.'

And then he's off. I stand watching the taxi as it speeds out of sight. Taking a deep breath I come to an obvious conclusion. Yes, there's no denying it. I, Lara Hope, have finally fallen in love.

Chapter Sixteen

When you're single your mobile phone is just a mobile phone. It's a useful gadget, just like a radio, or a tv or a fridge. It's very handy in that you can use it to text people you don't want to talk to, text others to cancel dates, or say you're running late. And at Christmas you can text your greetings to everybody instead of sending cards, and wish people luck in their exams without having to physically speak to them and waste time discussing subjects you have no interest in.

The mobile phone is great little invention, except that it's a lethal accessory of course when you've had too much to drink. Have you ever been in a nightclub at 3:00am and heard what you think must be the funniest joke ever? Have you then decided to ring your nearest and dearest to tell them in case you forget the joke in the morning? I have. I have also rang ex boyfriends and either been all lovey dovey or exceptionally abusive, depending on what tipple I've been drinking. Gin puts me in a black mood where I just want to go home, curl up in a corner and cry, whereas drinking champagne makes me want to text everyone in town to find out where the party is at.

However, when you meet somebody you fall madly in love with, the mobile phone suddenly becomes a weapon. When it remains silent, you stare at it full of doom and gloom, and constantly check to see if it's switched on. And when there's a text message from 'him' it can genuinely make your day.

Dave didn't call or text the day after our date. I was gutted. I composed many many messages to him. Some were witty, some were romantic, some were desperate. None were sent.

Then yesterday, when I was in work, I got a text from him. It simply said 'Thinking of you.' Of course I analysed it to death. I scrutinised it about a million times. What did it mean? Was it a brush off? Did it mean something? Was he really thinking about me, and if so, how much was he thinking of me? Was he going to ask me out again and if so, when? It was driving me crackers. Why didn't he just ring me? I was dying to hear the warmth of his voice again.

I found it hard to concentrate in the shop. We had lovely new baby clothes in stock, and the latest range of prams and wooden cots but all of that seemed so insignificant now. I just wanted to know what the future held. Would Dave and myself live happily ever after? Would Gerri be moving out?

Would I be moving in? Was I ready for such a big commitment? Was he?

Of course I couldn't ring Sandy to get her to help me analyse the text. As far as Sandy was concerned, I hadn't met up with Dave again. I couldn't tell her I'd gone behind her back and arranged a secret rendez-vous with him. There was a time when I would have told Sandy anything. All that has changed now.

It's hard to believe that just a few short weeks ago I was plodding along with my uncomplicated single life. Now I'm in a state of turmoil. Why are new relationships always so messy? Why do I feel I'm walking on eggshells?

Although he texted me yesterday, I still haven't answered him yet. I don't want to appear desperate. It's better to come across as an incredibly busy, independent woman with a hectic social life. Alas, if only that were actually true! I mean I *am* busy but the old social life leaves a lot to be desired. Sandy, Karen and I are going out tonight and I'm not particularly looking forward to our 'mad night out'. When you're in love all you think about is spending time with 'him'.

Nights out with the girls are not always what they're cracked up to be anyway, but I'm trying to be enthusiastic as I root in my wardrobe for something appropriate to wear. Short skirts are out, as are high heels because I really don't fancy walking home in the freezing cold yet again. However if I wear a polo neck and jeans, I'll be comfortable but will I get chatted up? Then again, why would I even want to be chatted up by a random stranger when I have Dave?

We're meeting in my place for one or two before heading to Davy Byrne's. After that we're planning on doing a pub crawl. Already the night ahead fills me with dread. Pub crawls entail lots of drinking and I'm so sick of having hangovers. They really do seem to get worse with age. When I was younger I would quite happily get completely sloshed and then do it all over again the following night. Now I can't honestly hack the pace. Nor can I stand the thought of spending a full day in bed with the curtains closed, holding my throbbing head and regretting everything I said and did the night before. Most of all I hate opening my handbag and finding all these random phone numbers scribbled on bus tickets and receipts. I have an awfully annoying habit of writing down people's numbers but forgetting to write down their names as well.

Also I hate waking up to find a text message from a completely unknown number going 'how's d head?'

Actually I know what I'll do this evening. I'll have just a quarter bottle of wine and then switch to Diet 7-UP. Then tomorrow morning I can get up bright and early and do something healthy like go for a walk on Sandymount Strand.

I decide to stick on some music to get me in the

mood for going out. Anastasia belts her tunes out from my CD player as I try on outfit after outfit. I wish I was thin, I think for the zillionth time this month. I would love to wear jeans and a simple black top without constantly wondering how big my arse looks. I also hate the fact that while everybody else always leaves their jackets in the cloakroom, I tend to leave mine on and subsequently get hotter and hotter and sweatier and more irritated as the night wears on.

Karen and Sandy are coming over to mine, which is good, because one of my pet hates is waiting for people in pubs. There's only so much interest you can have in the 'Mind your handbag' signs when you're all alone. And I don't like ringing people on my mobile for a pointless conversation, just so I can look busy.

Maybe the girls can advise me on what to wear. Karen is pretty trendy and knows what looks good. Hopefully she can help me out now. Clothes are strewn all over my unmade bed and everything looks crap. I'm badly in need of a proper shopping spree. The trouble with working in a shop though, is that shopping is the last thing I ever feel like doing in my spare time.

My place is reasonably tidy. I say 'reasonably' because it's never actually perfectly tidy. I never have the time to get it spick and span. Well to be honest, whenever I do have any spare time I don't like to waste it doing something as mind-numbingly boring as housework. God forbid, I don't get these women who love a good spring clean. And as for those who swear that ironing is therapeutic? Give me a break.

I've bought some nice flowers, put them in a John Rocha vase and filled it with water. I've also given all the rooms a generous squirt of air freshener and the kitchen counters a good wipe. Now I feel I deserve a holiday! A bottle of wine is chilling in the fridge. I only intend opening one bottle for the girls. If I open a second one, they'll get so comfortable they won't want to go out all. I know. We've been there before. I remember Sandy once called over for a night out. Three bottles of wine later we were in no mood for hitting the town and ended up watching a video instead. Sandy passed out on the sofa half way through it and I'd had to drag her into the spare room fully clothed. I'm sure as hell not going to let that happen tonight.

At 8:15pm the doorbell rings. My heart sinks. I'm not ready. I haven't even finished drying my hair yet. It must be Karen. Sandy would never dare be this early!

I press the buzzer to let her in and seconds later I'm astounded to see Janine and her friend Ruth at my front door. What the hell is going on? Did I invite them over and forget about it or something? Surely my memory isn't that bad.

Janine looks shocked to see my face made up.

'Are you expecting somebody?' she asks before barging into my flat with her pal, Ruth, in tow.

'Just the girls,' I answer.

'Oh, a girls' night in then?' she looks around the place and sniffs the newly bought flowers.

'A girls' night *out*,' I correct her.

'Weally?' says Ruth.

Ruth is one of Janine's particularly annoying friends. She is also engaged. The two of us have never seen eye to eye. I always call her 'Wuth' behind her back because she can't pronounce her Rs.

'Are you going to a westewaunt?' she enquires. 'We can come along so, if you don't mind. I'm hungwy.'

'Well, *I'm* not hungry,' Janine says quickly as I try to suppress a smile. My cousin is obviously horrified at the very suggestion of going out for something to eat. 'Have you something to drink?' She plonks herself down on my sofa.

I'm lost for words. I can't believe the nerve of the pair of them just barging in like this. And why are they both so dressed up?

'We were at a chawity lunch,' says Ruth boastfully. 'It was vewy glamowous, wasn't it Janine?'

'Yes, everybody was there. We got our photos taken by a photographer so do look out for us in the society magazines, Lara.'

'I will,' I say, pretending to be interested. 'What was the lunch in aid of?'

They both look at me blankly.

'What was the charity?' I attempt to clarify the question.

'Oh I dunno,' Ruth shrugs. 'Something to do with poor people I suppose. All in a good cause. I love supporting chawities.'

'Well most charities are always looking for volunteers to collect outside the churches after Mass on a Sunday,' I point out. 'Maybe you should offer your services.'

Ruth looks horrified and swiftly attempts to change subject. 'This is a weally nice place you've got here. Do you live here all by yourself?'

I nod and then go to the fridge to retrieve the bottle of wine I've been chilling for Sandy and Karen. What a waste!

'Lara loves living here by herself,' Janine says snidely. 'She's very independent.'

'Oh I envy caweer women like you,' Ruth giggles as she accepts a glass of wine from me and immediately takes a large gulp. 'You're all so bwave. I used to be a nurse but it was vewy hard work.'

'Why am I brave?'

'You just are. I could never work now. I just wouldn't know where to start. I never twained in anything besides nursing and that was years ago. I don't know one end of a computer from another.'

Janine seems to think this is very funny. 'It's a difficult choice to make, isn't it Lara? Career versus family?'

'It's not a choice at all,' I shrug. 'Anyway, I certainly haven't ruled out having a family in the future.'

'Have you a boyfwend?'

'Yes,' I lie gleefully. I notice Janine's jaw dropping.

'Who is he?' she barks. 'Why didn't you tell me you had met somebody?'

'I met him though work.'

'One of the customers?'

'I'm not telling,' I say coyly.

'But you yourself said the only customers you ever get in the shop are fathers. I sincerely hope this man isn't a family man.'

I say nothing.

'Women who go after family men are the pits!' Janine continues talking in an unbearably loud voice.

'Yes, women who go after other people's men are absolutely widiculous!' Ruth chimes in.

'I don't want to talk about him,' I say firmly.

The buzzer goes. Seconds later Sandy is in the flat. Thank God she has arrived to save the day. She looks none too pleased to see Ruth and Janine however. I hope she doesn't think I've invited them without telling her. As if I'd be that twisted!

'Sandy, I hardly recognised you,' Janine stands up to air kiss her. 'You look different. I think it's your face.'

'Well I'm wearing a different lipstick to the one I normally wear. It's called *Blossom Pink*. I'm not sure I've got used to it yet.'

Janine squints at her. 'I don't think it's the lipstick,

no. I think your face has filled out. It really suits you, you know. It was too thin before.'

Sandy looks livid. She declines a glass of wine from the opened bottle. Instead she has brought her own supply of vodka and Diet Coke. She sits down and sips it in silence as my cousin and her friend yap on obliviously about their fiancés.

'I'm so glad I'm not out there on the scene anymore,' says Ruth, the alcohol beginning to loosen her tongue somewhat. 'I believe it's a jungle these days. I don't know how you single women cope!'

'We manage to get by somehow,' Sandy answers frostily.

Janine pretends she hasn't heard. 'It must be a pain though. I mean I read somewhere recently that there are over sixty thousand more women than there are men in this country alone. The competition must be fierce.'

Sandy gives me an exasperated look. It reads, 'What are these two twits doing here?' I just shake my head helplessly. I wish Karen would bloody well hurry up so we can all get out of here.

Janine and Ruth are fairly knocking back the wine. I must grab myself a glass before it's all gone. Have they no homes to go to? Why are they here anyway? It's Friday night. Why aren't they in the land of Couple Heaven with their perfect men instead of sitting here uninvited, ramming their opinions down our throats?

'Where are the lads tonight?' I ask casually.

'They're at a stag,' says Janine as if she couldn't care less.

'Oh really. Where's the stag on?' Sandy enquires with a mischievous glint in her eye. Uh oh. I know that look.

'They didn't say,' Ruth mumbles, shifting uncomfortably in her seat. 'Anyway Janine, tell us about this joint thirtieth party you're having. Are you getting catewers in or what? God, it's hard to believe you're both going to be thirty, isn't it?'

Janine purses her lips. It's a sore point that although Ruth is a good two years younger than us, she was also the first to get her own house and get engaged. But, Janine is thinner as she so loves to point out behind Ruth's back, has less grey hairs and her fiancé is much better looking than Ruth's. I must say, I'd have to agree with her on that. Ruth's 'Wobert' is certainly no oil painting. In fact when God was dishing out looks, 'Wobert' must have been standing in the 'wong' queue. Not that it seems to make a blind bit of difference to Ruth. *Any man is better than no man*, seems to be her motto.

'I think we'll have to get in caterers, alright, what do you think yourself Lara?'

'I suppose.'

I couldn't care less if we ate crisps off the floor to be honest. This party is going to be nothing short of a nightmare anyway. Just another chance for our Janine to show off in front of all her silly friends.

I'd be just as happy with a good old knees up round at my place.

'I've made a list of people that we're going to invite,' Janine informs us. 'And your name is at the top of the list Sandy.'

'Oh thanks so much,' comes the heavily ironic reply.

'I'll put you down for one, will I?'

'No, you can put me down for two.'

A flash of a surprise flashes across Janine's face. 'Why? Is there a man on the scene at the moment?'

'Not yet, but there will be soon if I've anything to do with it. In fact I feel very lucky at the moment. Put me down for three.'

Janine looks visibly pissed off. 'I'm serious Sandy. We're going to have to be very careful about numbers and all that. The marquee will only hold a certain amount you know.'

I nearly spit out my wine in shock. Marquee? What the hell is she on about?

Sandy's eyes nearly pop out of her head too.

'A marquee?' she exclaims, taking the words right out of my mouth, which is a good job as I'm practically speechless. Nobody has a marquee on their birthday for God's sake! They have marquees for weddings though. Maybe Janine and Alan are planning on getting hitched on my birthday? Over my dead body, I think.

Janine's face remains expressionless. 'I want the

party to be very special. We're inviting a lot of friends we haven't seen in years.'

'And who'll be paying for all of this?' I gasp. 'Just out of curiosity.'

'We can split the bill between us,' says Janine, clearly not comfortable about discussing money matters in front of our friends. I'm annoyed though. She can't just spring a big party like this on me. I don't even want to host one. Most of the people there will be friends and colleagues of Janine and Alan's. I want no part of it whatsoever.

'But what about your wedding?' I ask suddenly. 'Won't you be having a big bash for that?'

'No,' Janine shakes her head firmly. 'We don't want much fuss about that. I'd say we'll go off to Rome and do it quietly.'

I'm about to open my mouth to protest when Karen arrives. She doesn't seem to notice the tense atmosphere in the room and goes around giving everybody a hug, even Janine and Ruth, although she doesn't really know them. I am so relieved that she is here.

'Gosh I didn't know there was such a big gang coming out!' Karen exclaims. 'Oh well, the more the merrier I suppose. There's a good gig on in The Olympia tonight but I've only got three tickets. Not to worry though,' she says fishing her mobile out of her pocket while Sandy and I look on in mild alarm. 'I'll just ring my contact and see if we can get another two. Shouldn't be a problem, although it'll be standing room only. The gig sold out weeks ago.'

She starts punching digits into her mobile but I interrupt. 'Hey Karen, you've got the wrong end of the stick. Janine and Ruth aren't coming out with us tonight at all. They just popped in to say "hello", isn't that right girls?'

I smile hopefully at the two lassies looking very comfortable on the sofa with their glasses of wine.

Ruth turns away from me. 'What's the name of the band Kawen?'

'The Devlins.'

'Oh cool. I really like their music,' says Janine. 'Go ahead and ring your friend and tell them there's an extra two people coming along. Jesus, I haven't had a good night out in yonks.' She holds out her glass. 'Do I have time for a refill?'

I can't believe it. Janine and Ruth never ever invite me to go out with them. And now they're gate crashing my girls' night out. The bloody cheek of them! I quickly refill my wine glass and then look at the empty bottle. 'Sorry Janine, there's none left.'

'Here, you can have some of my vodka and Coke,' offers Sandy, much to my astonishment.

Janine looks at the bottle doubtfully. 'I dunno about mixing my drinks,' she says. 'Should we?'

'Go for it. Let's go cwazy,' Ruth holds out her own glass. 'Come on Janine, when was the last time we went out and painted the town wed?'

Janine can't remember and when Sandy fills her

wine glass with vodka and coke, she doesn't even try and stop her.

At 7:45pm we arrive in taxis at the Olympia. We head for the bar at the back and Karen meets a guy who is apparently 'huge' in the music industry. I shake his hand. He may be big in the industry but he certainly has a beer belly to match. He asks me if I'm into music. I tell him I like The Devlins. He asks me if I can sing.

'No, I cant,' I tell him truthfully.

'Pity. You could look the part if you shed a few pounds.'

At first I think I must have heard wrong. I stare at the man in complete shock. Then I look at Sandy to see her reaction. Her face is expressionless though. I must have been imagining it.

'Would you like a drink Ladies?' the man with the large belly asks.

'We'd both like a vodka and Diet Coke,' says Sandy.

'*Diet*, is it?' the man laughs. 'Don't worry, I'll remember that.'

He waddles off.

'Did I hear what I think I heard?'

'Did he insinuate that we were fat?' says Sandy.

'I think so.'

'You're right. I think he did.'

'Jesus! How dare he! Who does he think he is going around insulting people like that? I've got a good mind to storm off.'

'Well just wait until we get our drinks first,' says Sandy determinedly. 'We might as well get something from the sleazy bastard.

The guy returns about twenty minutes later once the band have already started playing. I want to go out and listen to them and not be stuck in here talking to this insulting creep of a man. We drink up fast.

'So what do you do?' the man asks Sandy's boobs with interest.

'I'm a teacher,' she replies through gritted teeth, pulling her jacket around her.

'Ooh, and I bet you're dead strict and all. I used to fantasise about my Maths teacher when I was in school.'

'And did he ever find out?' Sandy raises an eyebrow.

'*She*,' he answers hurriedly, going a bit red in the face. 'Miss Higgins was a woman.'

'Oh I *see*,' Sandy starts to nod as if it hadn't occurred to her that his teacher might have been female.

I try to suppress a smile.

'And what do you do?' he turns to me with a leer. I notice the foam off his head of Guinness has stuck to his moustache. Ugh.

'Tax.'

'Tax?'

'Yes.'

He looks at me blankly. Good. It works every time.

'Oh right. Well, lovely ladies, I hate to abandon you but I'm just going to mingle a bit. Don't go away whatever you do.'

That is of course exactly what we do. Suddenly we spot Janine, Karen and Ruth over in a corner chatting to not one, not two, but three cute men. At least two of them are cute anyway. One is a bit hairy for my liking. I'm really not a big fan of face rugs. But I wouldn't kick the other two out of bed for a bag of nuts. Hey! How come we didn't spot them earlier?

I give Sandy a knowing nudge and we make our way over.

Karen introduces us immediately and hands are routinely shaken. The guy in the middle is the best looking one with dark hair, cut very short, and a cute smile. He's of fairly small build but everything's in proportion and he looks fit. His name is Frank and he tells me he is a film reviewer.

'Oh?' I feel my eyes widen with interest. I don't often meet men with careers in the media. How exciting! 'And what that does that entail?'

'Going to films and writing about them, that kind of thing, you know yourself.'

Actually I don't know. I can't believe somebody actually gets paid to go to the cinema. What a cushy number! How do you become a film reviewer? Is there a course that you do?

'And do you like that?' I ask, simply because I can't think of anything else to say.

He shrugs. 'Well, it's a job. It's not as glamorous as it sounds. But it's okay. You have to sit through the greatest load of shit sometimes though.'

'Well it beats working for a living, I suppose,' Sandy pipes up. 'And handy when you have a hangover. You can just go into dark cinema and fall asleep for the morning.'

Frank looks a bit put out. 'It's not really like that,' he explains. 'You've got to concentrate, read between the lines, and work out what the director is trying to achieve with the scenes.'

'I see,' says Sandy, looking like she's sorry she's opened her mouth now.

With that, Karen suggests we all go outside and show a bit of interest in the concert. The music is brilliant and I have to say I haven't enjoyed anything as much in a long time. These guys really know how to play a live crowd. After they're finished I'm in a really good mood and don't feel like going home just yet. Karen suggests we all move on to Brogan's next door. She says that you never know who you might meet in there. The place is always full of musicians, actors and artists apparently.

Alas, once inside I don't recognise anyone famous, except for a guy who I think might have once been in Ballykissangel. And no, unfortunately it isn't Colin Farrell. Karen spots a corner seat and we all shove in. The guys buy their own pints and we buy ours.

Karen whispers to us that one of the guys, Bert, is a gossip columnist and therefore isn't liked very much around Dublin. He has an angry face and his small roundy glasses have a habit of steaming up as he speaks. I wonder what makes a man become a gossip columnist. I mean, bitchy gossipy women are bad enough, but now that men are getting in on the act I'm wondering where it will all end?

I ask him how he likes gossiping for a living. He doesn't take it very well.

'I write features as well,' he almost spits.

Right. Well, I won't probe any further. Poor guy. You'd almost feel sorry for him. No wonder he's angry at the world. Nobody ever liked the gossips at school. I mean, it was weird. Secretly, you'd want to know all the gossip so you'd listen to it, but you never actually liked the bearer of all the salacious news, did you? And you'd always be paranoid that the minute your back was turned, their damaging titbits would involve you. Imagine being a gossip columnist for a newspaper though! People would always worry that you were going to stitch them up. Probably, the only people who'd be nice to you would be self-centred egotists willing to sell their souls just to see their names in print.

'That gossip columnist is so bitter he looks like he's just swallowed a whole jar of beetroot juice,' I comment to Karen when we're safely in the Ladies out of earshot.

'You're telling me!' Karen laughs as she reapplies her mascara in front of the mirror. 'Bert is eaten up with self-hatred. He thinks his job is degrading. I mean, imagine hanging out at celebrity events all week, knowing that you're not a celebrity yourself and that you never ever will be. His job is to kiss their asses to get stories. But he knows deep down that if he ever gives up his job, the same celebrities wouldn't spit at him on the street. No wonder he's so miserable. Imagine always being the one on the outside looking in? Imagine going to the beautiful luxurious homes of the stars to interview them and knowing that you have to return to your poky cold little flat afterwards to write up the ramblings of the rich and famous people who automatically forget your name as soon as you walk out their door?'

'Actually I couldn't imagine anything more humiliating. But why on earth do *you* entertain him?' I ask.

Karen sighs. 'Unfortunately, we need him. The band managers are always breathing down our necks asking us to get more and more publicity for our bands. So we make up some half hearted cock 'n' bull story and then phone Bert and pretend we're giving him an exclusive.'

'Is that how it works?' I ask in amazement.

'Ah sure you wouldn't realise the half of what goes on. It's a funny old game this,' Karen says giving her shiny hair a flick. Luckily for us though, Bert, spiteful and vindictive as he is, can be bought.

Post him a few VIP tickets and a bottle of champagne now and again and he drools all over our bands and writes that all of our singers are stunning and talented even if they're actually not. But it suits us though. The bands themselves are over the moon, the managers are happy enough, and it makes my life a hell of a lot easier. And hey, I don't have to live with the guy! Come on, let's go back out there. We're wasting valuable drinking time.'

By the time we get back to our seats, Bert has disappeared. I ask Frank, the film reviewer, where he's gone.

'Home, I suppose. Would you like a drink?'

'Sure, I'll have a vodka and Diet Coke. Thanks.'

Frank then offers everybody a drink. I'm completely taken by surprise. After all, as far as I can remember, Frank was the very one who suggested we should all by our own drinks when we first sat down. After he goes off to the bar, Sandy whispers that the lads told her they've made a pact of not buying rounds until Bert goes home. Apparently he has stuck them just once too often.

Myself, Sandy and Karen end up having a great laugh with the guys. One fellow is a wine critic for one of the Sunday broadsheets and Karen seems to think this is hysterical. 'I would *love* that job,' she keeps saying over and over again while managing to spill half her own glass all over the table, much to the disgust of Janine and Ruth. They have been virtually ignored for most of the evening. Every time I glance over I spot one of them yawning or looking around, obviously bored senseless in each other's company. You see, the problem with Janine and Ruth is that they only want to talk about their men but don't actually want to listen to one another. I keep waiting for them to make their excuses and leave. No such luck however. And when Janine stands up to buy a round, I nearly fall off my chair in shock. Surely this is way past her bedtime.

After that round the girls insist they want to go on somewhere else. They want to go somewhere with music. Hmm. Obviously they can no longer bear listening to each other. As long as we don't head for Temple Bar, which let's face it, is like a mini theme park for Newcastle lasses on hen weekends, I don't mind where we go.

I must admit I'm not overly fond of smelly old pubs with no locks on the toilet doors and no mirrors. Then again I don't exactly love 'trendy' bars full of self-absorbed poseurs with Burberry bags thrown over their shoulders either.

Janine suddenly gets it in to her head that she wants to go to Cocoon in the Hibernian Mall. It's quite a distance on foot from where we are but as it's not raining I'm quite happy to walk. Janine and Ruth won't hear of such needless exercise however, and immediately flag down a nearby taxi. Karen decides to go with them. The rest of us come to a mutual decision that a bit of fresh air won't do any harm. Dublin of course, being a Friday night, is littered with chavs over for the weekend. They all look identical. Straight dyed-blonde stringy hair, thick eye make-up, low-slung jeans with a white, lime green or baby pink belt with matching bag, or else a ridiculously short skirt with legs streaked with orangey fake tan tucked into nasty furry boots.

Sandy and Danny, the wine critic, walk ahead. They seem to be getting on very well. At least their body language would suggest so anyhow. When Sandy trips on an empty Burger King cup, Danny catches her before she crashes to the ground. Her bag falls to the ground though and Danny helps her to gather the scattered contents. As they kneel on the ground, their heads are very close together.

'Don't they look cute?' Frank comments with a chuckle.

'Yeah, you wouldn't think they'd just met, would you?' I laugh. I'm in good form. The vodka has gone to my head and I'm feeling quite light-headed. I'm even finding the chavs vaguely amusing as they link arms and scream into their mobile phones, 'We're in Dublin, it's wicked, yeah!'

'Would you look at that?' Frank suddenly stops dead in his tracks. His face is a mixture of amusement and bewilderment.

'What?'

'Danny and what's your friends name again?'

'Sandy! What the f . . .!'

Sandy and Danny are practically eating the faces

off each other. I am stunned, and more than a bit embarrassed. They've only just met for Chrissakes! Frank starts to laugh. He seems to think this is the funniest thing ever. I don't find it half as amusing. I hope Frank doesn't assume he's going to get the same display of public affection from me! We walk past. I'm about to say something to Sandy but Frank takes me by the arm and says it's best to leave them be.

'But Sandy doesn't know what she's doing!' I protest weakly. Frank isn't buying that however.

'She's a big girl,' he says.

As soon as we enter Cocoon our ears are assaulted by the sound of loud music. The place is literally throbbing with young beautiful people and there are a lot of spiky haircuts everywhere. Still we manage to spot the girls up at the bar. They're surrounded by men. Well, *that* was quick anyway. Lucky girls. At least I think they're lucky until I notice one of the guys is Garry. My heart almost misses a beat. Oh my God! No I'm not imagining it. It *is* him. Garry, the doctor. I get an awful shock when he turns around and waves at me. He looks pretty fantastic but I don't care. I simply blank him. I haven't forgotten his behaviour at the ball. As far as I'm concerned he's a womanising creep.

I pretend I haven't seen himself or the girls and I make Frank sit with me in the far corner of the room. Frank doesn't protest. In fact, I think he's secretly pleased to have me all to himself.

We chat away. About films. No surprises there. Frank is going on about some sci-fi film which to be perfectly honest sounds like a load of crap. But because he seems so genuinely interested in the subject, I pretend to be too.

'It's a fairly complex flick. Really, it's only after you watch it maybe four or five times, that you begin to make sense of it all,' he explains earnestly, staring into his pint of Guinness, as I just sit there nodding, wondering what's the point in it all. If I don't 'get' a film the first time I'm not going to torture myself by sitting through it a second time, never mind a third or a fourth. Roger, a guy I used to date years ago, had a very annoying habit of always sticking on 'The Life of Brian' video after a night out. Himself and his pals used to watch it nearly every single weekend with a few cans of beers, rolling around in amusement while myself and my girlfriends used to look on in bewilderment. What is it about men? Why don't they ever grow up?

Anyway, I don't really mind sitting here listening as Frank painstakingly dissects every film he's seen this week. At least he isn't sitting here talking about himself. You wouldn't believe the amount of guys who do nothing but self promote themselves on a date! It's like they're at a job interview and trying to cram all their life achievements into a fifteen-minute conversation. Don't they realise that most girls on dates just want to have fun and that the last thing they need to know is that the man sitting next them got an A in Applied Physics in the Leaving Certificate?

Eventually Frank excuses himself to go to the bathroom. I sit alone toying with my glass of vodka and Diet Coke. Should I go up to the girls? Will they think myself and Frank are being anti-social for avoiding them? I'm still deliberating my next move when suddenly I look around to find Garry sliding into the seat next to me.

'Well hello there, stranger!' he says smiling and goes to give me a kiss. I offer my cheek reluctantly. He looks better than I've ever seen him before, wearing a classic navy suit and a crisp turquoise shirt that brings out the piercing blue colour of his eyes. He smiles, revealing Hollywood star type teeth. What a good-looking bastard! And what a pity he just happens to know it. If he were a box of chocolates, I'd bet he'd eat himself.

'Hello Garry,' I say suddenly wishing I didn't feel so tipsy. I'm sure I'm not looking that great. I haven't touched up my make-up since we left Brogan's and I wasn't even looking that hot back then. It doesn't matter how much foundation you slap on after a certain point in the night. After a few drinks even the dimmest bar lighting can be cruelly unforgiving.

'Did you enjoy the ball the other week?' he puts a territorial arm over the seat behind me.

'Yes,' I say rigidly. 'Very much. And that girl you were with was lovely, I have to say.'

Garry looks at me oddly. 'What girl?' he frowns as I just look at him in disbelief. Is he for real? Does he think I'm stupid?

Just then Frank comes back and looks anything but pleased to see Garry has taken his seat.

'Excuse me,' he says to Garry.

Garry looks from me to Frank and suddenly doesn't look too cocky anymore.

'Oh forgive me,' he says. 'I didn't realise that you two . . . that you two . . .' he gives an embarrassed cough.

'Yes,' I say vaguely as Garry stands up reluctantly. 'Well it was very nice of you to come over. Take care now. Enjoy the rest of your night.'

Garry offers Frank his hand. He shakes it disinterestedly. Then they both stand looking at each other until it becomes awkward and uncomfortable. Eventually Garry offers a final goodnight and disappears back into the crowd of funny haircuts.

'Was that a friend of yours?' Franks asks me in a sort of flippant manner.

'Not really. I just know him to see.'

'Well he certainly knows you to see. He hasn't stopped staring at you all night.'

'Really?' I ask, momentarily thrilled, but then immediately berate myself for getting excited about such a cocky bastard. So what if he was staring over? He was just trying to make a point. Huh! He obviously couldn't bear the fact that I didn't run over to hurl myself at him.

'I know that type,' Frank says dismissively. 'Fucking suit. He should get himself a real job.'

I try not to laugh at the irony of that. I mean, Frank spends his days in darkened deserted cinemas eating popcorn and trying to figure out the meaning of life through the eyes of off-the-wall film directors, while Garry, for all his devious womanising, at least saves lives for a living. But why am I even thinking about him, never mind sticking up for him? I would never fall for somebody like Garry no matter how tempted I was. Yes he's handsome and charming, but he's a sleaze and plays women. It's such a pity. I glance over at the bar again. Once again Garry has taken centre stage and I can see Karen and Janine lapping up his charms. Jesus, don't they know any better?

Suddenly I wonder is it simply a coincidence that Garry and his pals just happen to be in the same bar as Janine. I put the thought to the back of my head though just as quickly. I'm being ridiculous. Bad and all as Janine is, surely, surely . . . mind you, she did seem fairly delighted with herself when Garry texted her. In fact she couldn't wait to share the good news with me in order to ruin my day. I look over again and she is sitting very, very close to him. Too close. I see no sign of Ruth. Sensible girl. She must have decided to go home early. And as for Janine, well she's obviously making the most of her last few weeks as an official singleton . . .

I'm bursting to go to the toilet. I excuse myself

and push my way through the crowd to get down to the bathroom. I walk down the stairs carefully, terrified that I might fall. In the Ladies there's a predictable queue. I cross my legs and silently urge the others to hurry up. Why do women take so flipping long in the cubicles anyway? If we all just took a few seconds, then there'd never be any queues.

I hate queuing for the bathroom. It's as annoying as standing in the queue for the Pass machine. I always end up behind some fecker who inserts his card and then stares at the screen instructions for about twenty minutes scratching his head. People like that should be fined for time wasting!

The bright blonde bombshell in front of me is even more impatient than I am. She starts hammering on the nearest door. 'Would you ever hurry up in there? My bladder's about to explode!' she yells in a not-so-ladylike manner.

'I'm not weady,' replies a faint voice. It's so weak I can barely hear it. But I definitely recognise that voice.

'Ruth. Is that you in there?' I ask, horrified.

'It is Wuth. I'm not weady.'

The bombshell is not impressed.

'She's obviously plastered,' she says scornfully as she hammers on the door again.

'No actually, she always speaks like that,' I tell her ignoring the filthy look being thrown at me.

Luckily one of the other cubicles becomes free and

the bombshell disappears, thank God. Bathroom scraps are regular occurrences when you're a teenager. Once you're approaching thirty however, they're definitely best avoided.

'Ruth?'

'Yeah?'

I can barely hear her. I hammer on the door again but she doesn't answer. Fuck it anyway. Thankfully the bathroom has cleared somewhat now, and when the cubicle next to Ruth's becomes free, I go in, stand up on the toilet seat and peer over the partition. Ruth is on the toilet seat with her head leaning against the wall. She looks completely out of it.

'Ruth!' I yell, and she opens her eyes momentarily before shutting them. Oh sugar, how the hell am I going to get her out of there? I definitely don't want to go upstairs and have to ask the staff for help. And Janine wouldn't be able to wake her up any more than I would.

'Ruth! Jesus, would you ever open the door?' I call in exasperation.

'Okay,' she says and stands up shakily.

I jump off the toilet seat.

'Sorry about that,' I tell a girl waiting sympathetically outside. If I wasn't so worried about Ruth, I'd be mortified. This is the kind of carry-on you'd expect at a school disco, not here.

As soon as I get Ruth out of the cubicle, I make sure she splashes her face with cold water. She's in a right state. No wonder! Herself and Janine have been drinking since this afternoon.

I haul her upstairs and sit her down, while I go and fetch Janine. As I don't want to announce Ruth's business to the world, I whisper in her ear.

Janine comes over to where Ruth is sitting, visibly displeased about being torn away from Garry and his cronies.

'Ruth?'

'Mmm?'

The girl's eyes are practically rolling in her head. Janine looks at me and then throws her eyes to the ceiling.

'She always does this,' she mutters. 'Ruth can't hold her drink at all. You can't take her anywhere. Look at her trying to ruin our night!'

I'm appalled by Janine's selfish outburst. Ruth is supposed to be her best friend. And besides, she isn't trying to ruin anybody's night. It's obvious just by looking at her. Ruth doesn't even know where she is.

'We need to get her into a taxi and home fast,' I tell Janine grimly.

'Fine. If you take her outside to Dawson Street, there's a taxi rank there. Mind you,' she says looking at her watch, 'it's late. You might have to flag one down.'

'Janine,' I say firmly. 'She's your friend. I presume you are coming with me.'

Janine face falls. I feel like smacking her.

'I mean it. You're coming with us, do you hear me?'

'Right so,' she says sulkily, obviously realising she's not going to get out of this one. 'I'll just get my coat then.'

She flounces off.

'You're going to be okay,' I whisper to Ruth. 'We'll have you home in no time.'

Suddenly Janine is back. I look over to where I've been sitting with Frank but I don't see any sign of him. Where could he have disappeared to?

Myself and Janine manage to haul Ruth out of her seat and out into the night. As we're walking towards Dawson Street, we hear footsteps approach us. I swing around to see Garry catching up with us.

'Is she okay?' he asks, his voice full of genuine concern.

'She's fine,' says Janine. 'Don't worry. You go back to the bar. As soon as we have her safely in a cab, we'll be back.'

Garry takes a good look at Ruth who isn't doing a very good job of remaining steady on her feet. 'You can't put her in a taxi like that,' he says. 'And besides, no taxi is going to take her. She might get sick, or worse, pass out.'

'Well what do you suggest we do then?' demands Janine, clearly irritated.

'I'll drive her home,' Garry offers.

'But you've been drinking,' I protest.

'I've only had two pints. My last two drinks were cokes.'

Janine and I look at each other.

'Honestly, I'm sober. I'll drive her home. I've got a clinic in the morning so it's time I was heading off anyway. You go back to the bar, girls. I promise I'll look after her.'

'I'll come with you,' Janine suggests, much to my surprise.

'No, there's no need for that. Go on back to the bar,' he says and this time it sounds like an order.

'Fine so.' Janine grabs my arm. 'And thanks Garry. Give me a ring tomorrow, won't you?'

We get back to the bar. I can't help thinking how decent Garry was tonight. Maybe I misjudged him before. Now, I can't find Frank anywhere. He must have gone home. Sugar. I never got to say goodbye. Karen is still at the bar, getting cosy with one of Garry's pals. Our little group just keeps getting smaller as the night wears on and people drop off. Janine suddenly decides she wants to go to a nightclub. Karen and her new 'friend' are all for it too. Personally I'm not sure it's such a great idea to prolong a night that has already seemed to go rapidly downhill. I'm persuaded by the others however and soon Karen is leading the way to a nightclub around the corner. Because she seems to know the manager, we are whisked inside and up to the VIP area.

Garry's friend is visibly impressed and although I hate to admit it, so am I. As I look around I spot various familiar faces from the world of small tv. I half expect to see Colin Farrell here as I've read somewhere that he's in town this week, but no such luck. I do spot one or two newsreaders however, and a couple of models that you always see in papers promoting scratch cards and alcoholic drinks.

The fawning hostess immediately finds us a private booth. She obviously thinks Karen is mega important. And I suppose she is in a way. Even by her own admittance, the music industry is pretty incestuous. And when some of the biggest music stars are in town, it's Karen's job to decide where to take them around. As a result she gets free admittance into, and reserved seating, in any club in town.

It makes perfect business sense for the clubs because if Karen's protegés are 'papped' coming out of a club, it's fantastic publicity for the owners. And publicity like that leads to more promises of endless supplies of bubbly for Karen any time she decides to pop in. Like tonight, say.

The hostess takes a good look at myself, Janine, and Garry's friends, but if is she is disappointed we're not famous, she certainly doesn't let it show.

Garry's friend orders champagne from the wine list. And soon we're all raising our glasses to toast the night. I actually don't know how Janine has the stamina to keep going. Her stomach must be made of iron or something. After a while she receives a text from Garry to say that Ruth has been safely delivered home. Funnily enough, Janine seems more pleased that Garry has texted, than with the knowledge that her best friend hasn't died of alcohol poisoning. Sometimes I wonder about Janine. I mean, how our mothers could be sisters? How can we share the same blood? We couldn't possibly be more different. Although I'm trying my best to enjoy the night, I'm struggling to keep my eyes open at this stage. I feel bad about having deserted Frank, and I feel bad for the way I imagine Ruth will be feeling tomorrow. And as I look around the bar I see how drunk everybody is, and how the sleazy men in suits are chatting up the hard-faced, dyed blonde women on the wrong side of forty, I suddenly remember why I'm not particularly fond of the Dublin club scene. When you haven't been out for a while you always think you're missing out on the fun nights. Sitting here however, is a stark reminder of reality.

Half way through my glass of champagne, a tanned man with dark spiky hair slips uninvited into the seat beside me. He's good-looking in a kind of obvious kind of way. He looks a bit like Charlotte Church's rugby playing boyfriend, Gavin Henson.

'Hello?' he says cheekily.

Janine gives him a withering look.

'How are you girls enjoying your night?'

'It was going great until you came along,' she says wearily.

The spiky haired one doesn't seem to hear. He turns his attentions solely on me.

'What's your name?'

'Lara.'

'I'm Jonathan.'

He shakes hands with myself and Janine.

'What do you do?' he asks.

Oh here we go again. What is it with men in clubs? Why do they try and place you straight away? Maybe I should start carrying around copies of my CV to save me from having to explain myself to every second bloke.

'I'm a beauty therapist,' I decide to tell him, just for the hell of it. Hopefully he'll just sod off then.

No such luck however. His eyes widen with interest. 'Oh really? Do you own your own salon?'

'We both own it,' Janine joins in with a smirk. 'We're business partners.'

'So next time I'm looking for a back, sack and crack I'll know where to go,' the guy says and starts to laugh like it's the funniest thing he's ever said in his life.

'C'mon Lara,' Janine suddenly grabs my hand, 'let's go and dance.' We leave the uninvited stranger in the company of Karen and Garry's pal, who have just started to indulge in a game of tonsil tennis. He won't stay long there, I reckon.

'What a creep!' Janine shouts to be heard above the music. 'Men like that shouldn't be allowed into the club to hassle us. It's a pity 'cos he was good-looking. There's no other good-looking men here at all, is there?'

'No.'

'I'm glad I came though. It just reminds me of how lucky I am to have Alan.'

I grit my teeth and start jigging to the music. We're the only people on the dance floor but that doesn't matter. Given enough drink most people usually think they can give Britney a good run for their money. And I, unfortunately, like most inebriated folk, tend to leave my inhibitions with the cloakroom attendant, along with my jacket.

We're not alone on the dance floor for very long. A tall lanky fellow in a loud check shirt and tight black trousers joins us for some Travolta style dancing. He's actually quite funny until he tries to grab Janine's arse. She dodges his lunge, he falls flat on his back and is promptly removed by security as we look on in amazement. Jesus, I hate to admit that Janine is right, but being single really is like negotiating your way around the jungle. One false move and you'll be bitten by a slithery snake. It's weird, you know, you read articles about why now is a brilliant time to be single, but I bet those articles are written by housewives who do a bit of freelance magazine writing to help pay the grocery bills. I mean, there is no way genuine singleton journalists think bopping around seedy joints like this is a laugh.

I continue dancing around in a daze. I honestly dunno what's going to become of m all. I mean, obviously I have high hopes for Dave and myself.

But just suppose it doesn't work out and I am forced to hang around nightclubs week after week looking around anxiously for somebody who seems relatively normal? I don't think I could bear that to be honest. I mean, it's such hard work finding someone in the first place, but then when you finally nab someone, it's even harder trying to keep them! Karen and I often talk about this. She once said to me that the difference in studying for exams and trying to make a relationship work is that at least with studying, you know you're going to achieve something at the end of it all. And she's right. If you put in the hours and hard slog, you'll get the results. But the harder you chase a man the more he seems to run in the opposite direction. And the more heavily you invest in a relationship, the more you worry that your other half is simply going to throw it all back in your face and that your 'love account' will be emptied of every last cent.

Karen and Garry's friend are leaving now. They say they are tired. Er . . . right. Whatever. We all say good-bye . . . and then there were two.

Janine is like the bloody Duracell bunny bopping up and down on the dance floor. I don't know where she's getting all her energy from. I look at my watch. It's almost 3:00 am. I must say I'm a little bit disappointed with the VIP area in this place. I thought it would be a lot more glam. I mean where are U2, Liam Neeson and Gabriel Byrne? That's what I want to know. To be perfectly honest, if I hadn't been told this place was so cool, I'd be forgiven for actually thinking it was quite boring.

Any man who has tried to chat us up has been a sleazebag or off his head on something. All the girls are wearing designer dresses and vacant stares. The atmosphere in here is about minus one. Maybe it's time to call it a night. My head is telling me that anyway, even though my feet are determined to keep dancing. So are Janine's. Every time I go to sit down she pleads 'Oh just one more song, please!'

She's like a teenager who has sneaked out from home without her parents knowing. I'm seeing quite a different side to Janine tonight. Oh, don't get me wrong, I know she's still her same selfish spiteful self, who had no qualms about letting friend Ruth get into a cab completely sloshed, but she's certainly letting her hair down tonight. For a girl who's about to be married she looks like cookbooks, DIY tips, soft home furnishings and wedding lists are the last things on her mind.

'Do you want to go outside to the main dance floor?' I ask Janine.

'Why? What's out there?'

'The non VIPs,' I say, trying not to laugh. 'You know, the ordinary people who pay to get it in?'

Janine agrees. 'Yeah, it might be more fun. Who are all these VIPs anyway? There isn't a real celebrity within a hare's sniff of this place.'

We head downstairs to the riff-raff, who, believe it or not, are slightly more civilised than the VIPs.

There are also far more men than women in the room, which is also a bonus. In fact it's not that surprising. I have always maintained that if you're serious about looking for a fella, then Friday night's the night to do it. It makes sense when you think about it. Most men go out for a few pints straight after work on Friday. Of course, I don't think they actually plan to dance the night away in their suits. And they I'm sure they don't envisage scoffing kebabs on the street about ten hours after they leave the office either. But that's just the way it goes.

You know yourself. You leave the office, it's a nice evening, you've had a very stressful week and you can't wait to forget about it all over a drink or two. And anyway bonding over a couple of bevvies is a good way to keep in with the crowd work. At least, if you're standing in the middle of your colleagues, there's less chance of them verbally savaging you in between pints. Everyone knows that some poor sod is usually slated during after-work drinks. With any luck, if you're standing within earshot, it won't be you.

So there the guys are, standing around the pub, trying to buy the boss a drink and look like they're well in with him. The boss, if he has any sense, will leave after a couple, while the rest hang on for another to dissect him. It's around this time, they half think about going home but then the barman miraculously comes around with crisps, cocktail sausages and a few sambos on a tray. This satisfies the hunger pangs and now they're on to their fourth or fifth pint. If they last this long, it's highly unlikely they'll be going home. Anyway what's there to go home to? A man without a partner faces a long lonely night in front of the telly with a takeaway on his lap. It makes much more sense to keep going and when the pub finally closes, it's onto a night-club.

Women, on the other hand do it all differently. After a stressful week in work all they want to do is go home, take off their uncomfortable suit and high heels, remove all their make-up, have a nice bubble bath and then watch the Late Late show wearing a face pack and sipping a nice cool glass of Carmen. They decide they'll hook up with the girls on Saturday night instead. Yes. That way they'll be nice and rested, get their hair done in the after-noon, maybe get a nice top in town and finish off the day's shopping by relaxing in a fancy restau-rant somewhere. After that they'll hit a few pubs and notice how many women there are in Dublin.

Because you see, all the girls have had the same idea. They're all disappointed and then spend the night in girlie groups moaning about the fact that 'there are no men out there'. They're wrong. You see, there are men out there alright. But they're not out on a Saturday night. Why? Well, because on Saturdays the guys are all partied out, have their feet up on the sofa and are watching the TV with a few cans of beers. So my advice to all the single gals out there is, no matter how wrecked you are on a Friday, get those dancing shoes on!

But anyway, there I am going completely off the point. Back to the club. Here we are in a sea of jiving suits. The party's in full swing and we're partying like there's no tomorrow. The men are flocking around us. Janine looks like she's in her element and if I'm being honest, so am I. God, I wish life was always this much fun. It's a pity we wasted all that time in the VIP area.

But suddenly as we're at the bar, and some man we've never met before is insisting on buying us drink, Janine freezes. As I've had quite a lot to drink now, I'm not exactly sure what is going on but I notice her eyes are fixed on a couple in the corner. A man in a grey suit and a rather tubby girl with a black sequined skirt riding up her leg and showing the world a bit too much of her thighs. Nothing too unusual there. At this time of night anything goes. But then I realise why Janine looks like she's just found herself in the middle of a horror flick. Recognition sets in like a slap in the face. The guy takes a breather from snogging the girl, turns around and Janine's hand flies to her mouth to suppress a scream. We know that man. Both of us know him. It's Ruth's fiancé. Not somebody who looks like him, but the very man himself. We both stand rooted to the spot.

'Jesus! I don't believe my eyes!' I gasp.

Janine's face has gone a shade of unhealthy purple.

Her eyes are bulging so much they're in danger of popping out their sockets. She looks too angry to speak.

'Isn't he supposed to be out with Alan?' I shout to be heard above the throbbing music. 'You didn't know they were going to be here, did you?' I add, suddenly becoming suspicious. Is this the real reason why Janine has been refusing to go home all night? Did she have a sixth sense about this or something? Christ almighty, it hadn't even occurred to me that we might have bumped into the lads.

But where is Alan? My eyes search the room. He must be in here somewhere. And then I see him. On the dance floor. He's with somebody. They're slow dancing. And Alan's hand is placed firmly on the girl's skinny arse. I am momentarily stunned. But before I can shield Janine from the scene, she spots him too. I try preventing her from making a scene by grabbing her arm but she wriggles free. And like an uncomfortable scene from EastEnders, she's marching over there, all fired up. I watch open mouthed as she drags her fiancé away from his new-found friend, draws back her fist and then punches him right in the mouth.

Everything happens so fast, and before I can even manage to get my head around the ugly scenario, we have all been kicked out onto the street. Alan is now sporting an unsightly bloody nose, and despite his protests to 'keep it down and stop making a scene', Janine is screaming at him like a common fishwife.

We're all outside now and a crowd of curious on-lookers have gathered around. People always love a bit of a scrap after a night's drinking, especially when there's been nothing much doing all night. Tonight the crowd is only too delighted to be provided with some last minute entertainment on their way to Abrakebabra or the NiteLink or wherever. The doormen are warning us that if we don't move on immediately, the police will be called. Things are going from bad to worse. I think I'm feeling an early hangover coming on already. I cannot believe that only moments ago I was bopping around the club without a care in the world, marvelling at all the fun I was having, and wondering why I didn't do this sort of thing more often.

Chapter Seventeen

Breakfast

> Fried eggs
> Baked beans
> Toast and butter (about 500 slices)
> Hash browns
> Lucozade (2 bottles)
> Biscuit and raisin Yorkie
> Salt 'n' vinegar crisps
> Ice cream
>
> Total calories: A million.

I wake with the sun glaring through the thin blinds. My clothes are hot and sweaty because the room is so hot, and they stink of stale cigarettes. A fly is buzzing somewhere in the room but not near enough for me to lash out and swat it. I feel like shit. I am honestly never drinking again. Christ, I can barely raise my head. I would pay any amount of money now to just feel normal.

Janine slept in my bed last night because she was too upset to go home. And too devastated, obviously, to sleep on my couch. Instead I was the one who woke up on the living room sofa with a creek in my neck, the lights still on and last night's make up still caked on my face. There are five missed calls on my phone and an empty bottle of champagne lying sideways on the floor. Jesus, we must have drunk that when we came home. Odd. Last night was hardly a cause for celebration. I have absolutely no recollection of opening anything anyway.

I check my phone to see who the missed calls are from. One is from my mother, three are from Alan and the most recent one is from Dave. Funnily enough, I'm too hungover to even care and I certainly don't have the strength to ring him back. Instead I listen to my messages. My mother is wondering if I'd like to go and visit some garden centre with her and Dad. Well, obviously not. Not unless she wants to see me vomiting into the plants and shrubs. The three messages from Alan are all the same. He's wondering if Janine has stayed with me last night and, if so, is she still in my place. Well she is, sort of. At least she's here in body, if not in mind. And Dave is just ringing to simply see how I am. Aaghh. I snap the phone shut. He doesn't need to know how I am. I need a new head. I feel somebody is driving an electric screwdriver right through the middle of it. When will I ever learn?

Last night was supposed to be fun, so why am I suffering? Never ever again. I know I've said this a zillion times before but this time I really, really mean it. I'm getting way too old for this kind of carry on.

Janine surfaces just after lunch looking like she's just been woken from the dead. Her face is deathly white but make up free. How did she remember to take her make up off and I didn't? How can somebody be drunk and disciplined at the same time? God, I can't even remember coming home, never mind being able to scrape the muck off my face. And judging by the furry tongue hanging out of my mouth, I didn't even remember to brush my teeth. My mouth feels like bread mould.

'There's loads of food in the kitchen,' I mumble at her. 'Help yourself. Alan keeps phoning my mobile by the way. What will I tell him if he calls again?'

'Tell him he can go to hell.'

'Right. How's your head anyway?'

'Don't ask. Have you coffee?'

'It's in the dark green jar, next to the microwave. You can go ahead and make me a cup while you're at it.'

'Sure.'

Gosh, I hate to be sadistic or anything, but Janine is actually nice and mellow this morning. I can't believe she's even agreed to make me a coffee without putting up a fight, bless her. Hangovers obviously suit the girl.

Minutes later, she returns with two steaming mugs of strong black coffee. She has even washed two saucers to put them on. I am so, so impressed. Imagine being able to actually fill a sink and wash things with a hangover. She sits on the rug on the floor with her coffee and stares into it as if in a trance.

'Are you not having anything to eat?' I ask, as I'm able to hear her stomach grumbling.

Janine shakes her head. 'I'm not hungry. I'm too sick to eat.'

Too sick to eat, I think jealously, suddenly feeling disgusted with myself for pigging out earlier. How come I'm never too sick to eat, eh? You've got to hand it to her though. Janine is disciplined right to the very end. She should have been in the army.

She sits there motionlessly. Neither of us speak for a while. And then, trying to make her feel better, I say, 'it'll all be alright Janine. Don't worry. These things happen.'

But instead of being grateful for my well-meaning words, she looks up at me, her face full of contempt.

'You're taking the piss, right?'

I'm taken aback by her confrontational manner. I'm only trying to help, aren't I? Trying to ease the pain and all that. Jesus, would she rather I sat here laughing about the whole thing?

'Things are never as bad as they seem,' I reply

hoping I don't come across as a painful know-it-all.

'This time they *are* as bad,' Janine says in a very quiet voice, as if she's talking to herself. 'It really doesn't get any shittier than this.'

'So . . . so do you think that it's all over?'

'You were there. You saw him molesting that tart. What do you think I'm going to do? Go over there and hop into Alan's bed and make up with him? Not if he were the last man alive.'

'He was drunk.'

'Yeah, well we were all drunk. But I don't recall either of us misbehaving,' Janine says huffily.

I don't disagree. Janine wasn't exactly an angel herself last night but I don't think this is a good time to remind her that she was practically sitting on Garry's knee in Cocoon. Nor do I jog her memory about the way she called after him on the street to ring her.

'At least he didn't snog her,' I point out, trying to be optimistic.

'That's because we got there just in time,' Janine practically spits. 'Who knows what might have happened if we hadn't happened to arrive when we did? Himself and Ruth's fiancé might have gone somewhere for an all out orgy and we would have been none the wiser.'

'Jesus, I'd forgotten about Ruth's fella. Do you think she knows?'

'Of course not,' Janine scoffs, rubbing her eyes

with tiredness and yawning. 'You don't honestly think he phoned her this morning to tell her the good news, do you?

'Well, no. So, are you going to tell her?'

'Are you mad? Of course I'm not.'

I look at Janine in disbelief. I can't believe she's not going to tell her best friend what we both plainly saw.

'But you can't let Ruth be in the dark about this,' I protest.

'If you're so concerned, why don't you tell her?'

'Me? Sure I barely know the girl. That would be ridiculous.'

Janine shrugs. 'Ruth wouldn't believe me anyway. Women never do. They don't believe things like that even when it's staring then in the face. I'm sure this isn't the first time that guy was unfaithful. Ruth's not going to call her marriage off over anything I decide to tell her. If I'm the messenger, I'll be the one who gets shot. I'm just not prepared to take that chance.'

I understand where Janine is coming from. Sort of. I wonder if I'd like to know if I was being cheated on? I mean, I'm pretty damn sure that I would but, yes I probably would hate the person who told me. It's a tricky one that. No wonder the wife or girlfriend is always the last to know in these situations.

Janine drains the last of her coffee, stands up and stretches, revealing her taut tanned stomach. Even after a night on the booze, she doesn't seem to have added a flabby ounce to her midriff. I'm so envious. Life is so unfair. She's wearing a pair of my old jeans, which haven't fitted me in years. I bought them in a sale, determined to fit into them one day. That one day never came. And now those same jeans are hanging off her.

'I suppose I'd better get a move on,' she sighs, 'and decide what I'm going to do with the rest of my life, now that it's suddenly fallen apart.'

'Don't be so hard on yourself,' I say kindly. 'You're just feeling a bit hungover and miserable. Go on home, get into bed, and sleep on things.'

'Sleep?' Janine looks at me like I've suddenly sprouted a pair of horns. 'I don't have time to sleep. I'm off to the gym to do a good five miles on the treadmill. Now that I'm single again, I'll have to make damn sure I get my figure back.'

Her figure back? I shake my head in amazement. When did it ever go away? Well, there's a girl who refuses to stand around while the grass grows under her. She's bloody fantastic.

I let her out. At the door, her face softens for a split second. 'Thanks for letting me stay pet. You've been very kind. But please don't tell me again that things have a habit of working themselves out. It's just so annoying.'

I open my mouth to say something but she sticks out her hand and covers it swiftly.

'I mean it,' she says with determination. 'Another

positive word out of your gob, and I'll clock you one.'

And after seeing her in action last night, I decide I'd better not take a chance.

Chapter Eighteen

My diet has resumed. They say that even if you have a bad day you should never give up. So I won't. I have been very good today so far, but considering it's only 10:00am in the morning, maybe I shouldn't be celebrating just yet. Yesterday was a total wipe-out. An absolute disaster.

Although I thoroughly admire Janine's sense of discipline, when I'm as hungover and depressed as I was yesterday, the fridge becomes my best friend. Even the 'fat' photo stuck on the front did nothing to prevent me from opening the door and raiding the contents. But now it's Sunday and I'm back to my normal self.

I'm not sure why I felt so low yesterday. But I did. Everything just seemed a bit negative and hopeless. I felt bad for Janine and even worse for Ruth. I didn't feel at all smug about the bad behaviour of their men. I didn't think how lucky I was to be single. No. I just felt kind of disillusioned about the whole relationship game, and realised how many people out there were living a lie. Seeing the behaviour of those guys made me think that you just can't trust any men. I feel almost as depressed as I did when I read about Brad Pitt and Jennifer Anniston splitting up. I mean if they can't work it out with all their fame and money, how can I manage?

Sometimes I think about my mum and dad and how devoted they are together. Like my grandparents were before them. People long ago didn't seem to mess around as much as they do now, did they? Men went to work and came home and their wives were waiting for them with a nice dinner or whatever. The women weren't out working, nor were they hanging around bars. Anyway, I suppose they didn't have the money back then to socialise in clubs till all hours.

I wonder is there such a thing as a faithful man? Somebody once told me that the only men who didn't have mistresses were poor men because poor men couldn't afford them. At the time I thought it was one of the most depressing things I'd ever heard. But is it true? For crying out loud, surely there are *some* people out there who make the vows, utter the words 'forever' and actually mean it.

I wonder was Dave ever unfaithful? Did infidelity split them up? If he cheated on her and subsequently broke her heart, then how can she bear to live under the same roof as him? How does she even cope now knowing that he is dating other women? Or does she even know? Has he told her? Can I trust him when he says he's telling the truth?

Indeed it has crossed my mind that Dave's ex might deep down be hoping for a reconciliation. I certainly couldn't have lived with any of my ex boyfriends after we'd split up. Their whole set-up is a bit unconventional I must admit. It's doing my head in. Why can't I find a normal man with no baggage? Granted, once you reach a certain age, most people you meet are going to be carrying a certain amount of baggage. But unfortunately for me, most of the men I meet seem to towing a couple of caravans full.

Although Dave phoned yesterday he didn't leave a message. I wonder why? I wonder what he did with himself over the weekend. I wonder did he think about me? And if so, was it a little or was it a lot? Man, I'm driving myself crazy thinking about him.

I'm giving my apartment a bit of a spring clean this morning. A cluttered place is the sign of a cluttered mind, or so they say. There's little I can do about the state of my mind, but if dusting the windowsills can help, then I'm all for it. I stick on my oldest tracksuit and tie my hair in an unflattering bun. Now I'm ready. But God, where will I even start? Maybe I should get myself a housekeeper. Next time in the supermarket I definitely must check the notice boards.

I think I'll start with a bit of dusting as that's

not too strenuous, but just as I begin to take the picture frames off the window sills, the buzzer sound loudly, almost giving me a mini heart attack. Who on earth could that be? As it's Sunday, it's obviously not the postman or somebody selling something. And my mum thankfully always calls in advance. Janine was only here yesterday so it's hardly her again. I wonder if it's Sandy. I haven't had sight nor sound of her since she met that rock critic . . . or wine critic or whatever the hell he was.

I press the intercom.

'Hello?'

'It's Wuth. Sowy to disturb you but I was wondering if you were fwee for a chat?'

Oh Jesus, Mary and Joseph, I don't fucking believe this! What the hell is Ruth doing here? And what does she want? How can *I* help? I feel myself breaking into a cold sweat. I am so not prepared for this. Has she come to confront me? Will she interrogate me about her fiancé's behaviour? What am I supposed to say? How much has she heard? Has somebody tipped her off? Will I tell lies? What has Janine been saying? This is terrible. How will I look her in the eye? I'm as readable as a newspaper. I don't do fibs very well. Why doesn't she go and quiz her fiancé for fuck's sake?

'Lawa? Are you still there?'

'Oh yes Ruth,' I say in a small voice. 'I'm still here, sorry. Come on up.'

With shaky fingers I buzz her in. What on earth have I got myself into now?

Ruth walks into my flat, head held high. She is done up to the nines and looks a bit like Yasmin le Bon in her youth. It's easy to see how she's one of Janine's best friends. Immaculately dressed in blue understated jeans, soft black shiny leather boots with a staggering heel, fitted black cashmere jacket and crisp-white blouse, she exudes elegance. Her glossy chestnut hair is swept off her face, and she wears enormous Jackie O type sunglasses. Leaning forward she gives my scrubbed make-up free cheek a kiss.

'I see you're doing a spot of cleaning,' she says looking around and sounding suitably impressed. 'Good for you.'

Personally I don't know whether it is good or not. It's more of a necessity than anything else. I'm certainly not one of those women who goes around claiming that ironing is therapeutic – they should really be prescribed something! As Ruth looks around the room with interest, I hope she doesn't notice the cobwebs beginning to form in three of the four corners of my living room. If she does, she doesn't say anything however, and sits herself down on the sofa, crossing her long legs in front of her.

'I'm afraid I'm not the best housekeeper in the world,' I say light heartedly, trying to make a joke of it. I think I would be an interesting contender on *How Clean is your House?*

Ruth gives a little giggle but looks distracted. I sense she is fairly nervous. She pulls at her fingers awkwardly and fiddles with her engagement ring.

'Would you like a cup of coffee?' I offer hospitably, thankful that I ran out to the shops earlier and picked up a packet of fig rolls along with the Sunday newspapers. Normally I'm not that organised but I hadn't a crumb in the place earlier after my enormous bingeing session yesterday, during which I managed to shove almost all of the contents of my kitchen down my throat.

'I'd love a cup of tea actually,' Ruth stands up. 'Don't you move. I'll get it myself. I don't want to cause you any twouble at all. In fact I feel tewible for barging in like this, especially it being a Sunday and all. You go on with what you were doing. We can chat as you clean. I don't want you to be putting yourself out for me.'

'Oh, you're not disturbing me at all,' I tell a blatant lie. 'Not at all in fact. I'm delighted with the bit of company.'

'That's vewy kind,' says Ruth blushing slightly. 'After the other night I was afwaid none of you lot would ever speak to me again. I would have wung you to see if you didn't mind me calling over, but I didn't have your number and Janine doesn't seem to be answewing her phone at the moment.'

'Oh really?' I say, raising an eyebrow. That's just typical of Janine. When the shit hits the fan she runs for cover. Isn't she a great help altogether?

I pick up the duster awkwardly and start on the mantle piece. This spring cleaning isn't exactly living up to expectations. The plan was to clear my head and now it's all gone haywire. My mind is swimming with confusion. God, please let me find a way out of this uncomfortable situation.

'Is that you?' I hear a screech from the kitchen.

My heart sinks. The 'fat' photo again. I really must start hiding it before I let visitors into the apartment.

'Oh that? That picture was taken ages ago,' I call out, struggling to inject a bit of enthusiasm in my voice.

'It doesn't weally look like you. It must be quite an old photo.'

'It is. Thank you,' I say, somewhat relieved. At least she doesn't think it was taken last week or anything.

Ruth comes back in with a pot of tea and two cups. I tell her that there's fig rolls in the press.

'Oh yes I saw them,' she smiles. 'But I don't really like sugawy things. Oh sowy, did you want one yourself?'

'No!' I say somewhat forcefully.

'Oh I forgot, you're on some kind of diet at the moment, aren't you? Janine was telling me about it.'

Was she now? I wonder what else Janine has been saying about me.

'In fact I was going to bring you a small box of

chocolates,' she says, putting down the pot and rooting in her handbag. 'But then I wemembered about your diet so I bwought you this instead.'

She hands me a small gift-wrapped box. I take it in astonishment. What's all this in aid of?

'It's just vewy small,' Ruth says apologetically as I unwrap the gift. It's Chanel No. 5 perfume. Not eau de toilette, but the real thing. I'm not sure what's going on. Does Ruth think it's my birthday or something?

Before I can protest, she stands up and wraps me in a tight bear hug. I can barely breathe. I would so love to know what's going on. The suspense is killing me. As is this hug. Eventually she lets go and I resume breathing.

When she sits down again I see that she's very emotional. She opens her mouth as if to speak, and then shuts it again as if she's physically unable to get the words out.

'Is everything okay Ruth?'

'Sure,' she says with a sniff and wipes her eyes. To my horror I see that she's about to cry. Oh my God!

'Listen, it can't be that . . .'

'No, it is that bad, it weally is . . .' she interrupts, and with that the tears start to flow down her fragile cheeks.

I feel I'm in the middle of a bad dream. How can this be happening?

'Take your time,' I say, offering her a tissue.

'Thanks.'

We sit in silence while Ruth tries to compose herself.

This is such an uncomfortable situation. I don't know how the hell I'm supposed to be involved, but I certainly seem to be. So much for a relaxing Sunday. Then finally Ruth manages to get the words out and tells me exactly what's on her mind. I listen, flabbergasted. I cannot believe what I'm hearing.

She tells me that her fiancé Robert isn't speaking to her because she got so drunk the other night. She then goes on to tell me how she woke up vomiting and then spent the entire morning on the toilet with the runs, which is frankly more information than I need to know. I say nothing however and continue to offer the tissues. She's nearly got through the entire box at this stage.

As I continue to listen, dumbfounded, Ruth confides in me that she didn't even start feeling normal until about seven o' clock yesterday evening. I nod sympathetically. I can relate to that all right. But what I cannot stomach is the irony of it all. Robert isn't speaking to her? Robert is berating her for drinking too much? How dare he! I'm incensed by the injustice of it all. What an out and out bastard. That fellow should be strung up by the balls!

'The funny thing is, I don't even like dwinking,' she wails before blowing her nose loudly. 'I don't know what got into me. I'm a disgwace.'

'Now, hang on a minute,' I say reaching over and patting her head. 'Don't you dare go beating yourself up over the other night. We all go out now and again and let our hair down. We all get drunk and do things we regret, but you didn't do anything wrong. You got a taxi home and that was that. I'm sure Robert was er, you know, drinking and having fun too. Wasn't he on a stag night or something?'

Ruth looks at me, her face masked with confusion. 'You mean you don't know? Didn't yourself and Janine meet him?'

Oh shit! I feel a slight panic attack coming on. How much does she know? What did he tell her?

'Oh, yes,' I say backtracking furiously. 'We met him in the club. I forgot.'

'You forgot?' she looks at me suspiciously.

'Yes, how could I have forgotten? Of course. I remember now. We met him in the club but we'd all had so much drink taken at that stage so it's all a bit blurry.'

'All a bit bluwy?' she echoes. 'Wight. So you won't really be able to help me then,' she says quietly examining her fingernails.

Help? What kind of help was she looking for? Does she want me to come forward as a witness? Did she expect me to describe Robert's fancy woman to her? To be perfectly honest all I can remember was that she had fairly chunky milk white thighs and was wearing a skirt that was offensively short. I know I definitely didn't get to see her face. I certainly couldn't pick her from a line-up or anything.

'Um, what kind of help do you mean?' I ask nervously. I hope to God she doesn't expect me to play the part of a private detective or anything. Maybe I should stop avoiding the issue and tell her truth. Maybe I should just say it, just blurt out the whole incident and get it over with. I take a deep breath. I can do this, I tell myself.

'I'd weally like you to wing him.'

'What?'

'Wing him and tell him the twuth. He needs to know.'

The truth? The truth about what? What is the girl on about? She's wrecking my head, so she is.

'Listen, do you mind if I make another pot of tea?' Ruth asks suddenly. 'I think I need one.'

I think I need something a lot stronger. I'm normally not used to so much drama on a Sunday morning. I look at my watch. It's now 10:45am. Is it too early for a vodka?

While the second pot is brewing, Ruth lets it all spill out.

'Wobert said he saw yourself and Janine in the club but obviously I wasn't with you. I explained to him that I had gone home early on my own in a taxi, but he said that sounded vewy stwange. He said he didn't believe that I would have gone home all by myself.'

'Really?'

I listen open-mouthed and patiently wait for her to continue.

'He said it didn't make sense that I would leave alone while the two of you continued the night on without me. He said that I probably sent the two of you into that club to spy on him.'

'Did he now?'

'Yes, but that actually couldn't be further from the truth. You know that. I had no idea the lads were even going to a club. I would never ask him where he was going because I think what the lads do on a night out is their own business. I'm not at all possessive like that.'

'Indeed.'

How very convenient!

'But he just wouldn't believe me.'

'Why wouldn't he believe you? I don't get it. Does he think that people can't go out without being unfaithful? That says more about him than about you to be honest,' I say, but my obvious hints seem to fall on deaf ears.

'You see there's a pwoblem,' Ruth picks up the teapot and slowly pours us both a fresh cup of tea. 'And it's a big pwoblem. I don't know how it happened but it did and now I have to do my best to wesolve the pwoblem. That's where I need your help.'

Jesus, would she ever get to the fecking point? What is the 'pwoblem' and what the hell does she think I can do about it? God, I'm bad enough sorting out my own problems without taking on those of other people.

'It's all Gawy's fault,' Ruth suddenly says dropping another spoonful of Sweet 'n' Low into her cup and stirring it thoughtfully. 'It's all a big mess weally.'

I nearly drop my own cup in shock. My blood pressure has suddenly shot up. What is she trying to tell me? Was she with Garry? Did he make a move on her? Oh my God! The bastard! I trusted him to look after her. She didn't know what she was doing. She probably couldn't even have told you her own name when I left her in what I thought were Garry's safe hands. If he has gone and laid a finger on her, I swear to God, I will personally seek him out and murder him!

'What did Garry do?' I ask, trying to keep as calm as possible, but inside I'm shaking.

'Oh he didn't do anything bad,' says Ruth, taking a slow sip of her tea.

This conversation is a bit like pulling teeth.

'Did he make a move?'

'Oh no,' she shakes her head as I feel a tremendous relief. Then I feel bad about automatically presuming the worst about him. Maybe he's not such a cad after all. I shouldn't always be so quick to point an accusing finger.

'But he did do something naughty,' Ruth adds, dropping another bombshell. I feel my heckles rising again.

'He tried to come in for coffee?'

'Oh no, nothing like that.'

God, I would rather play Mastermind on live TV than play this game again. No wonder she's Janine's best friend. Nobody else could stick the pair of them!

I take a deep breath. This is no time to lose my cool.

'So what happened?'

'Well, the next morning Wobert called awound with flowers for me.'

'Really?'

And she didn't smell a rat?

'Yes. And I was so sick I could bawely speak to him. He was vewy concerned and wanted to know if he could get me anything fwom the shops. I told him I had some pawacetemol in my bag, and asked him to put a couple of tablets into a glass of water for me.'

'And then?' I ask, anxiously trying to hurry the story along. At this rate we'll be here all bloody day and I haven't started to get into my spring clean properly.

'Then he found the number. It was in my bag. I didn't even know it was in my bag.'

'Whose number? Garry's number?' I ask, shocked.

'Yes!'

Oh my God! Was it not bad enough that he was chasing Janine all around the pub? Why did he have to give her best friend his number too? Jesus, you couldn't keep up with the guy. Is he on a mission to stuff his number into as many handbags he possibly can before he dies? What a ridiculous individual! He must have seen that 'Click' ad with Ben Affleck once too often.

'I'm twying not to wead too much into it,' says Ruth. 'I mean I know he gave Janine his number too so it's pwobably his thing. He pwobably didn't even fancy me. I mean, I was hardly looking my best by the time I left the bar,' she adds with a giggle. 'As I said, it's pwobably just his thing.'

'It does seem to be his *thing* alright,' I say hotly.

Ruth's hand flies to her mouth. 'Oh my God! Don't tell me he gave you his number too! I'm so sowy Lawa. I didn't mean to wain on your pawade or anything. I'm sure he just gave me his number out of politeness. If he gave you his number it's pwobably cos he genuinely likes you.'

'Er, no actually, he never gave me his number,' I say hurriedly, feeling a bit foolish now.

'Phew!'

'Yes, phew!' I laugh, although I'm not finding any of this remotely funny. The cheek of Garry never asking for my number! Does he think I'm not good enough, huh? I mean, why did he single me out as the *only* woman in town that he decided not to give his phone number too. Oh well, as if I care! I'm better off. In fact I should be flattered that I'm not his type. The way I see it, he just seems to go for women who are already taken. I'm so much better off without that loser. The fact that the feeling seems to be mutual is, of course, beside the point.

'I knew absolutely nothing about Gawy putting his phone number into my bag. All I wemeber was that he gave me a lift home. When I said this to Wobert he went mad and kept asking me who this Gawy person was. But I couldn't even weally wemeber how we met. I think he knows Janine fwom way back but I'm not sure.'

'Yes. Way back. We both used to fancy him actually. Until we saw sense.'

'Weally?'

'Yeah. There's no attraction left though,' I add hastily. 'At least where I'm concerned anyway. Obviously I can't speak on Janine's behalf.'

'But Janine's getting mawied!' squeals Ruth excitedly.

'Oh yes, so she is. I keep forgetting haha. But anyway, back to what we were talking about, why didn't you ask Wob, sorry, Robert, to phone Janine about the mix up?'

'I did but for some reason he didn't want to do that.'

I'll bet he didn't.

'And now, I can't get thwough to her myself. So that's why I need you to wing him and put the wecord stwaight, as it were. I know it's a huge favour to ask but I weally wouldn't be here if I wasn't despewate.'

She gives me her phone but all I can do is stare

at it as if it's an atomic bomb about to explode in my hands.

'You want me to phone him now? I mean, right *now*?'

She nods with a pleading look in her eye.

'Now? Oh Ruth, I can't do it now. I just can't.'

'Why not? Look, he won't believe me but he'll pwobably believe you. You've got to tell him I wasn't with anyone. I'll be eternally gwateful.'

'Are you sure this is such a good idea though Ruth? It's not good having this level of mistrust in a relationship. I know I'm single and all, but even that's kind of obvious to me.'

'I don't know what else to do' she says hopelessly and all of a sudden she looks so fragile that I don't want to refuse my help.

'Okay, tell you what. You give me his number so and I'll ring him later on,' I suggest as a sort of compromise. 'Honestly Ruth, I couldn't ring him now with you standing over me. I'd be too nervous. I'd be afraid I'd say the wrong thing.'

We shake on it and Ruth then stands up to leave. 'Thank you so much,' she says gratefully, giving me a huge hug. 'Because of your kindness I now know I have a chance of getting my welationship back on twack. Wobert is my life. I don't know how I'd live without him. I'll make sure you're the guest of honour at our wedding Lawa.'

Hmm. I might just have to strangle the groom first.

'Thank you,' I say grinning like I've a full corn on the cob stuck sideways in my mouth. 'I love weddings. Right then, I'll see you down to your car.'

But as I open the front door of the apartment, I'm met with an unexpected shock. The colour rapidly drains from my face as I stare ahead. Because standing outside, wearing a pale blue t-shirt and a dark pair of sunglasses sweeping back his hair, is Dave. I look at him, frozen with horror. I don't think I have ever looked so disgusting in my entire life. In fact I'm sure I look positively vile. And what's worse is that I don't think he has ever looked so good. Damn him anyway.

I want to run away and hide. How can I let him look at me when I'm looking this revolting? My hair is so greasy you could use it to oil car engines. And my tracksuit is not one of those fancy velvet Juicy Couture ones that all the stars seem to wear to the gym. No, it's more like one of those ones you see people wearing outside the criminal court, waiting for their friends to be sentenced for joyriding, and giving the fingers to camera crews. I actually can't believe he's seeing me like this. Of course I know he has already seen me in my swim-suit but at least I had my fake tan on that fateful day! Today I am white as a snowflake, but unfortunately not half as pretty.

Funnily enough, Dave looks just as shocked as I feel, which you know, is really rather weird. I mean, he knows I live here, and he's obviously come to see me, so why does he look so completely startled?

'Dave!' Ruth and I exclaim in unison.

'Girls!'

Ruth and I look at each other. Our surprise is mutual.

'Do you two know each other?' she asks almost accusingly.

'Yes, well, Dave er, helped me out when I was er, unwell,' I stammer, the words tripping over themselves. This is surreal.

'Oh, I see,' Ruth laughs, almost sounding relieved. 'He's your doctor! God, it's a small world, isn't it?'

I have to agree. Sometimes it's too small for comfort. What are the chances of these two people knowing each other?'

'How's Gewi?' Ruth asks pleasantly.

Gewi?

'Oh fine, fine. She's in great form.'

'Did she have the baby?'

'Yes, he's almost a year old now. Little devil. I'm mad about him though.'

'Plenty of sleepless nights then?'

'God, don't talk to me!'

'Well if he looks anything like his mother I'm sure he's a stunner. Anyway, congwatulations to both of you. Tell her I was asking for her, won't you?'

'I will do.'

'I was in nursing school with Gewi many moons

ago,' Ruth explains to me with a big smile on her face.

I just nod, feeling totally bewildered. The expression on Dave's face gives nothing away. What on earth is going on?

Ruth then says, 'Well I'd better be off then. Thanks a million for everything Lawa. You're a star!'

And with that she gets into her blue Ford Ka and speeds away.

Chapter Nineteen

'What was that all about?' I ask Dave.

'What do you mean?' he asks wrapping his arms around me and nuzzling my neck. 'That's not much of a welcome, is it?'

He tilts my chin up with his finger and kisses me softly on the lips. I close my eyes and cherish the moment. I wish I could forget about the conversation I just heard.

'Are you glad I called?'

'Very,' I smile at him.

'How do you know Ruth?'

'She's a friend of Janine,' I say.

'Good-looking girl.'

'Yes, yes she is. She was er . . . a friend of your ex?'

'That's right.'

'You never told Ruth she was your ex. Why not?'

Dave stares straight ahead. It's impossible to read him. 'It's easier that way. She'll probably find out eventually. I don't feel comfortable talking about the split to people I haven't seen in years. It's hard to explain.'

'But you were talking as if the two of you were still together?' I protest weakly. I hate all this skirting the issue.

'Come on Lara,' he squeezes my hand. 'Don't be putting pressure on me. It's going to take time, okay?'

'Sure,' I mumble.

As it's such a nice day, Dave offers to drive us both to Powerscourt so we can hang out for the entire afternoon. I take him up on it. Powerscourt Gardens have to be the most beautiful romantic surroundings on this earth. I can't think of anywhere I'd rather be when the sun is shining. And certainly spending the day strolling around such magnificent surroundings with Dave appeals a lot more than spending the day alone with a duster, rubber gloves and a bumper bottle of Domestos.

I take a quick shower and try and make myself as presentable as possible. I decide to wear a pair of beige cords and a chocolate-coloured cashmere polo neck. I also bring a cream bomber jacket with me as it's still March and there can sometimes be quite an unforgiving wind out in Powerscourt.

It doesn't take us too long to get to the gardens and the woman on the gate asks me if I'm a student, which fairly makes my day. It's a long time since I was a student. My woolly hat must have done the trick.

Dave and I are totally relaxed in each other's

company. I have filled him in on all my news. On the journey here I told him all about my weekend so far with Ruth and the girls. However I leave out the bit about finding Ruth's fiancé in a compromising position with some tart and the fact that Ruth wants me to make everything right between them, because I still haven't quite decided what to do about that. I need to think about it carefully. There's no way I'm going to let that Wobert off the hook.

After rambling on for about a half an hour I decide it's time for me to shut up. I don't want to come across as self-obsessed. My grandmother has always told me that men love nothing more than to talk about themselves and that if you're a good listener, most men will find your company simply marvellous. I try to bear this in mind as I ask Dave how his weekend has been.

'Oh, very uneventful so far,' he laughs. 'Compared to yours anyway. I spent the day yesterday with Matthew at the zoo.'

'Was that fun?' I ask, my heart melting at the thought of Dave pushing the little buggy around Dublin zoo pointing out the baby monkeys to little Matthew. Suddenly I'm overcome with a strange emotion. A little yearning for a mini me whom I could dress up and wheel around for people to admire. I wonder does Dave want more kids?

'And where is Matthew today then?' I ask. 'You could have brought him along with us. I wouldn't have minded at all.'

'His mother has him all day today.'

'Gerri?

'Yes.'

'Did she do nursing with Ruth?'

'Yes, but as far as I know Ruth didn't stay in nursing very long. She went off travelling to Australia or something and the girls lost touch. Ruth was always a bit too glamorous for nursing. Or at least she certainly thought she was.'

'Is that how you met Ruth and Gerri? Through hospital work?'

'That's right,' he says vaguely trailing off. He's fiddling with the radio dials now.

Okay, I get it. I know I should stop asking questions now. It's not the healthiest of pursuits, you know, trying to find out stuff about your boyfriend's ex. But I can't help but being curious about this woman who lives under the same roof as Dave and is the mother of his child.

Dave, however, is refusing to elaborate. And as he turns up the volume on the radio, he is making it clear that this line of conversation is one he is not anxious to continue with. I try not to take it personally.

In Powerscourt, we stroll along happily, wandering down to the Japanese gardens hand in hand. The sun has come out to play as if on cue, and despite it being a Sunday, it feels as though we are on our own. Alone with mother nature; the vibrant-coloured flowers, exotic trees which are hundreds of years old, and babbling brooks flowing by in a hurry. It's like being transported to another world.

I'm like a different person to the girl I was yesterday. Twenty-four hours ago I was hungover, depressed and disillusioned. I couldn't see the use or the point in anything. If that's what a night on the booze can do to me, then maybe it's time I thought about giving it up. I wish there were pubs that had a three drink rule. That no matter how much money you flashed at the barman he would absolutely refuse to serve you any more, and that if you continued to argue, you were promptly rejected from the premises. Think how much healthier we would be as a nation if the pubs adopted this military style rule. And don't knock it. They said that the smoking ban wouldn't work. They said people would never accept it, not in the winter anyway, when it was raining outside. They said that old lads who had been smoking in pubs for years were too set in their ways to accept the ban and that it was a crazy idea. Publicans were on every television and radio station claiming that pubs would lose money, that punters wouldn't comply and that everyone would just stay at home. They were wrong.

Of course they were wrong. As if the punters were going to stay at home for the rest of their lives just so they could smoke their brains out in the comfort of their own living room! Now, I like the odd cigarette myself but I must say there's nothing more vile than sitting in a restaurant, about to tuck into a mouth-watering meal, when the punter next to you, having finished his dessert lights up with his coffee. Now, when I visit friends in the UK, I just can't get over the fact that this still happens!

Personally I think the ban has been a most welcome addition to the dating scene in Ireland. Before it arrived, everybody just sat smoking at their own tables and people didn't mix. Now I almost feel sorry for the non-smokers as these are the poor sods left inside minding the coats and drinks!

'A penny for your thoughts,' Dave pulls me close to him and kisses the top of my head. 'You seem to be lost in a world of your own.'

'Oh I'm just thinking about the smoking ban,' I tell him, at the same time realising that I must sound pretty dull. After all, here I am strolling in Ireland's answer to paradise with the man of my dreams, and all I can think about is people standing outside pubs puffing on smelly nicotine.

'Really? How odd.'

We both start to laugh and then we stop and hug each other. It feels like we are the only people standing in the world. Dave smells delicious. I nibble gently on his neck. He tastes even better. This feels very right. It's as if I've been waiting for someone like Dave all my life and now he has been presented to me on a plate. He's so gorgeous, sexy and clever, and has a way of looking at me that just wants to make me melt. I feel safe in his arms and that's a nice feeling. I just wish I could get him to move out of the house he shares with his ex. After all, it must be painful for both of them to continue living with each other, having to see each other day after day. How can they possibly move on under those circumstances?

I feel so comfortable with Dave. It's as if I've known him all my life. With so many other men I always felt I was treading on egg shells, worrying that I was going to rub them up the wrong way. I used to fret about saying the wrong thing or worrying that if I made one false move they were going to pack their bags and flee. Which is exactly what they all did. Eventually. God, when I think of all the men I have dated in the past – what losers they were compared to my Dave! I can't believe I threw away so much precious time with them. Going for long boring walks when all I wanted to do was curl up with a good book; attending football matches where I wasn't even sure what team we were cheering for, and listening to guys who used to tell me 'I *know* what I'm talking about', as they readily poured scorn on my own life. To think that I stood back and accepted their advice because they were men, or a couple of years older than me! I should have known better but hindsight is a wonderful thing.

It's funny, but when you're seeing somebody there is a huge pressure to spend 'quality time' with that person. At the time you kid yourself that you're investing in a relationship. But when the market collapses, you're left with an unbelievable mess. To sum it up, the 'quality time' you once spent with that person you now look back on as simply a 'waste of time.'

After a while walking around, Dave suggests going up to the restaurant in the main house for lunch. As my stomach has started to rumble I welcome the idea. I'll just have a nice salad or something. Nothing too heavy.

When we get our food we sit outside to catch the last of the afternoon rays of sunshine. The view of the lake with its impressive fountain is mesmerising. I could sit here watching it all day long. Then again, I think I could quite happily sit in rush hour traffic as long as Dave was safely by my side. I haven't felt this happy in a long, long, time. And then it hits me. As Dave leans forward, his stare penetrating mine, and casually pushes a stray hair off my face, I want this to last forever.

Chapter Twenty

'Hello? Is that Robert?'

'Yes. Who's this?'

The voice at the other end of the phone sounds paranoid. Aggressive even. This ain't going to be easy, I can tell you.

'This is Lara.'

'Lara?'

'Lara Hope. Janine's cousin.'

'Oh right. Yes, right. How are you?'

'We met the other night. Briefly.'

'Oh yes. Er, can you just excuse me for a minute? I'd like to take this call outside, thanks.'

I'll bet he would. It's six o' clock. He's probably having Sunday roast with Mammy and Daddy, the spoiled brat!

'Hi Lara. Sorry about that. So what can I do for you?'

Gosh he sounds so formal! Does he think I'm calling him for a bank loan or something?

'I'm ringing on behalf of your girlfriend, Ruth.'

'I see.'

He sounds suitably less arrogant now and a tad confused. Good.

'I'm ringing just to let you know that Ruth felt very unwell on Friday night.'

'I know that. But she's fine now. I was speaking to her yesterday.'

He sounds fairly baffled now.

'So anyway,' I continue regardless, 'I just wanted to get something clear. You see, myself and Janine were going to see Ruth home in a taxi, but fortunately for everybody, Garry, a very *old* friend of ours, very kindly offered to drive her home to door, so that she'd be safe.'

'Oh, oh I see.'

'So that's why she wasn't with us when we, you know, happened to stumble across you in the club.'

'Oh, well thanks very much for looking after her,' he says nervously.

It sounds like he's anxious to get me off the phone now.

'In fact, if anything,' I add, almost beginning to enjoy myself now, 'it should be *you* apologising to her, don't you think?'

'What do you mean?'

'I think you and I know exactly what I mean,' I say calmly. 'But let's not go back over the weekend's mistakes. We all get drunk and make fools of ourselves sometimes, *don't* we? Unfortunately though, some of our little mistakes happen to occur in public.'

He doesn't answer. I do hope I haven't given him indigestion. Actually I take that back. I hope I have.

'So anyway, thanks for taking the call, Robert. I hope I've cleared the air. I don't like to see friends blamed for crimes they haven't committed, do you?'

'No,' he says sulkily, obviously admitting defeat.

'Well goodbye now,' I say, before adding cheekily, 'and enjoy the rest of your weekend.'

I put down the hall phone, and only when I have done so, do I realise that my hand is shaking.

'Who was that?" Dave taps me on the shoulder giving me a fright.

'Jesus! Don't walk up behind me like that,' I scold him. 'Oh that was nobody. Just an old friend.'

'But not a very *good* friend I imagine. You sounded pretty cross with her on the phone.'

'Did I? Oh, I was just taking care of business,' I laugh, giving nothing away. It's my turn to be secretive now. Two can play this game.

'Ok, little Miss businesswoman, let's crack open this bottle of champagne.'

Oh, I forgot to tell you earlier, Dave has brought a bottle of Piper Heidsieck with him. He's so generous, but I'm reluctant to open the bottle as I've an early start in the morning. Anyway, I'm still on a high from this afternoon so I don't need alcohol to add to the fun. If Dave's driving, that means he'll probably just have the one glass, while I'll end up polishing off the rest of the bottle myself. That would give me some hangover tomorrow. Just as we're about to start our mind-numbingly boring week of stocktaking tomorrow. Hmm. I think I'll pass.

'Are you sure you want to?' I ask dubiously. 'I have a horrific week ahead workwise. How about yourself?'

'Well, I have a week's annual leave so I've nothing to get up for tomorrow, thank God.'

I catch his eye. Is he saying what I think he's saying? Is he asking in a roundabout kind of way whether he can stay the night? I feel a wave of uncertainty wash over me. Am I ready for this? Is it not a bit too soon to get physical?

'I can sleep in the spare room if you like,' he says gently placing both his hands on my hips.

I can't look at him. I'm afraid to. I'm terrified my feelings will show in my face. I don't want to appear vulnerable. Sleep in the spare room? After the day we've had together? Somehow I think both he and I know that's not even going to be an option.

In the end I decide to light a small homely fire. Dave sticks on some classical music and then we crack open the champagne. The good thing about my apartment is that it's on the third floor so I have a chimney. A real fire is always a lot nicer than a gas-powered one, don't you agree? And of course, I love the smell of burning briquettes. It reminds me of being on holidays in the west of Ireland.

The mood is clearly being set and the evening

ahead is full of anticipation and promise. Although I haven't done much cleaning today I'm not that bothered about it now. Seriously I was never going to be a contestant for housewife of the year anyway. The housework can wait. There are more pressing matters to be taken care of right now, I think, as my hormones run riot.

At the pace this relationship is racing at, maybe this time next year Dave and myself will be married and I'll be buying recipe books and signing up for sewing classes, while he takes up an interest in gardening. There'll be plenty of time for housework then.

We lie on the rug in front of the fire, relaxing and warming ourselves as the flames spring to life. I wish to God I didn't have to go to work tomorrow. I would love Dave to stay with me here forever. I never want him to leave. This apartment is big enough for two people. There's no need for us to be apart. Suddenly I don't want him to go back to the house he shares with Gerri. It's not normal that he's still living under the same roof as his ex. But then again, if it's meant to be, it will be. In that case nobody, not even the mother of Dave's child will ever be able to come between us.

I must remember not to rush this relationship though, I warn myself. I have a terrible habit of always diving into the deep end of relationships, only to find myself swimming to the top gasping

for air. Slow down, Lara, I tell myself. And stop
fretting. Live for the moment, things will work out.
They have to. They just have to.

By the time we are half way through the champagne, the room has noticeably heated up. Whether
this is simply thanks to the fire or due to my
hormones, I have no idea. Certainly the champers
is going down an absolute treat. Dave asks if I mind
if he removes his t-shirt. I give him a shy smile.
How could I possibly object? There are women
who'd pay him to do that. Suddenly I remember
how good his body looked back at that spa. I can't
wait to get another look.

He peels off his t-shirt and I look on in admira-
tion. What a view. His body is taut and tanned and
what's this I see? A tattoo? What the f . . .? How
come I didn't notice *that* in the steam room?

I examine the tiny star on his shoulder blade and
run my finger slowly over his skin.

'What's this? A symbol of love?'

'More like a symbol of stupidity,' he laughs.

'I didn't think doctors got tattoos done,' I say.
'Do many of them get it done?'

'I dunno. It's not exactly something I go around
talking about or showing to the consultants at
medical conventions,' Dave admits. 'I got it a long
time ago when I was student backpacking in
Thailand. I fell in love with a beautiful American
hippy girl called Kelly who played mesmerising tunes
on her guitar. We were inseparable for three weeks

and thought we were going to be forever. You know how it is.'

'Do I?'

God, suddenly I feel jealous of this stranger that I've never met.

'We made love under the stars on the beach every night, and after three weeks of being totally inseparable, we got matching tattoos under influence of gallons of alcohol and we vowed to never ever part.'

'So what happened then?' I find myself asking, slowly massaging the back of his neck as he speaks.

'We parted shortly after the tattoo thing. In the light of the day it didn't seem so romantic after all. She went back to America and I never heard from her again,' he says wistfully.

I don't get it. How could any girl in her right mind walk away from Dave? She must have been nuts, whoever she was. Still I'm very glad she did go back to America.

'I was broken hearted for weeks afterwards.'

'Really?'

I can't help feeling envious towards this Kelly woman who packed her bags and disappeared into the sunset. She'll probably be his dream woman forever and ever. The one who got away. Men always long for the woman who made off their heart . . .

'And so you were left with this tattoo as a reminder?'

'Yes. Well it's a reminder as to how young and

foolish I was. I vowed I'd never let a women break my heart again. I don't do that anymore. I lend it out now and again but I never give it away.'

'Maybe you just haven't met the right woman?' I suggest.

'Maybe . . .'

'I'm sure you've broken quite a few hearts in your time yourself,' I tease him, ruffling his hair playfully.

'I hope not. And would you stop messing my hair up? I spent all morning trying to get it just right,' he joked. 'Beckham's hair care routine is child's play compared to mine.'

'Oh really?' I chuckle, ruffling it even more. 'God you're so vain!'

He swings around, grabs my wrists and wrestles me to the ground. I try and fight him off but don't do a very good job of it. He is now on top of me and I can feel his broad chest through the fabric of my top. His lips meet mine and we kiss slowly, and then a bit more passionately. Our legs intertwine and we roll over. Now I'm on top. And when Dave lifts up my top and pulls it gently over my head I don't stop him.

Maybe I'm crazy. Maybe I *should* stop him. Maybe I *should* wait until I know exactly where I stand before we get intimate. Maybe I *shouldn't* let him get away with avoiding questions about his personal life. Maybe I *should* reread The Rules and follow them down to the last page. Maybe I *should* take things a bit more slowly before I get in too deep. Maybe I *should* hit the panic button before the alarm goes off all by itself. Maybe I *should*, of course, do all these things.

But I don't.

Chapter Twenty-one

'How many calories an hour do you burn while having sex?' I ask Sandy as we power walk along the Phoenix Park, arms swinging by our sides.

'Why?' she looks at me with sudden interest. 'Have you had sex?'

'Well of course I've had sex,' I laugh. 'I'm about to hit thirty. Did you honestly think I was still a virgin?'

'I mean recently,' she flings at me with an air of suspicion. 'Have you slept with somebody recently?'

'No,' I say vaguely staring at the road ahead. 'I was just wondering, that's all. Just wondering . . .'

'No, you weren't,' she counters. 'How could you just be wondering? We've just spent the last twenty minutes discussing your boring stocktaking day in the shop and then you suddenly start talking about sex? That's not normal, Lara. People don't do that.'

'Oh just forget about it,' I brush her off good-naturedly. 'I was just wondering, that's all.'

We carry on walking, inhaling the fresh air. I'm so glad that Sandy insisted we go to the Phoenix Park for a change. It's always a bit more interesting to vary the walks. God knows we walk around Herbert Park often enough, as it's convenient to my apartment. The Phoenix Park, however, is near enough to Sandy's place in Castleknock so we're here for a change. And we've agreed to go to Myo's for one afterwards, which I'm looking forward to.

'You didn't have sex with the film critic, did you?' Sandy asks anxiously as we stroll on working up a thirst.

'No!' I burst out laughing. 'No, of course I didn't. I don't sleep with men I've just met, you know. What kind of a dirty bitch do you think I am? I have morals, you know.'

'I slept with my man.'

'What man? The wine critic? No way.'

'Oh my God, I didn't think you'd be so shocked. Do you think I'm a slut for doing that?'

'No Sandy,' I say mentally kicking myself for being so flippant. 'Of course not. Not at all. Listen, people sleep with each other all the time.'

'But you said . . .'

'I was *joking* Sandy.'

But between you and me though, I am a little bit surprised. I mean, I know I slept with Dave last night but I kind of consider him my boyfriend now. In fact, I think he might even be The One. But

Sandy and Danny? Jesus! Talking about getting straight down to business.

'I didn't mean to sleep with him,' Sandy says in a small regretful sort of voice. 'It was just one of those spur of the moment things.'

'Well, I hope you took precautions anyway.'

'Lara,' she stops and stares at me dramatically. 'Lara, I didn't!'

'What? Are you crazy?'

'The condom burst!'

I stop dead in my tracks and stare back, horrified.

'It what? Oh Jesus! You're joking.'

'As if I would joke about something as serious as that,' Sandy seems appalled. 'Don't panic though. I took the morning after pill.'

'When?'

'Yesterday. The morning after. I was as sick as a dog.'

'God, you poor thing.'

'Yeah, it's bad enough having to take the tablets but I had a massive hangover to boot.'

'Did you go to the hospital?'

'Yeah, it was really embarrassing. Danny went with me, though. It was very nice of him.'

'Very nice indeed,' I scoff. 'If it wasn't for him you wouldn't have had to go to the hospital in the first place. Was it terrible?'

'Well, it was terribly embarrassing, if you know what I mean. I couldn't tell the doctor at the clinic that myself and Danny had just met and he was asking us loads of personal stuff, like what kind of contraception we normally use.'

'Crikey. So how did you leave it? Are you going to meet up again?'

'I'm sure I'm the last person Danny will ever want to see again after what we went through yesterday. I won't forget that hospital visit in a hurry. Luckily the doctor was really nice though. He was youngish and good-looking.'

Suddenly I remember what Garry said on Friday night about having to go home early 'cos he had a clinic the next day.

'Was his name Garry?'

'I don't know. It was Doctor something. He didn't give his first name.'

'What did he look like? Tall, dark and handsome?'

'I suppose so. But as I said I was hardly in a flirtatious mood asking for the morning after pill. He could have been George Clooney for all I cared.'

Jesus! I bet it was Garry. OhmiGod that'll be really embarrassing now if myself and Sandy ever bump into him around town.

'Anyway Danny rang last night to see how I was but he didn't suggest meeting up again,' says Sandy dully. 'So that kind of tells me. Why? Are you meeting your fella again?'

'What fellow?' I ask

'The film critic. You two were getting on like a house on fire.'

'Were we?'

'Yeah, he was quite cute actually. If I hadn't gone and fucked everything up with Danny, we could have met up again as a foursome.'

'Oh yeah,' I say nonchalantly. 'Well whatever . . . anyway don't you go berating yourself about what happened. You didn't have sex on your own. It takes two to do the wild thing.'

We both start to giggle simultaneously, and after a half an hour's walking we hop into Sandy's car and head for Myo's.

The place is quiet enough, which isn't that surprising really given that it's a Monday evening. We grab a seat in the corner and try piecing together Friday night's events we wait for the barman to take our order. Sandy is gobsmacked when I tell her about Janine and Alan.

'You mean it's all off between them then?' she asks goggle-eyed. 'God I don't believe it!'

'I don't know if it's completely off,' I shrug. 'Janine doesn't exactly confide in me at the best of times. I haven't heard from her since the other night. It's like she's disappeared off the face of the earth.'

'But is your joint thirtieth birthday party still going ahead?'

'I've no idea. Hopefully not. I can't think of anything worse than throwing a joint big bash with Janine to celebrate us hitting the big 30. I'd be just as happy with an intimate dinner with a couple of really good friends, you know yourself.'

'So any more news?'

'Nah,' I lie. I can't bring myself to tell her about Dave. I know she'd ask too many questions anyway and to be honest I don't even know the answers myself.

'So is work really awful?'

'Oh don't ask,' I sigh. 'Stocktaking is so boring. Honestly, it's the most excruciating task in the world. I don't think anybody outside the retail industry can even imagine how mind numbingly awful it is. Every single item in stock has to be checked and ticked off against the official charts. Of course it doesn't help that half the staff usually decide to phone in sick during stocktaking week either . . . You wouldn't believe Sandy, the amount of staff who actually phone in complaining of period pains! It drives me round the flipping bend. I'm a woman too, you know? But even when I'm menstruating, I turn in for bloody work. Managers don't get sick or suffer cramps. We can't afford to.'

'Same with teachers,' Sandy agrees. 'We can't just take to the bed for a few days once a month, much and all as we'd like to.'

'Teachers get a lot of bad press but to be honest I don't know how you do it. By the way, whatever happened about that little girl who came in with the bruises? Did that get sorted out all right?'

'Oh yeah . . . well social workers were sent out to the house. It would seem that the father – who actually happens not to be the girl's biological father at all – has an alcohol problem and the little girl is now living with her grandmother. I don't know how she got the bruises but at least I'm in the clear again.'

'And how is she?'

'Poor mite! She seems to be doing fine now. She made me an angel out of silver tin foil on Friday, God love her. My heart really goes out to disadvantaged kids, you know? I often wonder where they're going to end up. I do my best as a teacher but I can't play God with their lives.'

'I know,' I say contemplatively. Then I start thinking about how lucky I am that my parents are normal enough. I mean they're not *totally* normal (if there even is such a thing). I mean, my mother does have an extremely annoying habit of ringing me at ridiculously early hours on a Sunday morning to ask me how I am, and loves to start meaningless conversations which usually end up in a fight with her going, 'if you *knew* the sacrifices I made for you . . .' and me retorting with '. . . would you ever feck off? I never asked to be born, did I?' And as for Dad? Well he doesn't even really see the point in talking to me at all, unless I make a particular effort and accompany him around the garden quizzing him about the various plants and shrubs.

But at least when I was a kid they did make an effort to help me out with my homework and paid for college fees and that. I suppose they did their best.

'Do you want another drink?' Sandy asks, nodding at my empty beer glass.

I wish she wouldn't tempt me. 'No, I'd better get going,' I say. 'Long boring week ahead. I'll get a taxi home. I don't want you to have to drive me all across the city.'

When I finally get home I'm fit to collapse. I'd have expected at least a reassuring text or something from Dave but so far I've received nothing. As soon as I'm in the door, I check my home phone but the long unblinking glare of the red light tells me that nobody has tried to get in touch and nobody is wondering what I am up to.

Oh well . . .

I wish Dave would phone though. I'm feeling vulnerable now, not knowing why he hasn't been in contact. There was a time I would have rung him, just to hear the sound of his voice. There was a time I would have phoned, enquiring whether he had been trying to get through to me, and if not, then why not? There was a time when I would have humiliated myself by making these calls, usually after reading an upbeat article in a woman's magazine about how women should take the plunge and not be afraid to take initiative.

But I'm older and wiser now . . .

Chapter Twenty-two

Okay, it's day two of the dreaded stock take. And looking at my watch I'm relieved to see it's almost lunchtime. Good. That means I technically only have three and a half more days of this crap to get through. Thank God. The weekend can't come fast enough. Not that *I* have any plans to do anything of course. Dave hasn't phoned or anything. To tell you the truth, I'm beginning to get a bit paranoid about it at this stage. Was it because I slept with him? Should I have waited longer? Will he now think I hop into bed with anyone who asks? They say when you sleep with a man, that you love him a little bit more while he loves you a bit less. I wonder is there any truth in that? I also wonder at what stage does the game playing end? When can you just go 'this is me, now take it or leave it'?

As I'm on my knees counting the baby shoes, Millie, one of the staff members, taps me on the shoulder and says there's a woman at the customer service desk looking for me.

I look up with feigned interest. 'Did she ask to speak to a manager?' I enquire, suddenly bracing myself for the tirade of abuse. People who usually ask to speak to the manager don't do it because they want a nice little chat.

'She asked to speak to somebody about communion wear,' she informs me.

Oh God, that's all I need, I think to myself as I get to my feet, brush myself down and then make my way over to Customer Service. The recently delivered communion wear hasn't even been put out on the rails yet. And not only that, but we are under strict instructions from the area manager that nothing new is to be put out on the shop floor until the stock take is finished. Trust some old biddy to come looking for it now!

I look around for a woman with a young child waiting to try on the communion stuff. But the only person at the customer service counter is a smart looking, well-groomed girl, probably in her mid twenties. She appears to be alone. She certainly doesn't look like she's old enough to be mother of a toddler, never mind a seven or an eight-year-old making their First Holy Communion.

I notice she is smiling over at me. Slim with blonde highlighted hair scraped back in a chignon, she is wearing tight-fitting navy jeans coupled with a purple and gold kaftan top. The girl makes her way towards me, hand outstretched.

'Hi, I'm Lara,' I say in a friendly but business-like manner, shaking her hand. 'How can I help you?

'Are you the manager of the store?' she asks in a sweet, softly spoken tone of voice.

'Yes'. I'm taken by surprise. Most people demanding to see the manager usually shout, 'ARE YOU THE MANAGER?' in a loud, aggressive voice, while usually shaking damaged goods in my face.

'Good, just the person I'm looking for then. Would you have a spare moment?'

I haven't really, but I say I do anyway. The customer always comes first and all that. After all, they're not to know we're in the middle of a stressful stock take, are they?

'My name is Antonia Kennedy. I'm a researcher with *Fashion for Now* on RTE. Are you familiar with the programme?'

'Er, yes, indeed I am,' I reply, wondering if this Antonia girl has found herself in the wrong shop. *Fashion for Now* concentrates on high street fashion for the modern woman. It's a hugely popular daytime programme, repeated on Sunday mornings. I always tune in on my day off. But to be honest, I wouldn't be setting my alarm for it or anything. I love my fashion tips, but not that much.

'Well Lara I have a proposal for you. Do you have a minute to talk?'

A minute? I have the rest of my life. My head is spinning. What's all of this about?

'As you know, in a couple of months time we'll be in the middle of the popular communion season. Therefore we are looking for somebody to come on the show and discuss the various options children and parents have when choosing something to wear for the big day.'

'Really?' I say, my eyes nearly popping out of their sockets. Jesus, is she suggesting what I think she's suggesting?

'Of course we'd need different dresses in different price ranges. Obviously not all our viewers would have hundreds of euro to spend on an outfit that's only going to be worn for just one day . . .'

'No indeed,' I nod enthusiastically. 'Well, all our new communion wear is still in boxes in the stock-room at the moment but I'd be happy to courier samples out to you. We have some fabulous designs in this year, most of them very reasonably priced.'

'Great,' Antonia beams enthusiastically. 'And of course we'd like to show some outfits for the little lads too on our programme.'

'Sure. That'd be no problem. We have suits for boys in stock too. They're smashing. I'll send some of those over to you if you like.'

'Fantastic.'

'So is this a new direction for *Fashion for Now?*' I ask out of curiosity. 'You've never done children's wear before, have you?'

'Not really,' Antonia admits taking out a folder and pen. 'But it's something the producers are getting very excited about. We reckon the slots will prove very popular with our audiences, so,' she says beginning to scribble furiously onto the sheet in front of her, 'if I could just get your details . . .'

I'm happy to give them all to her. Antonia, whether she knows it or not, has just gone and brightened up my day. This will be great publicity for the shop. My area manager will be thrilled at the prospect of getting our clothes advertised for free on a popular fashion programme.

'And you wouldn't have a problem appearing on the show yourself to go through the clothes for our viewers?'

'No, I'd love it. What a challenge!'

'Maybe you could give tips on how stressed out mums and dads can prepare for the big day.'

'I certainly could,' I assure her. 'God only knows, when you've been working in children's retail for as long as I have, there isn't a thing you don't know about parental stress!'

Antonia laughs dutifully. 'Well thank you so much for your time,' she says, snapping her folder shut and offering a slender hand for me to shake. 'You've been most helpful. I'll be in touch shortly.'

'No problem at all. Lovely to meet you.'

As soon as she leaves the shop I approach Millie, who is busy counting baby bibs.

'Millie, would you ever hold the fort for a minute please? I have to go upstairs for a little while.'

She nods her agreement. Millie is the only staff

member I can genuinely trust. The others give her a hard time 'cos she's quiet and doesn't shout about her sexual conquests in the canteen over curried chips or ask for a cigarette break on the hour, every hour, like some of the others. But she's a damn hard worker and I honestly don't know what I'd do without her.

I make my way up to my little office upstairs beside the stockroom, and once I have safely shut the door, I let out a scream that'd curdle cheese. I, little old Lara, am going to be on the telly welly! It has just hit me. Wait until I tell all my friends! I am so excited I can hardly contain myself. I give myself a big bear hug before deciding I'd better get back downstairs and back to reality.

Chapter Twenty-three

I haven't eaten a thing today. Well I couldn't because of the excitement of everything, could I? It has all happened so fast. I can't believe I'm going to be on TV. Me? Lara Hope. Who would have believed it? I've come along way from kindergarten now I can tell you. Back in those days I remember a film company coming to our school to audition for fairies for a real life Hollywood flick. It was being filmed partly in Dublin in a not too far spot from where I lived. Janine and my sister Carly got blink-and-you'll-miss it parts after numerous auditions but, as for me? I wasn't even called back for a second audition. In hindsight, that was probably because when the director asked all the would-be fairies to dance in a clockwise circle, I went anti-clockwise instead and messed the whole thing up. But it was still no consolation to me at the time. When my name wasn't read out on the call-back list, I was truly devastated.

I remember coming home and howling my little heart out over the injustice of it all.

Mum then went out and bought me a pink furry pencil case to make me feel better. That did the trick alright. I cherished the pencil case and told myself that one day the film would be long forgotten, but nobody would ever take the case away from me. I still have it somewhere in the attic, if it hasn't been eaten to death by moths.

Oh well, that was a long, long time ago. And boy have I come a long way since then. I decide to relax, kick off my high heels and walk around my carpeted bedroom floor barefoot. Oh the relief! My feet are absolutely aching from standing around all day. I'm wondering whether I should indulge in a little foot pampering. A few years ago I got a foot spa for Christmas from my sister. You see I'd wanted one for ages, thinking that there must be nothing more luxurious than watching TV at the end of a hard day's slog, with my feet soaking in warm water in one of those yokes. But to be honest I've only ever used it about twice 'cos, when my feet are that tired, the last thing I want to do is start hauling that damn foot machine into the bathroom and begin filling it with hot water – the weight of it for a start! Also, you have to go and clean it after every use so that's *way* too much hassle for my liking. Now I use it to store things like airline ticket stubs, buttons, loose coins, concert tickets and flyers from local Indian take-aways. I always think those flyers may come in handy one day if I suddenly have a sudden urge for vegetable samosas.

I slip my poor weary feet into my fluffy baby-pink slippers and plonk myself down on the sofa with the phone on my lap. Now who will I ring first to tell my good news? Of course naturally I would like to phone Dave but as he still hasn't phoned me, I'm sure as hell not going to phone him either. Difficult and all as it is to refrain, I've got to retain some dignity. I suppose I'd better ring Sandy. She'll be thrilled for me anyway.

Sandy takes ages to answer her phone and when she does eventually pick up she sounds out of breath. God, she's really taking this exercise thing very seriously, isn't she? Fair play to her though, I think almost guiltily. The only exercise I intend doing this evening is putting my feet up.

'Sandy?'

'Yeah?'

'Where are you? Are you out jogging?'

'Er, no.'

'Oh . . . oh, are you alone? Can you talk?'

'Er, not exactly,' she says. She sounds like she's panting.

'What do you mean not exactly? Have you company?'

'Yes.'

'The wine critic?' I ask in astonishment.

'Yes. He called over with er, a bottle of wine.'

'Oh. Oh I see.'

Suddenly I don't think it's good idea to tell her about my good news just now. There's a time and a place for everything. And obviously I'm the last person on Sandy's mind at this very minute.

'Was there something important you wanted to talk to me about Lara?'

'No, nothing important. Ring me later when you're, you know, finished.'

'Will do.'

Crikey! That was quick. Hope they don't go bursting another one . . .

I ring my parents.

Dad answers.

'Hi Dad!'

'Lara, is everything okay?' he asks suspiciously. Dad thinks the only reason I ever ring is when I'm looking for a loan or a lift, which isn't exactly true. I ring for other reasons . . . like when my washing machine floods. Or all the fuses in the apartment blow and I need Dad to come over with his torch.

'Everything's fine. I'm going to be on TV, Dad.'

'Oh good for you. Well your mum's playing tennis so I'll get her to ring you when she comes in and you can tell her the good news yourself. Was there anything else?'

'No Dad,' I say somewhat dejectedly. 'No, there wasn't.'

As I put down the phone, a feeling of deep disappointment creeps over me. He didn't even ask me why I was going to be on TV. For all he knew I could have been going on one of those late night programmes with my voice altered, admitting a

serious crack addiction or that I was a prostitute
or something. Huh!

I ring Janine. But she's at a bridal fair and can't
hear me above the noise. *Bridal* fair? So does that
mean the wedding's back on? She says she can't speak
and tells me to ring back later if it's urgent. Hmm.
She can feck off with herself.

I ring Karen. But she's out on a date. Another
one. I secretly think Karen must be answering the
would-like-to-meet ads in the *Evening Herald*. I ring
Ruth, but her phone is switched off. I ring about
five more people and just get their answer phones.
I ring the talking clock and tell it my good news.
Actually I don't, but I'm tempted to. At least the
clock would answer the godamn phone!

I ring my sister as a truly last resort.

'What's the programme about?' Carly sounds
bored.

'Fashion.'

'You'll be talking about fashion?'

'Fashion for kids. Communion dresses and stuff.'

'Oh,' she says disinterestedly. 'You mean you're
on one of those afternoon slots watched by grannies
and the unemployed . . .'

'Yeah, well it's a foot in the door, isn't it?' I say
irritably, even though I'm not sure what I'm talking
about. A foot in the door? A foot in the door of
what?

'That's right sista. *Fashion for Now* one day,
Parky the next. You're on your way.'

That's it. She's just too cool for school. I vow that I'll never lend that cow any of my clothes ever again. I'll lend her nothing, not even a fiver. And God, will that hurt. My sister's still a student. She survives on handouts.

Just as I'm about to slam down the phone, Carly suddenly backtracks furiously.

'Ah Lara, you know I'm only taking the piss. I'm proud of you. Will you get your hair and make-up done for free and stuff? Will you, like, be able to get me and my friends into clubs and all for free now that you'll be a familiar head on the box?'

'Jesus, I'll only be on just the once,' I say, beginning to regret that I phoned now. The only reason I rang her was because literally nobody else was available to chat. Next time I won't bother.

I don't know if I told you before or not but there's a huge age gap between myself and my sister. Almost 10 years in fact. I'm more like her aunt, although she treats me like a grand aunt.

That's why Janine and I were brought up almost like sisters. We were the same age. Carly is like something from plant Zog with her wine-coloured plaits falling from her tight bandanas. She never wears anything but black and even has a stud piercing on her lower lip. It's always going septic and mostly I can't even bear to look at it. I don't know why my folks let her get away with dressing like a tree hugger. Carly doesn't even care about trees, but these days, if there's a march in town, you can guarantee to spot Carly in the middle of it. In fact she's been on TV loads of times herself for all the wrong reasons. I don't know why she's so fond of protests. She's doing it to prove a point I suppose, although what that point is exactly, is anybody's guess. I'd love a real girly sister whom I could go shopping with. Carly is no addition to the family. God my life was so happy when I was an only child. Back then there was just Mum, Dad and me. And sometimes Janine.

When Carly arrived (her conception was completely unplanned by the way) life was never the same again. Now she's studying philosophy in UCD, completely looks the part, and like most of her fellow philosophy students, doesn't know what she wants to do with the rest of her life apart from discovering the meaning of it all.

'It's still cool though. Will you need an assistant or anything? I could come along and hold the bibles up for the camera. Do kids still get bibles for their communion these days?'

'I don't know. I won't be preaching the Lord's word anyway,' I say, impatience beginning to rise within me. 'I'll be talking about fashion, not saying Mass.'

'Yeah well let us know when you're on, right?'

'Right.'

'See ya.'

She's gone. Just like that. Hmm. I check my phone

messages just to see if anybody else has called but
I'm sorry to say they haven't. Isn't that a bitch? I
just hate it when you ring so many people and
nobody calls back. Don't you just feel like a bit of
a loser when people don't ring back? I desperately
want to call Dave. I want to pour my little heart
out to him. I want him to throw his arms around
me and congratulate me. Doesn't he feel the same
special connection that I feel? If he does, then why
doesn't he bloody well phone? I mean, we're not
teenagers who met at the local disco, are we? We're
all grown up, so how come we're still messing about?
Why is he playing it cool? Christ, aren't we just a
bit too old for this kind of crap? I'd love to give
him a good shake-up and reassure him that he
doesn't have to play games with me. I've fallen for
him anyway. I'll tell him that for free. He doesn't
have to play hard to get. I'll love him anyway, no
matter what.

I switch on the telly, but there's nothing on. I
think I'll treat myself to a glass of wine. There's a
bottle of Carmen chilling in the fridge that's just
begging to be drunk.

As soon as I sit down and pour myself a nice
generous glass, my home phone rings. My heart
nearly leaps from my body.

'Hello?' I answer excitedly.

'Hey there,' comes the male voice. He sounds
different.

'Dave?'

'Who's Dave?'

'Who is *this*?' I answer, confused. I'm not in the mood for games. Who is this prankster? God, maybe I should hang up. They say you shouldn't talk to anonymous callers on the phone in case you encourage them.

'It's Frank.'

Frank. I frown at the phone. Frank? Not Frank from the other night? Not the film critic?

'Frank? As in Frank from the other night?' I ask suddenly. I hope I don't sound too foolish.

'That's me,' he says and he sounds like he's laughing. 'It's nice to know I made a good impression.'

'Well of course I remember you. But you ran off on me without saying goodbye. How did you get my number?'

'Karen gave it to me.'

Good old Karen, eh?

'She said you were Dateless in Dublin so I felt sorry for you.'

'God, she's so funny. Well I'm afraid this isn't a charity helpline. '

'But is it true? Are you single?'

'I might be.'

'That means you are.'

'It doesn't. It means I'm just not telling you.'

'Well do you want to go out?'

'Out where?'

'I've tickets to go to the opening of the new Colin

Farrell film tomorrow night. How about coming along as my guest?'

Oh my God! Colin Farrell. Will he be there? In the flesh? Will we get to rub shoulders, share popcorn, perhaps discuss the film afterwards over a glass of bubbly? I feel faint even thinking about it.

'Are you still there?' the voice on the other end of the phone wants to know.

'Oh yes,' I whisper excitedly. 'I'm still here.'

'So listen, I'll meet you outside The Savoy at seven thirty? How does that sound?'

'Sounds perfect. And listen Frank, thank you so, so much for thinking of me.'

I put down the phone. I can hardly breathe. Colin Farrell. Wow! I can hardly take in this news. First I hear I'm going to be a television star and then I hear I'm going to be mingling with A-list stars. God the excitement of it all! I'm tempted to jump up and down on the spot. The phone rings. Hmm. Who could that be? Don't tell me Frank has gone and changed his mind!

'Lara?'

'Dave!'

'Hey, how are you?'

'Fine,' I say somewhat coolly. He has taken his time in calling me so I'm not exactly going to sing for joy over his phone call.

'Is everything okay?'

'Everything's fine.'

'Listen, I'm just wondering if you're free for dinner tomorrow evening?'

'Dinner? Em? No, actually, no I'm not,' I say my heart sinking. Why is this happening to me? I sit in all fecking year twiddling my thumbs and nobody but people from phone companies call wondering if I want discount on all calls to South East Asia. And now I've two bloody great offers for the one night. I would so love to go for dinner with Dave. Of course I would. But Colin is Colin. I mean, come *on*, what would you do?

'I'm afraid I'm busy tomorrow night Dave, but any other night is fine with me,' I add cheerfully.

'Oh.'

He doesn't seem very happy. Well too bad, he should have phoned me yesterday. That'll teach him.

'Are you working late or something?' he asks.

'No.'

I'm not sure why I should explain my where-abouts. After all, until this minute I wasn't one hundred per cent sure that I would even be hearing from him again.

'No, I'm not,' I repeat firmly.

'Where are you off to?'

'The cinema.'

'And can you not go another night?'

'No, I'm sorry Dave, I can't get out of it. I'm meeting Colin Farrell afterwards.'

I'm greeted by silence.

'Are you still there?' I ask.

'I'm here. Did you just tell me you were going on a date with Colin Farrell?'

'Um, it's not a date. Like it's not just the two of us. There's a crowd of us meeting up tomorrow night. It was arranged ages ago. Can we not go to dinner another night?'

'It's just that my ex is away tomorrow night and I was thinking I could get a babysitter.'

'But what has your ex got to do with any of this?' I ask, pretty confused. What is going on? Why does she have to be told anything? Surely she knows about us anyway. He must have mentioned me to her at this stage. So what's the big deal then?

'Have you told her about us?' I ask suddenly.

I'm met with another long silence.

'Dave? You still there?'

'Yeah, I haven't told her. I'm waiting for the right time.'

'The right time?' I say, feeling exasperated. 'The two of you have long split up. Do you honestly think she'd give a fuck?'

'I don't know.'

'What do you mean you don't know? What's going on Dave? You'd better not mess me around. I won't put up with it.'

'I think she still has feelings for me,' he says in a voice so inaudible I can hardly hear him. My heart hits the floor. I really don't think I want to hear this.

'And do you have feelings for her?' I force myself to say the words.

'No,' he says immediately and relief suddenly washes over me. 'Listen Lara, can you not meet me tomorrow night?'

'I can't. I'm sorry.'

'The cinema means that much to you?'

Oh God, why do men always do this? Why do they always make you feel bad when you've done nothing wrong, eh? Well I suppose I don't have a completely guilt free conscience myself. After all I've just arranged a date with another bloke, like about ten minutes ago. But I can justify that. Yes. It's my once in a lifetime chance to hang out with Hollywood royalty so I'm not going to turn Frank down. Sure, I can go to dinner with Dave at any time. And anyway it's good to play hard to get now and then. Especially now. Now that Dave is telling me that his ex may still have feelings for him. Not only his ex but the mother of his child. God I'm not so sure I want to take on that kind of baggage.

'As I said the night has all been arranged,' I say distantly.

'Can I not come with you?'

Fuck!

'No!'

'You sound very definite about that.'

'I can't let my friend down. She's going through a rough time at the moment so I want to be there for her.'

God the lies!

'Yourself and Colin Farrell.'

I have to laugh.

'Are you going out with Sandra?'

'No.'

'Karen?'

See? He knows everything about me, even my pals' names. I know nothing about him except that he's still living under the same roof as his ex, he's a doctor and has a son. I don't even know what music he's into and what star sign he is. What kind of relationship is that?

'What star sign are you?'

'Pisces.'

'You should have told me.'

'Why?'

'Because I never go out with Pisces men.'

'Why?'

'Because they can never make their mind up about anything. And they're usually unfaithful too.'

'Goodbye Lara.'

'Hang on, you can't just cut me off like . . .'

The phone goes dead. Oh my God, I don't believe it. He has actually cut me off. I didn't think he would. Immediately I ring his phone but get his answering machine. Fuck. I really did insult him didn't I?

I don't sleep very well. I can't stop thinking about Dave. Why did he hang up on me like that? Was he just looking for an excuse? Was he pissed off that I wouldn't meet him for dinner? Or did I simply touch a raw nerve when I mentioned infidelity? How did I do that? I'm all confused and am losing sleep over it. This is bloody ridiculous. How can somebody like me lose sleep over a man? I'm not a flipping teenager any more.

'Hi Lara, just returning your call. Anything important?'

'Actually,' I tell Janine, my chest swelling with pride. 'I'm going to be on TV.'

I wait for her congratulations but instead I am met with stony silence. 'How come?' she says eventually, sounding anything but pleased for me.

'Well a researcher from RTE came into the shop and asked would I be interested in getting involved in a fashion programme.'

'Fashion!' she screeches so hard that I have to hold the phone a good ten inches from my assaulted ear. 'Did you say you're going to be on talking about fashion? That's absolutely ridiculous.'

I'm appalled by her attitude. Why is she being so nasty? It's only a once-off appearance on an afternoon show. Listening to Janine's outburst, you'd think I'd just been selected to play Brad Pitt's new love interest in a leading Hollywood production.

'I'm going to be talking about kids' fashion,' I

say suddenly feeling very disheartened. I want to get off the phone now before she has a chance to stick any more pins in my balloon.

'Oh right, anyway Lara I'm wondering if you are free tomorrow night. I'd like you to come in to Debenhams with me to try on some bridesmaid dresses.'

'Debenhams? But aren't you getting the dresses made?'

'I want to explore all options,' she says. 'There's no harm coming in and trying them on though. We'd have a good giggle.'

Hmm. Personally I can think of nothing less amusing.

'Can't Janine. I'm going to the premier of that new Colin Farrell film.'

'With who?' she barks.

'Frank.'

'Frank?'

'You know that guy we met the other night at the concert?

'Oh yeah, him. How come he has tickets?'

'He's a film critic.'

'That's right. I'd forgotten. Well you'll have fun at that I'm sure. He'll be sitting there criticising the film for the whole duration.'

'No, he won't,' I say defensively.

'What will he be doing then?'

'I dunno, I've never been to a premier before.'

'I have. Ruth's dad got tickets last year to one.

He gets loads of stuff like that through work and we went along. It was brilliant fun. We met Liam Neeson at the after party.'

'You did?' I gasp.

'Yup. Very nice man. Very tall, mind you. Now, what are you wearing tomorrow night? You'll have to look a million dollars at this thing if all the press will be there.'

'The press?'

'Of course, they'll be there, especially if they can write about Colin Farrell. Don't understand what all the hysteria is about that guy anyway. He looks like he needs to give his hair a good wash.'

'I bet you wouldn't turn him down given half the chance though.'

'I'm practically a married woman now Lara!' Janine pretends to be shocked. 'Don't be putting ideas in my head.'

'If you weren't getting married, would you go for Garry?'

'Lara!'

'Would you?'

'This is a highly inappropriate conversation Lara.'

'Would you though?

'I could if I wanted, but I wouldn't 'cos I have morals.'

'Has he asked you out?'

'He knows I'm getting married Lara.'

'Has he actually made a move though?' I quiz her.

'Garry and myself are just good friends,' she says coolly as if she's a Hollywood starlet drawing an uncomfortable interview to an abrupt end.

Chapter Twenty-four

Ohmigod, tonight was definitely one of the most embarrassing nights of my life. Janine had me so hyped about the premier that I was rooting through my wardrobe despairing of the rubbishy contents. How is it that no matter how much stuff I buy, I never have anything decent to wear? The only evening dresses I found in my wardrobe were my old debs dress (it's white, by the way), a silver sparkly number that was in vogue a decade ago but could now be mistaken for a kitsch disco ball, and a satin chocolate-coloured dress with one sleeve (it was made like that!). I also found a long chiffon baby pink backless dress, which is cute in summer but totally inappropriate for this time of the year.

In a complete panic, I rang Sandy who offered to lend me a stunning red dress with a slit up the side and a dangerously low cut designed to show off as much cleavage as possible. She had worn it to a hunt ball last year and said she felt like a man magnet. I sent a courier to her place that afternoon to pick it up. As soon as I put it on I knew I'd made the right decision. I felt like a goddess. The slinky showstopper clung to me in all the right places and I didn't even look fat. In fact I looked normal and dare I say, even a bit glamorous! If I don't get a second look in this, there's no hope for me, I smiled, giving myself one last self-satisfied twirl before calling a taxi.

I'm very surprised when the taxi pulls up outside The Savoy that there's no red carpet or anything laid out. Nor is there any sign of all the snappers I expected to see spilling out onto the pavement. Maybe I got the wrong place, I think panicking slightly. I give Frank a quick ring on the mobile. 'I'm just inside the door,' he says happily. 'See you in a sec.' He sounds like he's in great form. He's probably already had a couple of glasses of champagne with Colin. They usually have champagne at these things, don't they?' Assured that I'm definitely at the right venue, I give the taxi driver a generous tip and sashay up the steps into the cinema foyer.

And then it hits me. I am the only person in the room that is in any way dressed up. There's nobody here apart from a few studenty types and couples dressed in jeans or tracksuits. There is no sign of Colin Farell either, no young model looking types going around offering champagne on silver trays, no red carpet, no snappers, no star attraction. The only attraction appears to be me.

I want the ground to open up. I feel like a freak

show. People are looking over curiously as if I'm some sort of a novelty act. It's horrific. I wish I had lollipops or something to give them to make them stop staring. Then I see Frank, his face frozen in shock. He's wearing black jeans and a black shirt. He fits in. I don't. I want to run away, but where would I run to? Maybe I should run across the road to Penney's where I could buy a tracksuit and runners.

'Where are you going dressed like that?' Frank asks, astonished.

'Well, see the thing is . . .' I begin.

Frank looks at me blankly as I rack my brains for a plausible excuse.

'The thing is . . .' I continue, 'A friend of mine is having a birthday party later and I knew I wouldn't have time to go home and change, so I thought I'd just wear this into the premier and then that would save me time later.'

'What premier?' asks Frank, his face masked with confusion as both our faces suddenly start to look like the colour of my flamboyant dress.

I wonder if he's trying to be smart?

'The premier you invited me to,' I answer crossly.

'This is a press screening Lara. Not a premier.'

'Oh, I just thought they were the same thing,' I say feeling a bit thick. 'What's the difference?'

'One is glitzy with the hope of catching a glimpse of an A-list star, which is rare, and the other, like tonight is where a handful of people in the industry, like critics, turn up. You thought it was the former, didn't you?'

'Well, I wasn't sure . . .'

'You're friend isn't having a party, is she?'

'No.'

Frank starts to laugh.

'I'm leaving,' I say huffily.

He grabs my hand. 'No you're not. Come on.'

'Everyone is looking at me whispering,' I say self-consciously.

'Well, isn't it better than being ignored?' he says, not letting go of my hand.

Chapter Twenty-five

Frank is altogether too keen. He texted me last night to make sure I got home safely, even though he himself had driven me home to my door. He said he'd call today and true to his word he called this morning. Like at about 8:00 am. And then he called again at 10:00 am just to say hello. He said he'd really really really like to see me again which, to be perfectly honest scared the living daylights out of me. Now I don't find him at all attractive. Oh God, us women only have ourselves to blame when we go around moaning about men that don't call. But nobody should invade your space that much!

Last night after the film Frank wanted us to go somewhere and discuss it, but as you might appreciate I didn't really want to be seen around town in a ball gown. Imagine if I'd bumped into any of the Baby Bloomers staff!

Today I am pondering on the fact that I may never be happy. Why am I yearning for Dave and avoiding Frank's incessant calls? Why are nice men boring and why are good-looking men never nice?

Just as I'm about to bang my head off a nearby wall, the phone rings. It's Dave. My heart soars. He wants to take me away for the weekend. I pretend to think about my answer and try my best to keep the excitement out of my voice.

'This weekend? Let me see. It's all very sudden, but . . .' I do a little skip around the stockroom. The staff have all gone home so I can basically do anything I like among the prams and the playpens.

'It'll be great baby,' Dave says seductively. 'I haven't had you to myself for a while.'

'Yes,' I say, agreeing with a big smile spreading across my face. 'It will be fantastic to get away. Just the two of us. And I love Belfast too. The night-life there is brilliant. Last time I was there we had cocktails in The Apartment overlooking City Hall. It's a cool place to go on Friday evenings at around half five. Let's go there definitely.'

I pause for breath suddenly realising that I've been babbling on like an idiot.

'Actually Lara, it won't be just the two of us. It's a medical conference so there'll be lots of other medics there unfortunately. The weekend's being hosted by one of the big pharmaceutical companies and there's a dinner afterwards but we'll give them the slip at some stage and have a wild night of passion.'

'Oh, alright then.'

'Is that a yes?'

'Yes!' I practically scream. I can't wait to have my Dave back in my arms again. The dating game is no lark really. Frank was alright but his eagerness was frightening. He's like so many men who race to get married once they realise their hair is taking leave of absence. God forbid that I end up with someone like that. And as for Clive? Well if there was ever candidate to take a long run on a short pier . . .

'Cool. I'll order in champagne and strawberries. Nothing but the best for my favourite girl.'

Hmm. I wonder what he means by that. How many other girls are there? I should be the *only* one. I think when I go to Belfast I might try and get him to discuss his living situation. I mean how healthy can it be to see your ex every single day? God, I find it bad enough passing some of mine on the street!

Anyway I have to be positive. If there were other women in the picture, then he'd be inviting them to accompany him to this event. He must think an awful lot of me if he's prepared to introduce me to his colleagues and peers.

'I'm looking forward to it already,' I tell him.

'The hotel's gorgeous. I looked it up on the Internet.'

'Is it The Europa? I just love that hotel.'

'No, it's not The Europa, it's the Malmaison Hotel. It's newish. We'll have a great time there. What are you up to at the moment anyway? You're not still in work, are you?'

'I am. Our spring wear has arrived (at least some of it has). I have to try and make room for it all in the shop tomorrow. I can only really think when the staff and customers are gone. It's my favourite part of the day.'

'Well I hope they're paying you good overtime,' Dave laughs.

'Are you joking? The senior management at Baby Bloomers wouldn't know the meaning of the word.'

'Oh, I nearly forgot, how was the party last night with Colin Farrell?'

'It was er, er . . .' I struggle to think of something. 'Oh listen Dave, the battery's just going dead on the phone. I'll fill you in again, okay?'

''kay. Night gorgeous.'

'Night.'

I press END.

I am in love again.

Chapter Twenty-six

Racy underwear – tick
Fake spray tan – tick
Full leg and bikini wax – tick
Highlights – tick
Eyebrows plucked – tick
No eating for 3 days before Belfast – tick

Only one day to go now. I can't believe Dave and I are heading off for the weekend. It still hasn't really hit me yet that I'm about to spend an entire weekend with the man of my dreams. I hope we get on well. I'm sure we will. I mean, it's not like we'll be spending a week on a remote beach together struggling to think of interesting things to say to each other. Anyway, why am I even worrying about this? Everything will be fine. I should just relax. It's just a weekend away. No big deal. Oh God, I think, wiping a fresh film of sweat from my forehead, today has been one of the busiest days of the year so far and we're down half our staff. There's a big music festival on this week so I'd kind of expected a few people to skive off, but not this amount. At the moment, I'm tearing open boxes trying to get the new stock out for tomorrow morning. As soon as seven o'clock comes I'm out that door. Dave says he'll collect me, which is very handy. I'm certainly not going to take my work with me to Belfast. The place can fall in tomorrow as far as I care.

Just before seven the store phone rings. My first thought is to simply ignore it. After all, no normal customer would ring a baby clothes shop on a Friday evening, so what's the point in talking to some nut? With a skip in my step, I gather up my keys, turn off the lights and open the side door. The phone is still ringing. Oh feck it, I may as well just answer it. After all I'm technically supposed to be in the store until seven on the dot so maybe it's one of the UK managers checking up on me. They seem to have no concept of life outside Baby Bloomers. Honestly, at our last Christmas party the UK head office team flew in especially, got plastered drunk and still talked about Baby Bloomers all night long. Even when hotel staff had to physically carry Mr Jones, our boyswear buyer, off to bed at around five, I'm convinced I heard him muttering about next year's 'must-have school ties'.

'Good-evening Baby Bloomers. Lara speaking. How may I help you?'

Or not help, preferably.

'Lara, thank God I've caught you.'

Fuck, it's Mr Magee. My heart hits the floor. This is not good. My area manager is definitely not ringing to tell me a joke or to wish me all the best for the weekend.

'We've a problem on our hands Lara.

I feel sick. What does he mean by 'we'? I'm out of here. I haven't had a weekend off in I-don't-know-how bloody long.

'There's been a staff walkout in our Cork store.'

'What?'

'I've been ringing around all the managers. We all need to go to Cork first thing tomorrow to operate the tills.'

'How did this happen?' I ask distraught.

'I won't go over the ins and outs of it over the phone Lara. One of the staff was caught on CCTV camera with her hand in the till. We've suspected the stealing has being going on for quite some time and today we got the proof. She was fired on the spot and her colleagues have walked out with her in protest.'

'Shit. Sorry Mr Magee. Sorry, excuse the language, it's just that . . .'

My mobile starts ringing.

Shit, shit, shit.

'I understand that you've probably already made plans and I promise that you will be well compensated for the inconvenience at such short notice Lara.'

Compensated? Oh my God, you don't under-

stand, you silly man. It's not about the money or the time off!

'Oh I did actually have plans but . . .'

'Family commitments?'

Should I lie? Fuck, what would you do? I can't exactly tell him I'm scooting up to the North for a dirty weekend with a doctor. Dammit.

My phone rings off.

'Is there a car travelling to Cork in the morning?'

I mean Cork of all places. You don't get much further away from Belfast than that, do you? Why can't there have been a walk-out in our Belfast store?

'Yes, I'm driving down early in the morning. I can collect you at a quarter to seven Lara if you'd prefer not to drive.'

Suddenly I have a thought. If I drive myself down, then I might be able to get out early. Maybe they'll feel sorry for me and let me go home say an hour before closing time. That'd still give me time to drive up to Belfast. Oh I know I'd miss the meal and everything, but I'd still get to spend the night with the man I'm mad about. That's got to be worth something.

'No, sure I'll drive down myself.'

'Well, if you're sure. And once again sorry about messing up your weekend plans.'

'It can't be helped,' I answer resolutely. 'It's just one of those things, I know it's out of your control. I'll see you tomorrow then.'

And yes, you'd better bloody well make it up to me.

Chapter Twenty-seven

As predicted, Dave is not happy.

Well, that's actually a bit of an understatement. The guy seems devastated when he calls to collect me and I tell him I can't go. It breaks my heart to deliver the bad news. I sit into the passenger seat and explain the situation. After listening quietly he takes me into his arms and kisses the top of my head gently.

'My poor girl,' he says. 'You need a break from all of this.'

'I know,' I say rubbing my eyes from exhaustion. 'I'm shattered these days. Work just keeps getting tougher and there doesn't seem to be any let up. Maybe I'm in the wrong profession.'

'You need a holiday.'

'Desperately,' I agree. 'I'll have to see if any of the girls would come away with me.'

'Leave it up to me,' Dave says in soothing tones, stroking my hair.

'Huh?'

'I might be going to Thailand in a month's time.

How about you coming with me and leaving the girls at home?'

My eyes widen. Suddenly I no longer feel drained. 'Thailand? Are you serious?'

'Yep. Leave it to me. I'll work something out. As long as you can get the time off work.'

'I can definitely swing something. They owe it to me,' I insist, beaming.

I lift my head and kiss him full force on the lips. I would so love to be going to Belfast for the weekend, but a fortnight in Thailand with Dave would be well beyond my wildest dreams. I know he's always had a sort of love affair with Thailand. He goes there quite a lot. I suddenly remember what he once said to me about the girl he fell in love with over there, the woman of his dreams who broke his heart. Maybe the fact that he wants to bring me now, is a sign he's well and truly over her now . . .

'Take care,' I whisper reluctantly, opening the passenger door.

'You too,' he says as I swing my legs to get out of the car.

'Lara?'

I turn my head to look at him.

'I think I'm falling in love with you.'

Chapter Twenty-eight

I think I'm falling in love with you. I think I'm falling in love with you. I think I'm falling in love with you.

Oh my God I can't get those words out of my head. It's crazy. I should be concentrating on my work but instead I'm fantasising like a schoolgirl. The Cork shop is absolutely chaotic because apart from the Cork managers themselves, none of us know where anything is and the stockroom is like a maze. I'm just getting the hang of working the till now, thank God. It's really easy actually. You just sit and swipe, ask the customers if they have a customer value card, would they like any cash back, and whether they'd like their goods wrapped in a brown paper bag. God, I dunno how people do this all day for a living though. I'd crack up with the boredom of it. And I know I'll be repeating these questions in my sleep later.

Actually I won't be doing that. Let me take that back. I will be in Belfast tonight if all goes to plan and I'm certainly not going up for a good night's rest. Of course I haven't told Dave I'm planning to drive all the way up tonight. No. Just in case something goes wrong and I end up letting him down again. Anyway, I can't wait to see his face as he opens his hotel room door to me! That'll be some surprise for him.

The day in the Cork store passes without further hitches. At lunchtime I head around to McDonald's in Patrick Street to stuff my face. Feck the diet for today. After what's been inflicted on me this weekend I bloody well deserve a large fries and ice cream.

Yes, there's a God and he's up there looking out for me. I have just been informed by Mr Magee that I can leave at four o'clock. It is now exactly three minutes to four. I reckon it'll take me less than four hours to get to Dublin. There I'll have a quick shower to freshen up, change my clothes and then hit the road for Belfast. All going well I should arrive before ten and everything will be perfect. Okay, I'll miss the actual dinner but there'll be plenty of time for drinks and a laugh before we retreat for the night. I'm so glad everything has worked out for the best and that I didn't turn down the day's work in Baby Bloomers Cork shop. The senior management will think I'm such a dedicated manager and, who knows, I might try and push for a pay rise at my next assessment. Having said goodbye to everyone I hop into my car, hoping the Cork traffic won't be so bad and

I can get on the road without too much difficulty. I want to cover as many miles as possible before it gets dark.

By the time I reach Dublin I'm shattered. I just want to crawl into bed and fall fast asleep. Inside the apartment I splash my face with cold water to try and wake myself up. Then I make a strong cup of coffee and hop into the shower. It's almost eight o' clock by the time I'm ready to leave again. I take a quick look in the mirror and fish out my Touché Éclat to try and hide the dark circles under my eyes. I look wrecked.

I make good progress on the road and within forty minutes I pass the airport. I should be in Drogheda in half an hour. Thankfully it's Saturday night and there's hardly any traffic on the roads. I have Joni Mitchell crooning on my CD player all the way to Drogheda, and only switch it off when I park my car at the McDonalds drive through and pop in for a large diet coke and another large fries. Yes I *know* it's the second time I've scoffed McDonald's today but I need the energy. I've been up since five this morning. The place is full of teenagers stopping off for a feed before their night out. I sit in the corner looking out onto the busy road. I could have just driven through and ordered but I needed to get out of the car, stretch my legs and go to the loo. Besides when you eat take aways in the car, the smell just lingers unpleasantly for days afterwards.

I'm so tempted to text Dave to tell him I'm on my way but I don't want to spoil the surprise. I can't wait to see his face when I show up. He'll be over the moon. I empty my tray of wrappers into the bin and leave the restaurant. With any luck I'll be in Dundalk in about thirty minutes and I'll pull in somewhere there for a little rest. I'm not sure where the Malmaison Hotel is but I've written down the number for the hotel. Maybe I should just ring them now and make sure I know where to go.

The friendly receptionist gives me clear directions. I ask her about the medical dinner and she tells me that they've just been seated. I picture an empty seat beside Dave and my heart melts somewhat. Still I'll show up eventually. I, Lara Hope, am not a woman who lets a few little obstacles get in her way.

I sit in the car rubbing my eyes and yawning. Wouldn't it be so nice to have a private helicopter to whisk me off to Belfast? I switch on the ignition and get the car going. There's no point wishing for the impossible. The sooner I get back on the road the sooner I'll be there. I just have to imagine myself wrapped in Dave's arms to spur me on.

In Dundalk I pull into the car park of the old shopping centre. I can't keep driving. I check my mobile phone. It's nine o'clock. I'm making good time but the way I feel now, I seriously doubt I'll be in any mood for partying when I reach the hotel.

Suddenly a thought strikes me. Suppose Dave and

some of his colleagues hit a few of the bars in town after the dinner? It's not unlikely. After all, they're hardly going to hang around the hotel lobby all night talking about hospitals. Suppose I arrive at the hotel and Dave is out clubbing somewhere? Shit! Why didn't I think of that possibility earlier? What'll I do? I don't want to ruin the surprise but I sure as hell don't want this journey to be wasted either after all the effort I've gone to. I ring the hotel reception and they put the call through to his room.

'Hi, it's Lara. I'm on my way to Belfast and should be there in about an hour. Please don't go anywhere without me. I can't wait to see you. Call me back on 087-2557805.

And, Dave, I . . . I love you.'

I quickly press END. Oh my God, did I just say that? Just goes to show how exhausted I am. I'm probably delusional too! You should never tell a guy he loves you before he says it to you first. It's the cardinal rule and I've just broken it without thinking. Oh, well, I'm a passionate person I think, backing out of the car park. As I drive through Dundalk I see all the young people out and about enjoying their Saturday night. The main street is thronged with people spilling out of various bars and chip shops. I remember coming down here years ago and staying in The Fairways Hotel with a Louth guy I'd met in Gran Canaria. We'd booked a hotel because his mum said we'd have to have separate rooms if we were staying in her house. We'd felt so grown-up staying in a real hotel. I'd been so in love and we'd phoned and written letters until he met another Louth girl on another Canary Island the following summer. He'd told me it was best for him to see a local girl as he could no longer stand the long distance commute. Well I suppose two hours is pretty long if you're on public transport, but my heart was broken all the same. I would have done anything to make it work. I used to write him long love letters and spray them with my perfume so he'd be reminded of me. How sad was that? At least I learned my lesson years ago, I think as I put the boot down and head for Belfast.

I drive along with the music full blast to keep awake, listening to seriously dodgy pop tunes. Honest to goodness, I can't believe the shit that's in the charts now. Who buys it anyway? Mind you, people were saying that when I was an impression-able young teen with posters of Wham! and Duran Duran plastered all over my room!

When I finally reach Belfast, it's very, very late. I park the car and check into the Malmaison Hotel on Victoria Street. Its super trendy and the recep-tion is unlike anything I've ever seen. In fact it's more like a nightclub. I'm about to ask for Dave's room when to my complete and utter surprise a tall dark handsome man wanders out of the lift. My mouth almost hits the floor I'm so taken aback. What the hell is Garry doing here?

He looks just as astonished to see me. He stops

dead in his tracks and stares. It's very dark in the lobby so maybe he's not sure it's me. 'Hi Garry,' I smile at him.

He squints back, 'My God it *is* you! What on earth are you doing here?'

'What are *you* doing here?' I counter.

I'm at a medical conference,' he says lightly as I give myself an imaginary clatter across the forehead. How stupid am I! Garry is still standing looking for an explanation. I come clean and tell him about myself and Dave. I wonder does he know him. Maybe they're friends even.

'We know each other, but we're not friends,' insists Garry, his eyes almost darkening as he speaks.

'Oh,' I say a little awkwardly. 'Well do you know where he is? Is he in the bar?'

Garry steps in front of me as if to block my path.

'He's not in the hotel bar. He said he was going to either Café Vaudeville or The Pothouse. Are you sure he's expecting you?'

'Well, no, it's a surprise,' I say giving him a wink. God, he probably thinks I'm pathetic!

Garry still doesn't look happy. Maybe he's jealous of Dave. Or then again maybe I'm just deluding myself. After all Garry could have anyone on the planet. He's flipping gorgeous. And he must know that as well as anyone.

'Come on, let's go to Café Vaudeville to see if he's there,' Garry suggests.

'But aren't you with people already in the bar?'

'Yeah, but I'm sick of them already. All they do is talk about work. I fancy a change of scenery,' he adds cheekily, casually putting an arm around my shoulder. Mmm. He smells great.

It's a very short ride in a black taxi to the trendy Parisian-themed Café Vaudeville. We find a couple of bar stools and make ourselves comfortable. Garry then offers to get me a cocktail so I kindly accept. He wanders off into the crowd of trendy people as I scan the room to see if I can spot Dave. I try his mobile but it's switched off. Where the hell is he?

Garry arrives back with a Mojita for me and a Coke for himself.

'You not drinking?' I quiz him.

'Not tonight. We have a long day tomorrow with the conference and I want to have my wits about me.'

'Jesus, you're getting very sensible in your old age,' I tease, giving him a slight dig. 'Cheers anyway,' I raise my glass, still wondering where Dave has got to.

And then I spot him. My jaw drops open. Across the bar, his arm draped around the waist of a young blonde, Dave is standing there. In that one second my world seems to fall apart. I feel myself going into shock. Now I know why Dave's mobile phone is switched off. Everything suddenly seems to make sense. Garry sees my expression and winces.

'I'm so sorry about this Lara.'

'You knew?' I can barely get the words out. 'You knew Dave was seeing somebody else?'

'Somebody else? Dave always has at least three women on the go. I can't stand him. He has no regard for females whatsoever. His poor partner. I don't know how she puts up with him.'

'B . . . but he's not with her anymore,' I attempt feebly. 'They only live under the same roof for the sake of their child . . .' I continue, trailing off when I see Garry's pitying expression.

My pride takes another tumble as I feel the walls of the bar closing in on me. Suddenly I feel very hot. I need to get out of here fast and without Dave spotting me.

I see him up at the bar on the left with his back towards us. Garry takes my hand and we walk down the steps and out onto the street.

'We'll get a taxi back to the hotel,' says Garry.

'I want to walk,' I answer dully, crossing the street and making my way towards Donegal Place. Garry follows.

'You can sleep in my room.'

I stop and stare. I can hardly believe my ears. I stand outside the closed doors of Easons book shop and stare blankly at him.

'I didn't mean . . .' he runs his fingers through his thick dark hair.

'Oh yes, I think you did,' I stare at the ground fidgeting with my freezing fingers. This has been the worst day of my life.

'My car is parked at the hotel,' I continue walking.

'You can't drive home, not in the state you're in.'

'I can't stay here.'

'You can.'

'Can't.'

We walk on for another half mile until we're at my car. I open the door.

'Let me drive you home.'

'In my car?'

'Of course. You're not fit to drive.'

'What about your conference tomorrow?'

'I can get the train back up in the morning.'

My eyes are closing. I have never felt so exhausted. I hand him the keys of the car. 'I don't know why you're doing this for me. Is it because you feel sorry for me?'

I sit into the passenger seat. Garry starts the ignition. He doesn't answer the question.

Chapter Twenty-nine

I cry myself quietly to sleep as Garry listens to the radio and keeps the window down. He says it's to keep himself awake but when I wake up I'm shivering. 'Can you please turn up the window?'

'You're home,' he answers.

I look groggily out the window. He's right. I am home. I must have practically passed out on the way. It's lashing rain outside. The wind is howling. Suddenly I think of Dave and a wave of intense sadness washes over me.

'Thank you Garry.'

'It was no big deal,' he says stifling a yawn. His handsome face looks tired. I know it's been a very big deal for him. He has gone out of his way to help me.

'I won't try and kiss you because I don't want to be up for sexual assault,' he says. 'But I do expect you to thank me by treating me to a coffee sometime next week?'

'Okay, I promise.'

We swap seats. I drive Garry home. He lives in

a gorgeous artisan type cottage. Before he gets out he takes my mobile phone.

'What are you doing?'

'I'm putting my mobile number into your phone,' he says. 'You never know when you might want it.'

'Thanks.'

He squeezes my hand before getting out of the car. I watch his tall frame walk towards his front door, then I reverse the car and drive back to the apartment. I only live ten minutes away, thank God.

It has turned bitterly cold I notice as I fumble in my handbag for my door keys. The temperature has suddenly plummeted and there's frost on the ground. It's depressing. My freezing fingers search and search through the rubbish in my bag, through the bus tickets, torn beer mats, nearly finished lipsticks, but to no avail. The keys are nowhere to be found. For the second time tonight I burst into tears. It must be three in the morning now and I just can't take anymore.

Okay, I've got to think of something, but the only people who have spare keys are my parents and Sandra, and they live miles away. Also, I don't think they'd be too pleased if I woke them up at this time at night. I stare at my glass door in despair. There is a slight crack in the corner of one of the panes. If I could just push the pane a bit the glass should fall forward, and then I'll be able to put my hand in and open the door. I clench my fist and give it a knock. The pane of glass doesn't budge. I push a bit harder. No luck. Impatiently I give it a whack. My fist goes straight through it. So does my arm. It starts drowning in my own blood as the horror of what I have just done sinks in. I look down at my arm. It's like pasta salad in a rich red sauce. The blood is gushing out. I feel dizzy. I've slashed my arm to the bone. I take my mobile from my phone with my right hand. This is it, I think as I fall to my knees. My fingers are slithering across the digits of my wet mobile as I try and retrieve my contact list. I know my time is limited. This is probably the end. My eyes close as I dial Garry's number and then collapse in a bright red pool. The floor is like that of a slaughterhouse, filling with my blood. If he doesn't answer immediately I'm fucked . . .

Chapter Thirty

The lights in casualty are overbearing and the humming noise is constant. My mum's face is like death warmed up – she looks about 120 years old. My dad's face is stricken and my sister's face is a mixture of tears and streaked mascara. The only person who looks normal is Garry. He's holding my uninjured hand. My injured hand is bandaged but the blood is still managing to seep through the white material. My clothes are sodden and my sister asks me do I want to change into pyjamas. She has brought them in with her. They're baby pink with a picture of a rabbit on the front. I smile through the tears. They're tears of pain, not of sadness. I am in absolute agony.

My pulse has been taken, my blood pressure also, and there's a drip inserted in one of my veins. Garry assures my family that it's all right to go home and get some rest. He says it in such a calm way that they agree. They trust him. So do I. He says he will stay with me until I fall asleep. My family leaves amid promises that they'll be back tomorrow. I can barely hear them. My thirst is overwhelming. Garry, almost being able to read my mind gets me a cold glass of water and presses it to my lips. That's the last thing I remember before I drift off.

I'm awake again. I don't know how many hours I have been lying on the trolley. Somebody is hoovering under the trolley. I wish I had the energy to tell him to go elsewhere.

There's no sign of Garry. There's no sign of anybody. A couple of staff members seem to be having a break. They are sitting on the trolley opposite me discussing their holidays. I wish they'd shut up. I wish somebody would turn off the lights. This is torturous.

Garry is back. He tells me one of the doctors is going to look at my wound and that they'll get me a hospital bed as soon as one becomes available. The doctor, a smiley black man asks me to move my fingers. I can only move three of them. 'Can you feel this?' he asks. I look down at my hand where I can see he is touching my little finger, but I feel nothing. Nothing at all.

Chapter Thirty-one

Often when I've asked married people how they knew the person they chose was THE ONE, they'd smile and tell me they just knew as if it was some sort of secret code. I never really understood what they were talking about. Until now. Everything changed when I woke up in hospital after my operation. It lasted for 6 hours as I had slashed all the arteries, nerves and tendons. I was lucky I hadn't bled to death, the doctors told me. When I woke up I couldn't swallow because of the pain in my throat where they'd put the tube down it.

I was finally able to have a glass of water, which was amazing as I had been on a food and drink fast and was incredibly dehydrated. Garry had sat with me putting swabs on my tongue so I could at least get a few drops of water. Family members arrived at intervals with flowers and chocolates that I couldn't eat. Even my sister, Carly, apologised for being so rude to me a few days earlier, and offered to do my nails and make-up, which I gratefully accepted. I think if she hadn't, Garry might never have asked me out.

The plastic surgeon who operated on me told me my injury was very bad. She said that I wouldn't know for a year whether I'd ever get the use back in my fourth or little figure, but said that with constant physiotherapy, she hoped for the best. I was also told that if Garry hadn't reached me when he did, I probably wouldn't have made it.

I'm still off work, which isn't as great as it sounds, because I'm becoming addicted to daytime cookery programmes, and programmes about people searching for houses in tiny villages in the South of England. I've lost an awful lot of weight because for a long time after my operation I simply lost interest in food. I've actually discovered I'm the proud owner of a pair of cheekbones! The sad thing is that I can't wear any tight-fitting tops because of my cast, which looks like a toilet duck cleaner thingy.

When you pull through such a traumatic accident and face the man of your dreams, it's quite surreal. Heavily sedated with painkillers and pumped up with antibiotics and God knows what else, I didn't really know what was going on. However, when Garry asked me out, I think I finally smiled for the first time.

We're a funny old couple. I couldn't drink for the first few weeks because of all the medication I was on. I couldn't drive either. So Garry was my

chauffeur for a while and neither of us drank. We
didn't even kiss for the first few days because my
poor old severed arm was in the way!

Sometimes I think how lucky I was to have discovered the truth about Dave when I did, and that
Garry was there when I found out. If I'd been on my
own in that bar, I don't know if I'd have been able
to cope. I often think that the emotional pain I felt
upon discovering Dave with another woman, was
as bad as the physical injuries I suffered as a result
of the accident.

It's weird the way that my whole life has changed
since the accident. Every time I go out, people tell
me all about their own injuries as well as the injuries
of their friends, families and neighbours. I suppose
they think it makes me feel better but it doesn't.
The more gruesome their stories, the more I worry
about passing out at the thought of all that blood!

Yesterday was my birthday. I told Garry just to
get me something small so he did. The diamond
solitaire however looks huge on my finger. It's on
my right hand and as soon as my left hand gets
better I'll transfer it. I haven't really come down to
earth since Garry proposed. I truly feel like the luckiest girl in the world. Having long given up on the
dream, I finally got the perfect man. My parents
are over the moon. I think they always secretly
hoped I'd do medicine, so the fact that I'm going
to be a doctor's wife is the next best thing. I'm still
pinching myself that I am going to be Garry's wife.

Imagine me being a Mrs! I can't seem to get my head around it at all. I can't wait for the day I can turn around to somebody and say, 'my husband and I . . .' and look over at Garry. Have I already told you how gorgeous he is? By the way, I asked him why he gave Janine his number at the ball and do you know what he told me? He said he was hoping she'd pass it on to me. As if the silly cow would be so charitable!

Sandy incidentally has quit her job and is travelling the world. I desperately need to get in touch to ask her to be my maid of honour at the wedding. I asked Janine this morning but she refused point blank. She has still barely even acknowledged the fact that I'm dating Garry. Also, Alan seems to be having cold feet about their own wedding so they've postponed it for the time being. She grudgingly admitted that earlier this morning when I rang her with my good news. She didn't even congratulate me but I'll live, I'm sure. Carly also said she'd rather chew off her foot than be my bridesmaid but Garry's lovely sister said she'd love to be bridesmaid. I met her before at that charity ball I went to with Janine and Alan, though obviously I didn't know she was his sister at the time.

You're probably wondering whether Dave ever contacted me again. He didn't. Garry told him what had happened to me and he never so much as sent a text. It was a shock to find out how little I'd obviously meant to him, but at least he didn't manage to destroy me. Do you remember all that crap he was feeding me about living under the same roof as the mother of his child and them living separate lives? Well, apparently she knew nothing about this 'separate' life. Garry says it's a well-known fact that although Dave hasn't yet married the mother of his child, he'll never leave her because her family is loaded and the house they live in is in her name. Garry says she's a nice enough woman and that she's mad about him. Poor girl! I can't blame her for falling for him though. Muggins here did exactly the same.

Chapter Thirty-two

Mum announced our engagement in last Saturday's Irish Times. I didn't really want her to do it but she insisted it was 'the done thing' and went ahead. So naturally this afternoon I was inundated by text messages on my phone from well-wishers. Garry said he got the same amount of texts. My parents' phone was hopping too. Dad avoided answering any of the calls. While he is naturally delighted with my good news, he nevertheless does not want to be discussing it in great detail with the relatives and neighbours. I'm back living at home by the way, since my injury. I'm enjoying all the good food but I'm almost thirty for God's sake, so why do I have to keep telling my folks what time to expect me home?

Anyway, I'm over in my apartment this afternoon doing a few bits 'n' bobs. Heavy housework is out of the question, obviously, with just one arm but I still like to potter around and pretend I'm doing something useful. Unfortunately I was unable to do the guest slot about the communion wear but the television researchers for *Fashion for Now* have invited me back on to discuss summer essentials for kids, which I'm absolutely thrilled about, as are the Baby Bloomers bosses. Apart from that I haven't much to occupy my mind, apart from my wedding. I must grab a copy of *Confetti* magazine to get some ideas. I don't even know where to start! Maybe I'll start writing my wedding list now and get that over and done with. Everyone says the wedding list is a nightmare but I'm determined not to let it ruin my life.

Also, I'll have to see about buying a wedding dress. I asked Janine if I could borrow hers but she told me to fuck off. Oh well, maybe I asked for that! It probably wouldn't have fitted anyway.

To my surprise I suddenly hear a knock on my front door. That's funny, I'm not expecting anyone. I do hope it's not somebody trying to sell me a scratch card. I open the door breezily but nothing can prepare me for the shock.

I look into the face of the man standing at the door.

I open my mouth to speak but no words come out. He still looks heart-breakingly handsome. He stares at me with those intense eyes of his. He's carrying an enormous bunch of flowers.

I'm sure the colour has drained from my face as I struggle to find my voice.

'Dave, what on earth are you doing here?'

Chapter Thirty-three

I let him into the sitting room. With my permission he finds a vase and puts the flowers into it. He asks me how I am. He asks me about the accident, and when it happened. I tell him about Belfast and he looks at me, horrified. He kneels in front of me and rests his head on my lap. I stroke his head gently. I wonder if part of me still loves him.

Sometimes I wonder how you can love one man and still have feelings for another, even if that other person has treated you appallingly. I thought that being engaged makes you only want to be with that person.

Dave looks up at me.

'I'm sorry for what I put you through.'

'Are you?'

'You have no idea.'

'No, that's right. I cannot even begin to imagine the reasons for which you put me through so much pain.'

'I was in a very dark place,' he said. 'I was running away. Maybe from myself. Maybe the feelings I had for you were too strong. What happened was not your fault. I completely shoulder the blame. I think I was scared so I ran away.'

I say nothing. I wish he would stop. If he really loved me, he'd stop hurting me.

'Are you still fainting?'

I shake my head. 'I'm eating properly now.'

He fingers my ring. 'Is this what you really want?'

I take a deep breath. 'I think so. Garry loves me.'

'And do you love him?'

'Yes.'

Dave gets to his feet and brushes himself down.

'Are you still living with that woman?' I ask. I can't help wanting to find out.

'No, I'm not. I live on my own now. I've bought a bungalow in Dalkey overlooking the sea. It's beautiful. I'd love you to come out and see it.'

I give a weak smile. 'I'm almost a married woman now, Dave.'

'Are you one hundred per cent sure this is what you want though?' he asks, his eyes searching mine.

'I don't think anybody is ever one hundred per cent sure,' I answer honestly. My head is still reeling from the shock of his surprise visit. Nothing could have prepared me to for this. I close my eyes.

'You're tired,' Dave suggests.

I nod.

'I'm going to go now,' he says, running a hand through his dark blond fringe. 'I'm going home to make dinner for two. It will be ready at eight. If you're there, I know you still have feelings for me. And if you're not, I know I've lost the only woman I ever really loved and I'll just have to deal with that,' he says softly before leaning forward and pressing his lips to my cheek.

And then he's gone. I sit alone. I feel numb. I still can't believe this has happened. It hasn't really sunk in yet. Nobody changes that fast. He must be lying.

Two hours later I'm still sitting in the same spot. It's dark now but I don't have any inclination to turn on the light. It's cold, but I haven't the energy to light a fire. I am emotionally drained.

There are seven missed calls on my mobile phone. My phone has been ringing constantly but I haven't even checked to see who they're from.

At seven o'clock I've finally made up my mind. I switch on the light, get up and stretch my legs. I go into the bedroom, switch on the heater and open the door of my wardrobe. I want to look nice tonight. In fact I want to look my best.

Slowly I put on my make-up and brush my hair. I'm getting used to beautifying myself with one hand. I highlight my cheekbones with some light blusher and slap on some cherry-red lipstick. The one really annoying thing about only having one useful arm is that I can't put on my fake tan properly, but then again, I think if a man says he loves you, he shouldn't be worrying about your fake tan!

To finish, I dab some of Ruth's Chanel No. 5 behind my ears. I look at the time on my mobile phone. It's a quarter to eight. I still have time. I go into the kitchen and retrieve a bottle of Dom Perignon from the fridge. I won it at the Christmas office party last year. Until now I've never really felt the urge to open it. I put it in a brown paper bag.

It's now ten to eight. I pick up my mobile phone and dial.

'Garry?'

'Hey baby, I've been trying to get through to you all day!'

'I know, I know, I'm sorry. I was somewhat occupied. Have you plans for tonight?'

'Plans? Hey, I don't mind what I do as long as it includes spending time with you.'

'Have you any food in the house? I'll bring the drink.'

'Mmm. How about pizza and garlic bread? I'm afraid that's all I have in the freezer. Or we can go out if you prefer? Name a restaurant and I'll ring up and book.'

'No, let's stay in,' I say, smiling to myself. 'I don't feel like anything too fancy. Go and turn on the oven. Pizza sounds absolutely perfect.'

THE END